I0667580

THE WARLORD'S CONCUBINE

BOOK FOUR

By

PAUL BLADES

Dark Visions Publications
darkvisionspub@gmail.com

All characters and events portrayed in this work are
fictitious

Other books by Paul Blades:

军阀 外家
CHAPTER ONE

The crowd that cheered on at General Wang's victory parade was unprecedented. It seemed that all of Yeuyang had turned out as had the residents of every village within a half day's journey. Many villages too remote for their populace to appear had sent delegations.

The parade was led by the cavalry squad that had captured the Kuomintang general and all of his baggage train, including his beautiful, young whore. General Wang, and all his household, sat upon a high dais reviewing the proceedings. The lieutenant who had led the charge had been rewarded with the enemy general's white horse. He wore on his chest a bright, gold medal that General Wang had awarded him and in his pocket he had a bag of silver coins worth $500 American.

Next came Major Won, the warlord's second in command, and a company of his crack infantry battalion. Major Won had received a $1,000 gratuity for leading the main body of troops which had initiated the massacre of the Kuomintang forces. His chest bore a gold medal as well.

Following Won were six feisty, sleek thoroughbreds towing the half dozen six pounder canon that had been captured, a tall, smartly decked out cavalryman upon each one, and after them a group of smaller mounts leading the fifteen heavy machine guns seized at the end of the battle. Then came the rest of the warlord's army: the balance of his cavalry, his now battle tested regular troops and the blue clad militia. There even a delegation of war widows, all dressed in white, the wives of the militiamen who had been slaughtered like cattle at the beginning of the battle by the Kuomintang cavalry, or their bereaved mothers if the man had been unmarried. Each woman had been issued a small gold brooch memorializing her sacrifice and had been compensated by the award of a $25.00 yearly stipend, a small fortune to most of them.

After the war widows came the brightly bedecked armored car that had completed the rout of the invaders. Yellow and red streamers flowed from it dancing gaily in the breeze. Towed behind it was a wagon on which was mounted a gibbet from which hung the whore Wang had won. She was naked, her hands affixed to the gibbet above her, her ankles splayed wide and affixed to rings in the floor of the wagon. She was a tall, beautiful Eurasian woman, half Dutch and half Chinese. She had long, silky, black hair that ran down her sleek back and large, fluffy breasts that jiggled and danced as her wagon was towed over the cobblestone street. Angry red stripes covered her otherwise flawless body.

Wang had spent considerable time in the seven days between his victory and the parade tormenting her.

Major Won had been surprised when the warlord fled the battlefield so quickly following his remarkable and total victory. After quickly reorganizing his men, Won sent the captured woman, the $50,000 American found in the Kuomintang general's tent and the two hundred or so Kuomintang prisoners on a quick march back to the warlord's fortress. The officers had all been released so they could trudge ignominiously home and relate to their masters their inglorious defeat. But the enlisted men were a different story. General Wang would have a use for them. Construction on the road to the copper mines at Pingjang was about to start and the men would be put to work on one of the road gangs.

While Major Won prepared to conduct punitive raids into the territories that had supported the enemy forces on their march, he had Captain Huang take charge of escorting the booty to the Warlord's castle. Riders went out ahead of him alerting the rearward troops of the great victory, mostly militia who had been left behind to guard crossroads and food and ammunition depots. Word spread quickly amongst the villages along the way. To Huang's surprise, his little column was met by cheering crowds each time they entered one. The bedraggled prisoners were pelted with stones and rotten vegetables by the irate peasants, and young girls ran out to shower kisses on his men and hand them skins of the locally brewed brandy. Huang had the brandy quickly rounded up as they left each village so his men wouldn't get so drunk that the prisoners would escape.

The captured whore was led on the white charger seized from the Kuomintang general. Although they knew she was the warlord's property now, the ecstatic cavalrymen who had taken her prisoner had quickly stripped her of her dainty raiment so they could get an eyeful of her charms. To her great dismay, she was mounted on her horse that way, naked, her hands tied behind her and a rope around her neck affixed to the pommel of the horse.

She was the object of especial vitriol from the peasant women as they passed, a symbol of the venal National Government that had tried to plunder General Wang's domain. The Kuomintang cavalry had savaged two villages, raping and killing as they went, after they had crossed through the fateful pass, before returning to the scene of the battle and their annihilation. Word had spread quickly of their depredations. It got so bad that the captain had to detail several of his men to walk beside her horse pushing the angry women back.

When the column reached the fortress, the whore was sent directly to Wang's dungeon. The troops were greeted by Li Pao, the warlord's eunuch and factotum. Li was astounded at the news of the peasants' jubilation. He rounded up four horsemen and went out to see for himself. He met several squads of the warlord's men on their way back to the fortress and they all told him the same tale.

It seemed that the peasants preferred the devil they knew to the devils they didn't. General Wang was not what you would call a benevolent ruler. But he kept the right to despoil his subjects personal to himself. The officers and men of his army were well disciplined. And there was a general sense that his domains were ruled efficiently.

Li had made sure during the twenty years he had served the general that certain steps at public relations had taken place. This village had a well dug, that one received a dam to help with irrigation. Roads had been improved, mostly to facilitate the swift movement of troops, but these very same roads had been a boon to commerce. Men drafted into work gangs to build the various improvement projects were always paid, if not handsomely, at least enough to make their work seem one level above slave labor. Crimes against persons and property were swiftly and efficiently punished. Missionaries had been permitted to start several schools. Taxes, while heavy, were bearable.

It was after he had passed through the fourth jubilant village that Li got the idea for the victory parade. And for something else as well.

When General Wang learned that a beautiful Eurasian whore had been part of the booty captured from the Kuomintang forces, he insisted on seeing her immediately. He had just emerged from his impassioned victory tryst with his favorite concubine and was feeling refreshed and reinvigorated.

There had been two victories that day. The first had been against the Kuomintang invaders. That had been fortuitous and decisive. The second had been over the British slut who had been bedeviling him for the last two years. Well, it was not really a victory over her, although he felt that he had at last breached her defenses. And it was not a matter of defeating her as much as winning her over. Well, maybe not winning her over, but, well, he would think about it some more later. It was definitely a victory the way she had welcomed him to her bed. Him, not, in her mind, that upstart lieutenant she had been so enamored about. He felt that a new relationship was possible with her now. But what form should it take? She was not his equal. She was, after all, a slave. And she was a Westerner to boot. And the last thing he needed was another wife!

No, it would take much thought. Luckily, he had just the thing to take his mind off of it. He went down to his dungeon to inspect his new prize. He had the two attendants, the ones called by Violet Scylla and Charibdis, bring her out of her cell and string her up by her wrists. She was a fine prize. Her plump breasts were tantalizing, her hips graceful, her belly smooth and with just the right amount of roundness to it. Her face was much more than pleasing and her round eyes added a mysterious touch to her otherwise Asian features. At that moment, those features were a masque of fear.

The eunuch had forbidden the dungeon gremlins from working their cruelties on her until the general had his chance with her first. Her skin was as yet unblemished by the stroke of a whip. That would be remedied very soon.

Wang stepped up to the sniveling woman. He took hold of her delectable breasts and gave them a squeeze. They were soft and firm all at the same time. He pulled and tugged at her nipples until they were stiff and then pinched them until she moaned. Her thin, delicate lips were trembling from fear. She had a right to be afraid. Wang's victory over the invading army had not assuaged his need for revenge against them. Although not technically a part of the invading force, she had accompanied the vain and foolhardy Kuomintang general on what was to have been a holiday excursion. She was undoubtedly looking forward to a share of the spoils of victory. She deserved to be punished for casting her fortunes against General Wang's, a crime few lived to repent.

He stepped around her. Her long, jet black hair covered her curvaceous back. It ended just above the beginning of her soft, inviting rear cheeks. He took a skein of her hair in his hand and sampled it. It was soft and silky. He moved her hair aside and ran his hand over her back down to her buttocks. She flinched when he touched her there. It was something she would get over quickly unless she enjoyed being whipped to within an inch of her life. He brought his hand lower, pausing briefly at the little brown star that lay in the valley between her rear mounds. He wondered idly whether the Kuomintang general had ever pierced it.

The woman's legs had been spread and her ankles tied off to rings on the wooden platform on which she stood. It was an easy thing to do to slip his hand between her thighs and take possession of her pudenda. It had a finely trimmed border of soft, black pubic hair along its sides. That would have to go. He slid a finger along the crevasse between her love lips. She gave out a moan, not of passion, but of despair. She knew very well what was in her future. There could be no mistake about it. But she was as powerless to change her future as those dead men that had been left behind on the field of battle.

The dungeon had not yet been fitted with the electric lights that he was installing all over his castle. It was lit by large lanterns that flickered and cast a pale yellow light on everything. He would probably keep his dungeon like this. There was something otherworldly and ominous about the scant lighting. Shadows danced about, darkness loomed in the corners. It was like the dark place where some believed evil souls went after death. Surely this half Chinese, half European girl had heard of Hell. She undoubtedly grew up in one of the Christian orphanages in Nanking, since no respectable Chinese family would harbor a half breed.

He rubbed his finger up and down her slit, easing her outer labia gently aside. Her moisture came on, a defensive, automatic response, not necessarily one of arousal. Well, that would be fixed too. When the eunuch was done with her, she would water virtually on command.

For the moment, Wang abandoned his exploration of her quim. He stepped around again to her front, the sounds of the heels of his tall boots echoing off of the damp, shadowy walls. When he was before her once again, he stopped.

"*What is your name, whore?*" he demanded of her.

Her eyes widened as he addressed her. Her deep brown eyes flitted back and forth as if she didn't have the answer to the question and hoped desperately one of the other occupants of her subterranean prison might know it. Seeing only cold, callous faces, she looked back at the general. He was dressed in his well pressed khaki's, not a dress uniform, but one for everyday wear. Gold stars sat on the collar of his jacket. Red stripes ran down the legs of his pants. She would have guessed by now who he was. Had the tales of his depredations been told to her? Did she fear that she had fallen into the clutches of the devil himself? From her frantic look, he would guess yes. She withheld her reply to this perfunctory question as if speaking would make real this horrible nightmare.

Wang grew impatient with her reticence. He turned to his eunuch. "*Give her five blows with the whip,*" he ordered.

Li Pao sprang immediately into action. He had been holding a long, tapered switch in anticipation of just such a command. The long, thin instrument flew like lightening across her pale, enticing breasts.

"Ahhhhhhhhhhhhh!" she screamed. "*Nooooooooooo! I'll tell you! I'll tell you!*"

Another blow landed. This one across her graceful, tapered thighs. "Ahhhhhhhhhhhhhhh!" she screamed again. "*Please! Please! "Don't whip me! Please!*"

Ignoring her pleas, Li Pao gave her another fierce blow and then another and then another, in rapid succession. She danced and swayed and screamed. Long lines of red erupted across her breasts, her thighs, her belly and her tempting rear cheeks. "Ahhhhhhh! Ahhhhhhhhh!" she screeched at each kiss of the leather against her flesh.

"*My name is Xiu! My name is Xiu!*" she called out.

Li Pao had withdrawn and she stood there, her whole body trembling. Sweat was streaming down her torso, making her skin gleam.

"*When I ask you a question, whore, you will answer it immediately. Do you understand?*" Wang told her sternly.

"*Oh, yes! Yes!*" she answered desperately.

"*Do you know who I am?*" he asked her.

"*Yes! Yes!*" she responded pitifully. "*You are General Wang!*"

"*You are now my property by right of conquest. I am your master and you are my slave. Do you understand that?*"

"*Yes! Yes! I'll do anything you say! Please don't whip me! Please!*"

Wang turned to the jailors. "*Get me the flogger,*" he ordered.

"*Oh, no! No! Please! I beg you!*" the woman screamed.

Wang ignored her. Scylla, the fatter of the two heavyset men dashed off and returned with a seven tasseled whip with a short handle. The ends of the tassels were tied in tiny knots that had been soaked in vinegar and hardened. The girl watched the fiendish jailor hand it off to his master.

"Ohhhhhhhh!" she cried out in despair. "*Pleeeeeeease!*" Her voice echoed loudly through the dark dungeon, reverberating against its harsh, stone walls. Her pretty face, distorted by her anguish, reddened by the strain of screaming her futile supplications, was awash with tears.

"*Gag her,*" Wang commanded. The other jailer, Charybdis, jumped to obey. The implements of subjugation were never far away in General Wang's dungeon and he produced a thick leather prong affixed to a wide belt. He stepped forward, took hold of the woman's cheeks and pressed them hard, forcing her lips ajar. Her moan of dismay was cut off as he jammed the thick plug home. In a trice he had it belted behind her head.

General Wang swung the tasseled whip back and forth a few times in gentle arcs, to make sure that the strands were all loose and not caked up with blood from past use. He stepped up to the distraught Eurasian whore and let the long strands of leather run across her body, over her shimmering, sweat covered breasts, over her pleasantly plump belly, along the inside of her distended thighs.

The girl shivered and convulsed with fear as the rough surface of the tassels scoured her body. Her eyes were wide with terror. Undoubtedly she rued her lighthearted acceptance of the invitation to accompany her lover and patron on his jaunt. What had been billed as a pleasant holiday had turned into a horrific drama. Life would surely never be the same after today.

Satisfied that the girl's fear had risen to mindless terror, Wang stepped back. He addressed the girl.

"*Each time my whip strikes your body,*" he said, his voice ominous and powerful, "*I want you to etch deeply into your mind who it is you now serve. Your sluttish nature has led to your doom. You are nothing but an owned whore now. You will fuck me and those whom I shall grant permission to use you as if your very life depended on the pleasure received by those using you. You will be whipped for the slightest shortcoming. And when you cease being a thing of pleasure, I will have you brought back here to my dungeon and strangled.*"

The girl uttered a long, low, plaintive moan. Her body started to shake. As she saw the general's arm rear back in preparation for delivering a fierce, cruel blow, she screamed.

Wang delivered the first cut from the whip across her delectable belly. The girl's body tensed and she screamed again through her gag, the unintelligible sounds filling the dark room. He struck her breasts. They shuddered from the impact and bright red trails appeared across them. He struck her back and her rear, each time bringing the whip back so that he could deliver a powerful, flesh tearing stroke.

Blood was trailing down the girl's body from the impact of the hard knotted ends of the whip. Her eyes had rolled back into their sockets and she was moaning and screeching and blubbering and wailing. When Wang struck the insides of her thighs, her body jumped. When he reared back and swung the harsh instrument upwards between them, landing a blow directly upon her soft, exposed pudenda, she screeched even louder than before. He struck her repeatedly, covering the same, tender ground: her breasts, her belly and thighs, her rear and back, and the fragile mound between her thighs, more than once.

The warlord grunted and groaned as he delivered each devastating blow. He was expiating all of the tension and, yes, fear, that had stalked him while he scrambled to prepare his army for the fateful battle. Everything had been staked on the battle's outcome, everything, including the bedeviling flesh of his English concubine. The girl's howls of pain were a delight to his ears, the sound of the world succumbing to his will. Each stroke of the whip was proof of his continued mastery of his fiefdom.

By the time he was done, the girl had lost control of herself. She was slumped in her bonds. The floor was splashed with her urine which had been released during her bout of agony. Her moans had subsided. Trails of blood slithered down her marred flesh.

"*Release her,*" the warlord commanded.

The two jailors jumped forth and unhooked her hands from the chain that held them aloft. She collapsed to the floor, an inert jumble of flesh. The men watched her for a few moments as she sobbed and scrunched her damaged body up into a tight ball.

Wang looked at his eunuch and gave him a nod.

Li Pao stepped forward. "*Up!*" he yelled at the girl. "*Up on knees!*" He was dressed in his standard silver and blue sheath, a round cap of identical design upon his head. He was tall and thin, but very strong. He ran all of the general's affairs, including enforcing obedience in his whores.

The girl didn't move. Li's arm moved forward in a flash. He still had the long, thin whip in his hand. It made a loud 'crack!' as it struck her red lined rear. The girl's body jumped and she let out a howl. "*Up! Up! Up!*" Li screamed at her. She gave the eunuch a terrified look and scrambled to her knees.

Scylla and Charibdis leaped at her, one connecting her arms behind her back, the other removing the gag which had suppressed her woeful screams and sobs as she was whipped. When she was ready, the men stepped back. The general had released his stiffened manhood from his pants and he moved in front of the girl, about a foot away. He held his long, fat cock out, pointed at the girl like a weapon.

The girl immediately deduced what she was to do. Tears flowing down her face, she shifted herself forward on her knees until her face was inches from her new lord and master's rampant prick. Without hesitation, she subsumed it into her mouth.

As a Eurasian girl, there were few paths open for Xiu when she was turned out of the orphanage at 16, four years ago. Without family or friends, destitute, starving, she had sold herself to a man in exchange for a meal. She was still intact when she was delivered to one of the premier whorehouses in Nanking, although he had used her other orifices many times for several days. She had been trained in the exquisite arts of pleasing a man and her maidenhood was auctioned off to the highest bidder.

A little over a year ago, the Kuomintang general had purchased her contract from her brothel and set her up in a finely furnished, luxurious apartment as his mistress. She had wanted for nothing, was doted on by obsequious servants, had been clothed in the most resplendent finery. When her lover had insisted that she accompany him on what was supposed to be a frolic and lark, she had no choice really but to agree. She had heard the sounds of the fighting as she took her morning bath, but had thought nothing of it. She had just emerged, adorning herself with her silk robe, when the soldiers appeared in her tent.

An accomplished cocksucker, she was bringing all of her skills to bear on her new master's cock.

Wang sighed as the girl's tongue and lips enflamed him. He let his hands flow over the black, silky hair that covered her head. When she nibbled at the tip of his cock, he moaned. When her lips descended the length of his rock hard crank to its base, he inhaled deeply.

The only sounds were of the girl's slurps and moans and occasional sobs as she serviced Wang's prick. Two of the men looked on with anxious anticipation. She would surely have a lengthy sojourn in their subterranean world. That mouth and that tongue would dance on their cocks too, probably within the half hour.

The third man, the eunuch, was disinterested sexually in the girl, but admired her form and energy. She would be under his tutelage for a week or so and he would teach her the rudiments of true obedience. For him, it would be pleasant. For her, it would be strictly otherwise.

Wang's need was coming upon him. The girl's skillful mouth was delivering wave after wave of delightful pleasure to him. He felt his balls tighten and the tell tale tingling that signaled the imminence of his eruption. He could go on for much longer, but the whipping of the girl had been exciting and he desired completion.

Taking hold of the girl's coal black hair, he took command. He pulled her head back and forth at a forceful pace. He thrust his cock's tip deep into her throat each time, causing the girl to gag and squeal. Again and again, he fucked her mouth, thrusting his hips forward each time he brought her lips into contact with his belly. Finally, he could stand no more and his cock began to jet its thick, white goo in tumultuous spasms. He groaned and forced his cock deep into the girl's throat, holding her head there as his prick danced. She emitted muffled sobs and moans as her airway was blocked. Her bound hands writhed frantically behind her.

The warlord released a long, loud groan as he felt his orgasm begin to wane. The gurgling and coughing of the slut at his feet brought him back to consciousness of his surroundings. He drew her head back slowly, making sure that she kept a tight circle of her lips against his pole as it retreated, as any good whore would. Despite her frantic need for air, she performed ably.

That was seven days ago. He had penetrated her other two gates of pleasure in his bedroom at his leisure many times since then, in addition to his use of her well trained mouth. He had whipped her first each time. She was a skillful whore. After the parade, she would be delivered to his premier brothel in Yeuyang. The wealthy men of the town would line up to use her.

* * * * * * * * * * * * * * *

Now, seven days later, General Wang was standing high on a dais watching the parade and saluting his troops as they passed. It was taking place in the middle of his port city, Yueyang. Sitting on either side of him, on daises slightly lower than his, were the town dignitaries. On the level below him sat his two wives, reveling in the limelight. Kneeling on soft, plump cushions at their feet were the warlord's four concubines, all dressed in finery. Violet was, of course, among them.

She and her sister sex slaves had been escorted to the town by a squad of Wang's soldiers. They had been mounted in a brightly decorated ox-cart and driven down to the town earlier that day. It was quite a surprise to all of them. None of them had ever been out of the fortress since their embondment to the general. It was unprecedented. But their excursion was not meant to convey to them any loosening of the constraints under which they lived. They were accompanied by four of the dour, gray haired chaperones who were their constant companions and guardians. Beneath their bright, colorful silk sheaths, they wore chains connecting their ankles. Their hands had been bound to their waists by silken cords. And opium laced leather balls had been forced into their mouths to keep them docile and obedient. After all, their presence at the festivities was not for their benefit. They were, more or less, decoration to add to the general's glory. Their beauty and comeliness was just one more tribute to the general's greatness.

Violet knelt on her cushion, lazily watching the soldiers pass in review. She was rocking her hips back and forth unconsciously, setting in motion the small steel balls lodged in her crevasse. The eunuch had given all four of the women a fresh dose of opiate just as the parade was about to start and her mind was swimming.

Today was the first she had seen the warlord, her owner and master, since the day of the battle. After they had exhausted themselves in each other's arms, they lay together entwined for the rest of the afternoon. The warlord had fallen fast asleep. He had gotten little rest in the four days between his dramatic flight back from Shanghai and none in the previous 48 hours. Watching him sleep, the first time in her more than two year captivity she had done so, filled her with a kind of bitter sweetness. He was still covered in the blood of his own wound and the wounds of the men he had slaughtered. He seemed so much less the mighty warrior, the despotic ruler of over 350,000 souls, than a solitary man. In his desperate, frantic need to couple with her, she saw a side of him he had never dared reveal. All that he was, all that he had worked to build over the last twenty years was at stake in the battle. And she, she came to understand, was the living symbol of all that.

When he awoke, Violet called for her maids to bring soap and water so that he could be cleansed before showing himself to the world once again. She had bathed him tenderly, wiping away the traces of blood from his firm, manly body. Ting, one of her maids, brought some tea for him to drink.

All the while she was wiping away the traces of mud and blood that covered him, he said nothing. Li Pao, the eunuch had arranged for a clean uniform to be brought to him, and he donned it silently. When he was done, he ordered the maids out of the room. He turned to her and, taking hold of the sides of her head, gave her a deep, passionate, soulful kiss that left her gasping for air. When their lips broke apart, he laid her back down on the bed, had her spread her legs, and, after reinserting the ben wa balls into her crevasse, gently restored the steel lacings that bound her love lips together and fixed them in place by the closing of the glimmering, gold embossed lock that denoted her crevasse as his property. Then, without a word, he left.

Violet knew that something had passed between them during their frenetic coupling. He had revealed a human side of himself to her. Later that night, as she lay in bed, her ankles and wrists confined by chains as was now customary for her, she wondered what their moments of intimacy portended. She was still clearly his property. He had reasserted that relationship when he had rebound up her slit. Would he treat her differently now, confirming her humanity as she had confirmed his? Or would he retreat into his shell once more and continue his callous treatment of her?

The questions remained. He had used his other concubines during the last week, Iris, the beautiful, blond daughter of American missionaries he had purchased on one of his quarterly trips to Shanghai about six months ago, and the delicate Shu and her tigress of a sister, Hu, one or more of them every night. But he had not called for her. Did he rue the exposure of his vulnerability? Would he get rid of her, sell her on, rather than face her again? Violet knew that as harsh as life in the warlord's seraglio was, life elsewhere could be much harsher. Like the warlord's peasantry, she preferred the devil she knew to a new, strange and perhaps crueler one.

But it was more than that. The warlord had demonstrated his need for her. Was that the harbinger of love? Was the callous man capable of such an emotion? Violet realized that her chances at love in life had been dramatically reduced by her conversion to a whore, for that's what she really was, the general's whore. Even if she somehow won her freedom, no decent man would ever have any part of her, certainly no one of her class. To any subsequent owner, she would be used goods, suitable only for a brothel.

Two years was a long time to be a slave. Her life was sometimes harsh, but she had resigned herself to her fate. But if the general had fallen in love with her, wouldn't that mean that he would keep her? Would he treat her with respect? Could she love him in return?

He was up on the dais above and behind her. She could not see him, but she felt his presence. Had he taken notice of her? Was his reticence to use her a product of his uncertainty as to how to proceed with her now? Should she give him some kind of sign that she was ready to accept him, not as a master, but as a lover?

Below her, standing in rows, was the household staff, the maids, the male servants, even the cooks. Violet realized that her future relations with the general depended to a large degree on how it would be interpreted by them and all of his other subjects. She was British after all. Part of the joy the warlord had found in her ownership, she was certain, was based on that, a thumb in the eye of the great British Empire which had treated China so harshly. The people would understand that as well. And as she looked around at the happy, celebratory crowd, she realized that from here on in, "the people" would play a greater and greater role in how the warlord governed.

Wang was thinking the same thing as he watched the crowd cheer on his troops. And if there was doubt that his victory over the Kuomintang forces betokened a shift in his relationship with the people, that would be dispelled very shortly.

The wagon carrying the forlorn whore captured from the enemy general was not the last portion of the parade. Following her was a column of factory workers, mostly from the textile plants that would now be benefiting from the electricity he had brought to them. After them was a delegation from the shipping owners, its sailors and captains, then a delegation of miners from the coal fields he had taken under his wing last year. After them came a gay troop of children from the French orphanage and from the schools he had established under his eunuch's guidance. Then there was a column of peasant farmers, their hoes held on their shoulders like weapons. At the end was a troop of what would be his permanent construction brigade, primarily made up of the Kuomintang prisoners, organized by Li Pao.

All of the marchers, and much of the crowd, had been issued bright yellow pennants on which had been embroidered a red fire breathing dragon. Yellow and red ribbons were affixed in the hair of the children and of the women. Near the reviewing stand was a large banner proclaiming the victory of the 'nation' with the red dragon symbol beneath the slogan. Another banner proclaimed the wisdom and glory of their great leader and father, General Wang Ku.

A vast square had been cleared for the parade. Li Pao had arranged for the tearing down of sufficient structures in the town to accomplish this, suitably compensating the owners. The parade marchers, once they passed the reviewing stands, made a long circuit around the field, taking up positions all around it. When the last delegation had passed and were ensconced on the warlord's left, the parade came to a halt.

Li Pao had arranged for all the musicians that could be found to be combined into one large orchestra. They had been playing merrily, if somewhat inartfully, while the marchers had passed. Now they issued forth a loud fanfare. The crowd, there must have been more than five thousand of them, dimmed into silence.

The eunuch had arranged for the orchestra to play a popular folk song entitled, "May the Gods Bring Happiness and Prosperity to Our Village." He had had one of the local poets write new words to the tune and had distributed copies of it to all the marchers and amongst the crowd.

Wang stood as did all of the other dignitaries, including his wives and concubines. He waited until all eyes were on him and then he walked slowly down the steps of the dais until he reached the ground. He was bedecked in his best dress uniform, a bright, forest green with a red stripe down the legs of his pants. Glittery gold braid was sewn on his shoulders and on his officer's cap. On his chest he wore a suitable congress of bright, sparkly medals.

He walked slowly and with dignity to the middle of the parade grounds. There, in the center, was a tall flagpole that had been implanted the day before. Wang stood by it and came to attention. From the crowd emerged three people, a worker, a farmer and a child. Between them, they were carrying a large yellow and red cloth. When they reached the general, they stopped and bowed.

Wang took the end of the cloth and affixed it to the lanyard of the flagpole. When that was done, he slowly pulled on the rope, raising the cloth up towards the sky. As it rose, it began to unfold. It was the red dragon on a bright field of yellow. Above the dragon were stitched the ideograms for strength, prosperity and happiness.

When the flag reached the top, it began to flutter majestically in the breeze. Wang came to attention and saluted it. All of his soldiers presented arms. The civilian marchers placed their right hands over their hearts. And then the orchestra began to play. The marchers began to sing:

> *"From the rising to the setting sun*
> *The land brings us happiness and wealth.*
> *From the morning to night, our leader brings us*
> *peace and freedom.*
> *All the people rejoice for the benefits they bring*
> *us.*
> *May the gods and our leader bring happiness*
> *and prosperity to our nation."*

The voices were tentative and somewhat faint at first. The orchestra began discordantly but quickly came together and their music resounded over the square. As the music rose in volume and confidence, the voices of the crowd did as well. By the time the song got to the last line of the first verse, an immense swell of voices filled the air. There were three verses, the last line of which all ended with the imploring of the gods and General Wang for prosperity and happiness for the nation. The voices and music rose each time it was sung.

When the music ended, there was a momentary hush of silence throughout the crowd. A lone voice screamed out, *"Long live General Wang!"* The crowd erupted into a roaring cacophony of cheers. Wang saluted the crowd and marched to the foot of the dais. At a signal from the eunuch, the parade marchers began an orderly and proud exit from the field. As each unit passed, the warlord saluted them.

Li Pao stood proudly by the exit from the square. Now the general could no longer be described as a 'bandit', as the newspapers in Shanghai and Nanking often called him. He was the leader of a nation. A small one, perhaps, but a nation nonetheless. It would not change much from a practical point of view; General Wang would remain its despotic ruler. But it would give pride to the people and signal to the Mandarins in Nanking that their next incursion into Hunan would be met with a general uprising. The people might not fight for their warlord with passion, but they would for their country.

军阀 外家
CHAPTER TWO

That night, as General Wang sat propped up against the headboard of his soft, expansive bed, not a little drunk, he reveled in his new status as 'Father of the Nation'. Three of his concubines were with him. At the foot of the bed, Hu, the black haired tigress, was energetically plowing the love canal of the blond American, Iris. She sported a carved ebony model of her lord's cock affixed to her loins by a leather harness. The room was filled with the sounds of her impassioned grunts.

The American whore was writhing and moaning with pleasure. Her knees were up and spread widely, her beautiful, spun gold hair lay in a corolla around her head. Her face was a masque of delirium.

Hu's more demure sister, Shu, was laying across his lap. He had his hand buried in her quim and she was moaning fitfully as he teased it. He had fucked her already once while Hu had administered strokes of a flogger to the flesh of the American girl, her hands distended above her head and locked in place by a chain. Wang enjoyed watching Hu administer inducement to obedience to his other concubines. He never allowed her to mar them, that was his prerogative. The flogger, a seven tassled whip, did not create wounds, but instead raised a deep red hue upon the victim's flesh. Iris's breasts, belly, thighs and rear cheeks were a bright scarlet before he interrupted Hu's delight. The blond whore cried and sobbed as she received her due, a thrilling accompaniment to his violation of Shu's heavenly gate.

As he watched Hu work over Iris's sopping canal, he thought of the English whore lodged in his seraglio not more than 200' from where he sat. He had watched her today, during the parade, and all through the banquet which had followed it. The eunuch had kept her and her sister whores well plied with opium during the festivities and she had a somewhat vacant mien as her maids spooned bits of delicacy to her mouth. Her hips had been in constant, rhythmic motion, as the steel balls in her crevasse sent her reverberations of pleasure. Her face melted into an impassioned vision when her maid slipped her hand into her dress and caressed her breast. She turned and smiled at her and gave her a small kiss.

The memory of that smile made his heart yearn for her. His body still remembered how she had gently washed it that day after the battle. He was torn between leaving these memories intact or seeking renewed bliss in her arms. But what if it was not the same? It would destroy the ideali-zation of that day's encounter, render foolish his need for union with her. But if that moment could be renewed again and again, that would be bliss indeed! How could he know which it was to be? There was more than a little riding on that question. He had had his love of another cruelly dashed many years ago by a courtesan back in Shanghai in his younger days. Later, when he had come into his power and riches, he had bought her and watched while she was strangled in his dungeon. He knew that if the English-woman made a fool of him he would have no choice but to destroy her. And that was the last thing that he wanted to do. Maybe it was better to admire her from afar and let his memories of that afternoon suffice.

The deep, passionate groan of the American slut drew his attention from his reverie. Her legs were wrapped around the waist of her tormentor and her arms were dragging her body down fiercely into hers. The whores' lips were married and

Hu was pumping her hips furiously against those of the alluring, pale skinned woman's.

Wang felt his cock stir. The whore draped over his lap was panting heavily, her lust upon her. All of the women had been administered a dose of the passion inducing potion that was brewed up by the old witch from his native village before being brought to his room. He, himself, had taken a similar male potion and he knew that he would be capable of at least five explosions of lust tonight.

He pushed the dainty body off of his lap and ordered her to kneel in front of him, her legs spread, her breasts pressed against her thighs. He rubbed his hands along her smooth, curved back and placed himself behind her. Spreading her rear cheeks, he pushed the head of his long, thick cock against her brown tinted rear hole until the well used orifice gave way and he slid inside. Li Pao had all the whores properly greased before being brought to him so that this passage would be receptive to his desires. He groaned as the girl's ring clasped the stem of his cock tightly. She moaned too as the passage of his meat across the tender membranes inflamed her.

Slowly, Wang drew his rampant pole back and forth along the ring of flesh. The moist heat was heavenly. The Chinese girl beneath him moaned and sighed as he used her.

Iris's convulsions had eased and the two women were kissing each other lovingly. Wang issued several sharp commands to the idling duo. Hu quickly drew the harness from around her waist and tossed the faux cock aside. She scrambled over onto her back and, spreading her lithesome legs, slid her loins under her sister's panting lips. Obediently, Shu began to mouth her plush canal.

The still panting American waited until Hu was set and then, facing her master, crossed her leg over Hu's chest. She inched herself back until her pussy was in position over the Chinese girl's hungry mouth. She moaned and her eyes rolled back as the agile tongue began to work on her slit. She was leaning over Shu's back, her hands resting on her shoulder blades. Her impassioned face was within easy reach and Wang took hold of the back of her head and forced it forward until he could plunge his tongue inside her mouth. He groaned, as did she, as their lips clamped together.

A cacophony of grunts and moans arose from the bed as the four copulating figures writhed and thrust and sucked and licked each other into ecstasy. Hu screamed with pleasure as her sister's energetic tongue took her over the top. Iris moaned deeply into Wang's mouth as her pussy throbbed and contracted fiercely. Wang could feel Shu's tight little hole clench against his pole as even she reached a crisis.

He was pumping madly now into her. His juices were rising. He took a firm hold of Iris's blond hair and circled his tongue wildly in her mouth. He groaned, "Arrrrrrrrgh! Arrrrrrrrgh!" as his prick began to pump its seed deep into Shu's welcoming bowel. His body tensed with each exciting throb. His mind short circuited with pleasure.

When his crisis passed and his cock turned once more inert, the four bodies collapsed into a pile. Wang allowed his body to be smothered by the soft, feminine skin of his whores. The air was redolent with the odors of passion.

He rested for a while, savoring his recent pleasure. The women were slowly recovering their senses. He felt a hand circle his detumescing cock. He looked down and saw the devilish face of Hu staring back at him, her tongue washing over her plump, red lips. He rolled to his back. She squirmed free of her sisters and subsumed his manhood into her mouth. She suckled it earnestly and energetically until the blood began to return and he was hard once more. His lust resurrected, Wang ordered Iris and Shu to form a two backed beast, their faces in each other's loins. When they had complied and began to slurp and moan with lust, he pushed Hu off of his cock and turned her around. He crept up behind her, and with the delectable vision before him of the other two whores mouthing each other to pleasure, he mounted her lust canal from behind. Hu gave a great groan of satisfaction and began to thrust back feverishly at his plunging tool.

* * * * * * * * * * * * *

As her master frolicked with his other concubines, Violet indeed sat no more than 200' away from him in her room in the seraglio. She was sitting on a finely carved mahogany stool in front of her ornately decorated dressing mirror. She was not alone. By her side was her maid, Junjin, one of the three maids permanently assigned to be her companions and taskmasters. Junjin, a somewhat stocky, tall, peasant type was the most rigorous of them.

The room was small. Unlike the other bedrooms in the seraglio, which had walls of beautiful, hand painted rice paper, the walls to her bedroom were made of rough plaster painted a garish pink. It was part of her increased security arrangements following the invasion of the seraglio by one of Wang's lieutenants seeking union with her. Their night of passion was paid for by five lives and a severe punishment for Violet. Now, even if someone managed to breach the seraglio's security, they would find it extremely difficult to gain access to the British concubine.

She spent her nights behind a heavy, wooden door bolted and locked from the outside. The key was kept by the eunuch, Li Pao, who returned it to the seraglio every morning so that Violet could be released from her prison within a prison. As additional security, and as part of her continuing punishment, Violet spent every night locked in chains, her wrists and ankles bound together and a chain around her thighs. It was a discomforting arrangement for sleeping purposes, but the concubines rarely did more than loll around the seraglio all day and there was plenty of time for naps if need be.

The room was dimly lit by a single oil lamp set on a bedside table. The only other furniture was the mirrored dressing table at which Violet was sitting and the broad bed. The bed was soft and covered with a light green, satin sheet. There were several large, fluffy pillows covered in silk with colorful designs of pretty flowers. The floor was covered by a soft, maroon rug with oriental designs. Her clothes, the various silken robes that she wore from time to time and the more elegant dresses she was permitted on special occasions, like that of that day's parade, were stored away in a small closet.

Junjing was dressed in her maid's uniform, tight, off white canvas pants and a yellowish green pullover blouse. On her feet were the brown leather sandals that all of the maids wore. She had long black hair bound behind her head. She was, compared to Violet, small of stature, a little over 5'3", a full three inches shorter than her mistress. While plain, her features were pleasant. She was stockier than the other maids, but well within the limits of comeliness. As a maid in General Wang's employ, she was sometimes called to more carnal duties to satisfy him or one of his guests. And she could hardly fulfill her role as lover to her mistress if she were unattractive. This was her fourth year in General Wang's service, having been sold to him by her father when she was just 16. Her contract price went to feed her family and pay back taxes on their small farm. She had served the last two years as one of Violet's maids.

Violet was naked but for the black leather collar that she wore tightly sewn around her neck. It carried gold embossed ideograms denoting her as, 'General Wang's Concubine'. Her sole other adornment was the heavy, glittery steel lock that she carried on her loins. It captured and held fast a flexible, silvery steel cable that was wound through punctures in her outer labia. Imprisoned within her conch were three glittery ben wa balls that brought a tantalizing vibration to her pussy every time she moved. The lock too was embossed with golden ideograms roughly translated as 'Property of General Wang'. But this reference was not so much to her general person, but specifically to the crevasse between her thighs. It was another cones-quence of the seraglio invasion and another bar to her violation by any interlopers. It also served as a very dramatic reminder to its wearer of the warlord's mastery over her and her lack of rights as it pertained to her person.

As General Wang's concubine, Violet's life was organized to be focused entirely and solely on her lord's pleasure. She was, as were her sister concubines, treated much in the manner of a prized pet, or, perhaps, a delicate plant to be tended and pruned. None of the daily tasks normally associated with life were to be left to her. She was not allowed to feed herself, dress herself, bathe herself. Even her most personal functions were less of her concern than her ubiquitous maids', Wen, Ting and Junjing.

And never was a concubine permitted any solitary time. One or more of her maids was ever present, ready to serve her or, if she broke any of the myriad and complicated rules that governed her life, to betray her to her ultimate supervisors, the warlord's harsh eunuch, Li Pao, or one of the elderly chaperones that shared the seraglio with her and her sisters in bondage. A fierce punishment usually ensued.

But in spite of the maids' roles as informer and enforcer of the concubines' strict regimen, there formed a bond between them and their charges as strong and as loving as any more pedestrian relationship. Violet had come to love her maids, the child like Wen, Ting, the slender, sensitive one, and even Junjing, the most business like among them. They shared her moods, comforted her when she was beaten, even if their own acts of betrayal had brought it on, laughed and joked with her and made love to her often, making sure that she remained a finely honed sexual instrument.

It was Violet's bedtime, near midnight. Junjing was preparing her mistress for the night. There had been no need to undress her since, Zhu, the head chaperone, a cruel and haughty figure who dominated the seraglio like a rabid mother superior, demanding abject and complete obedience to her dictates, had ruled that the concubines must spend their days naked to encourage their sexual use of each other and to remind them that their charms were not theirs to hide. But there was makeup to remove, hair to be brushed, personal needs to be seen to. One of those needs was distressing Violet very much.

It was the practice that one of the concubines be kept in milk at all times for the enjoyment of the warlord and as a supplement to his diet. Usually, the obligation to produce the highly nourishing, semi sweet substance was rotated between his sex slaves. The duty was usually shifted whenever General Wang took his quarterly trips to Shanghai. The eunuch would, assisted by a potion concocted by the resident herbalist and potion producer, urge the new candidate into production by thrice daily massages of their mounds and suckling at their teats. For the last three months, Violet had done duty as the warlord's nursemaid. Every morning she was brought to the general's breakfast table where he would drain her breasts usually while stroking her to orgasm. Afterwards, he would order her to her knees to bring him off with her mouth, usually his first discharge of the day.

The Kuomintang's campaign to subdue Hunan Province for the national government had begun just as Wang had commenced one of his quarterly trips to Shanghai. It was planned that Iris would take her turn as the general's milk cow next and that she would be in full production when he returned. The trip to Shanghai was abruptly truncated, and for the better part of a week, the seraglio was on a war footing, all of its regular routines disrupted. Iris was never brought into milk; the eunuch had been too busy for that. Violet's maids were ordered to make sure that she remained in production, either draining her life giving essence themselves or ensuring that it was done by one of the other concubines.

Since the general had deigned to ignore Violet for the time being, she was not brought to his table each morning. One of the other concubines usually relieved her breasts' aching need in the morning instead, prefatory to a bout of sexual intimacy. In the afternoons and the evenings it was either another of the concubines or one of the maids. The last feeding was usually around midnight, just prior to bedtime, if the warlord had not called her to his bed. If he had, he often supped at her breasts before fucking her or sent her back to the seraglio after his use of her to be drained by one of her maids.

Tonight, like the last seven nights, and for the five nights during which the warlord was preparing his battle plans for his confrontation with the Kuomintang, she had not been called to him. Since he had demanded service from his three other sex slaves this evening, it was up to Junjing to alleviate her suffering.

She was most talkative tonight. She had prattling on about the parade.

"*Didn't the master look wonderful today, mistress?*" she asked while brushing Violet's long, shiny, brown hair. "*All the women were looking at him with desire in their eyes. And they looked at you too. I watched them. I am sure that many of them wish they could be in your shoes. It's not everybody who has such a glorious master.*"

Violet just gave out a little noncommittal hum by way of answer.

"*And the soldiers all looked so smart and handsome. Some day I hope to marry one of them. There's a corporal who teases me every time he sees me. My contract with the master is up a year from now. I'm hoping he will give me to one of his soldiers for a wife. I know I will make him very happy.*" Although slavery was formally outlawed in China since the fall of the Ming Dynasty, women were often kept in bondage through the fiction of 'contracts'. Their status was of little more than property anyway and many times they found themselves sold to brothels, or as in Junjing's case, as 'maids', by their families or by men who had kidnapped them. Often, when a contract expired, the woman was forced to sign a new one under duress if she was still desirable.

Violet was staring into the mirror watching the somewhat plain Chinese young woman perform her task. The strokes of the brush were comforting. *"Yes, little one,"* Violet replied laconically to Junjing's speculations, *"I hope so too."*

"But then I will not be with you, mistress, and that will make me very sad. Maybe I'll beg the master to let me stay. "

"No, Junjing," Violet rejoined. *"You should marry and have a family."*

It had been one of Violet's hopes when she had agreed to come to Shanghai and marry one of its successful businessmen, Robert Preston, to have a family, the same Robert Preston who betrayed her into slavery The fact that she would almost certainly never have one now was one of the bitterest aspects of her captivity.

"Well, we will see, mistress," Junjing continued. *"Until then, I will serve you well. You are the prettiest of all the master's concubines."*

"No, Junjing," Violet contradicted, *"the others are all much prettier."*

"I don't think so, mistress, and I don't think that the master thinks so either. I saw him looking at you today. He couldn't keep his eyes off of you."

Violet knew that it was part of Junjing's job to make her feel good and so didn't mind her lies. She knew too that it was a source of pride for her maids to have her be desired by their common owner. They were all very upset that he had not called for her for over a week.

"I'm sure that he will have you serve him tomorrow morning, mistress," Junjing continued. She paused in her ministrations to Violet's hair to sneak her hand around her chest and take hold of one of her milk filled breasts and give it a gentle squeeze. A few small drops of white liquid drained out of it, dribbling down Violet's belly. *"He loves to drink your milk, mistress. You'll see. Tomorrow he will call for you. I'm sure of it."* Junjing touched her finger to Violet's oozing nipple, taking up a small droplet and brought it to her mouth. "Mmmmmmmmmmm," she hummed. *"Your milk is so sweet, mistress. I don't think our master will be able to forgo it for much longer."*

Violet didn't reply. Serving the warlord the produce of her body was not high on her list of preferred activities. Now, her sister concubines was another matter. If she had developed a strong bond with her maids, her bonds with her fellow prisoners was much stronger. Especially Iris, the young American who had joined them a little more than six months ago. Although the speaking of English was for-bidden, Iris, the daughter of American missionaries, had lived in China all of her life and spoke Chinese like a native. Violet had learned to speak a pigeon form of the language over the two years she had been General Wang's slave, but learning it from people who knew no English was very difficult. Iris had an innate sense of the differences in the two languages and had already helped Violet progress a great deal, sometimes whispering to her the English translation. She learned more about tenses and syntax and the many colloquial sayings.

Sexual intimacy between the concubines was expected and even mandated. Their lives were served in a virtually perpetual sexual haze. Each morning and at regular intervals throughout the day, they were fed a potion that heightened their physical desires. They made love to each other out in the open, in the common room of the seraglio, with all the other women watching. Their sexuality was intended to be blatant rather than demure. And they spent almost all of their waking hours together, locked in isolation from the world, leaving the seraglio only for their daily baths or to perform their sexual duties for their master or, at his direction, for his guests.

This enforced intimacy and their shared experiences made them closer than sisters, closer than lovers often were. They knew every inch of each others' bodies, the inner core of each others' personalities.

But none of her sisters were around to ease the pressure on Violet's teats this night. It would be Junjing's task. Violet was hoping that she would quickly finish brushing her hair and relieve her of the dull ache in her breasts. Junjing's caress of her breast had made her emit a slight moan. The act of nursing had become so intertwined with her other sexual activities that it was hard to separate them. She knew that Junjing's emptying of her breasts would undoubtedly be accompanied by a trip up the mountain of arousal. When Junjing touched the end of her sensitive teat, she shivered and pressed her thighs tightly together.

The dutiful maid made note of her mistress's response and her need. Junjing delicately placed the brush on the table and pressed her front up against her mistress' back. She reached around her torso and took a light hold of her breasts from underneath them, lifting them gently from Violet's chest, giving them a slight squeeze while her lips caressed her in the nape of her neck.

"Mmmmmmmmmmmm, *my beautiful mistress*," she cooed. "*Touching you makes my heart beat stronger and my pussy hot. It's time for bed now and I'm going to suckle you and make you come.*"

Violet watched in the mirror as the girl's dainty hands encircled her full, heavy breasts. She saw her own lips part with incipient passion and her teats stiffen. The maid's promise of delight made her quiver with expectation. She took hold of her hands and brought them to her lips, kissing them tenderly.

"*I love you, Junjing,*" she said, her voice low and throaty. She could feel the young girl's breasts pressing against her back and her heat coming through her clothes.

"*I love you too, mistress,*" Junjing replied. "*Come to bed with me now.*"

Violet rose from her perch and obediently stepped over to the inviting bed where she laid across it. She watched as her servant stripped herself of her clothes, revealing her vibrant, youthful body. Along with her comparatively thicker frame came an asset of large, soft round breasts, somewhat unusual for a Chinese girl. They swayed and jumped as Junjing drew down her pants and pulled them over her legs. Violet's passion was already rising, not that it had ever been far beneath the surface. She and her sister concubines had been given a dose of the lust driving potion a little after eight o'clock and its effects were still with her.

Having relieved herself of her habiliment, the delicious looking young maid crawled up onto the bed where her mistress was waiting for her. They joined arms and matched their lips, giving each other a strong, impassioned kiss. Junjing squirreled herself along Violet's side, facing her, and while they kissed her hand floated over the skin of her torso, over her hip and then down her thigh. Violet, who had turned to her right side when her maid joined her, moaned at the contact. She used her left hand to caress the shiny, black hair of her lover and moved closer to her so that their breasts were pressing against each other's. Junjing moaned now too, her tone somewhat higher than the older, taller woman's.

They kissed for several minutes, their tongues dancing, their lips firmly pressed together. Junjing's hand slithered across Violet's lower belly and then moved between her legs, urging her long, tapered thighs slightly apart. Her fingers danced over her imprisoned love lips, lifted the heavy lock and then stroked the clean shaven surface. Violet's moan became a groan as the sensation of the delicate handling of her sex sent vibrations through her.

Hearing the unmistakable sounds of her mistress's arousal, Junjing eased their chests apart and then slid her body down. Instinctually, Violet lowered herself, turning her outer shoulder inwards, and presented her aching, loaded breast to the young girl's lips.

At first, Junjing gave the stiffened teat that Violet proffered her a light, delicate kiss. She circled the nipple with her tongue, washing the wide, smooth areaola. Violet's hand circled the back of her head, urging her on. Junjing opened her mouth and subsumed the already leaking nipple.

Violet gave out a long, deep sigh as she felt the hot lips encompass her. Within a few seconds the suckling mouth brought on her flow. She closed her eyes and reveled in the sensations of the fluid escaping from her breast. Her body became suffused with warmth and her mind became clouded with a soul encompassing pleasure.

As she worked Violet's engorged breast, Junjing kept a light stroke over her pudenda, over her belly and along her inner thighs. Violet had one leg propped up to give her lover full access to her most sensitive parts. As her passions rose, she brought the head that was suckling her closer in, gripping it tightly.

The sounds of Junjing's feeding, her slurps, her sighs of pleasure were the only sounds in the small room. Her loving attentions had turned Violet's prison cell, temporarily, into an island of harmony and love. As the first breast began to empty, Junjing took her hand and circled it, squeezing it gently to encourage its flow. When she had it fully drained, she nestled her head downwards, seeking its mate. Violet shifted, making her still full breast available. When the lips of her lover took hold of her other teat, she gave out another, long, satisfied moan.

Junjing quickly consumed the semisweet liquid that jetted though Violet's nipple at each pleasurable suck. Her finger had snuck inside the little gap at the top of Violet's bound nether lips and was circling and caressing the stiffened bud she found there. Violet moaned when she slipped her finger further through the narrow gap and caressed the slick ceiling of her canal, finding the spot where its sensitivity was the highest.

Overwhelmed with excitement, Violet moved so that she was hovering above the young woman, her legs outside of hers, her thighs rubbing against her hips. Violet's sexual organs had been rendered especially and dramatically more sensitive through the skills of a eunuch who had once been what was generally referred to as the Emperor's love master, servicing and rendering sexually voracious his bevy of concubines. It was a skill that had been handed down from master to master for over a thousand years and the art had been perfected. Through repeated, skillful manipulations and administration of special salves and potions, the nerve endings in her canal and around it, as well as the tips of her breasts and the tissue surrounding her rear entrance, had been rendered highly excitable. A caress or a kiss of these parts was enough to send Violet into a quickly rising heat. The stroke of a rigid cock along the walls and lips of her sexual tunnel or through the dainty star of her nether parts drove her into oblivion.

Junjing's suckling of her teats, her caresses of her pudenda and breach of the gap at the top of her love lips had the usual effect on the English concubine. Her breath was coming heavy and her loins were energized. She groaned as her passions rose inexorably. The hollow, gel filled balls in her crevasse bumped together and shifted back and forth as she rotated her hips. She clung fiercely to the head at her bosom.

When the breast was emptied, Junjing moved up to capture her mistress's lips with her own. She gently urged Violet to her back and crawled on top of her. She had begun to slide down Violet's torso, her tongue working actively on her taut, burning skin, when Violet took hold of her arm. "*You too,*" she murmured. Obediently, her own fires rising, Junjing swung her thigh over her mistress's chest and faced towards her loins. As she lowered her lips to Violet's pussy, she felt Violet's lips and tongue take possession of her own already engorged and lubricated love organ

Junjing moaned with delight as Violet's tongue and lips paid obeisance to her pussy. She had slipped her tongue through the gap at the top of Violet's and she was lathering the velvet passage as she suckled on the stiff nub of pleasure at its apex. The women groaned and their hips writhed, their hands gripped firmly onto each other's flesh. Violet came first and she let out a scream of passion as the convulsions of her cunt sent wave after wave of ecstasy through her. Her knees were spread open as far as they would go and she gripped the thighs of her lover as if fearful of being cast off of the bed. Her orgasm had lowered itself to a mesmerizing hum when Junjing's crisis came upon her. Her wail of pleasure, the tensing of her body, her hips thrust against Violet's mouth sent the English concubine's pussy into another round of heavy, delirious contractions.

The women were laying there together trying to recover their sensibilities when one of the grey haired chaperones came by. It was Chun, a heavyset, abrasive woman who took her lead on the way to treat the warlord's concubines from her mistress, Zhu, the head chaperone. Her hair was pulled up behind her head in a bun and she was wearing the dour, bluish grey kimono which was the standard uniform for the chaperones. Her face was wrinkled and she had steely, grey eyes. She looked into the room and saw the women lying face to foot on the bed breathing deeply.

"*Get up! Get up!*" she shouted loudly in a deep, rough voice. "*No more fucking today! Get ready for bed or there will be the whip!*"

Just as she spoke, the midnight gong sounded, the signal for all concubines not otherwise engaged with the master to go to bed. "*Did you hear that? It's time for bed! Get up!*"

Since Chun was the major domo of the seraglio for the night, she was carrying the fierce, flexible but hard, three foot long whippy stick that was the primary means of discipline in their hermetic world. She swung it now through the air, landing a fierce blow on the edge of the bed. "*The next one is across your backs!*" she snarled. "*Get up!*"

Junjing and Violet were scrambling to obey her command. Junjing leapt from the bed and began to dress. Violet sat up and began to arrange her large, fluffy pillows for the night. Seeing that her command was being obeyed, Chun walked off. She would be back in a few minutes to check the locks on Violet's chains, taking the key with her when she locked them both in for the night.

Junjing dressed quickly and stepped over to the bamboo box that contained the chains. She shook them out and returned to the bed.

Violet needed no instruction for this, the worse part of her nightly ritual. She rolled to her belly and placed her arms behind her back. Junjing had them cuffed and joined in a trice. Violet then brought together her ankles and raised them while Junjing affixed the shiny, steel shackles and connected them. The dutiful maid then connected Violet's ankles to her wrists with a two foot long chain, short enough so that Violet could not fully extend in the bed, but long enough to avoid extreme discomfort. When the lock clicked closed, Violet obediently rolled to her side, facing her maid. Junjing wrapped a leather strap that went around and between her mistress's thighs. She pulled it tight, forcing the thighs together and then locked it in place.

She was done not a moment too soon, for Chun appeared back at the door. She came into the room and placed her hands on Violet's bindings, making sure that they were all locked and secure. When she was done, she took the key which fit all the locks from Junjing, who gave her a bow of respect. Chun merely grunted and stepped from the room. Without comment, she swung the heavy wooden door closed behind her. It made a solid 'thud' as it closed. Violet and Junjing both looked at it as they heard the sound of the key turning the thick bolt that secured it. After that, there was silence.

The other concubines spent the night bound too, but their bindings were of soft, white, silken cords. No one wanted concubines wandering around the seraglio at night. Junjing grieved for the harsh treatment her mistress received. She had been trying to think of ways to speak to the eunuch to get him to soften her nighttime conditions. She had not yet found the courage. The difference between her and the eunuch in social status was akin to a man and a dog. She knew of maids who had received whippings for talking out of turn with Li Pao. No matter how much she loved her mistress, she didn't want to get whipped for her if she could help it.

Violet snuggled on her side against the soft pillows, trying not to let her sorrowful emotions at her treatment rise up. It did no good and made her nights stressful. She pulled lightly at the chain connecting her wrists and ankles, more out of habit than anything, and writhed her hands. She knew that they were going nowhere, but the response to being confined was almost automatic.

Junjing went to the bedside table and lowered the lamp so that only a very dim light shone in the room. She then leaned over and kissed her mistress. "*Good night, mistress,*" she said softly. "*And don't worry. Tomorrow the master will call for you. I'm sure of it.*"

She retreated to the stool Violet had been sitting on earlier and lowered herself onto it. She would watch over the concubine throughout the night. Within a few minutes, Violet was fast asleep.

军阀 外家
CHAPTER THREE

Violet, as usual, slept fitfully through the night. Often, while awaiting sleep to reclaim her, she thought of her strange fate. This night was no different. It was made particularly disturbing due to the uncertainty of her relationship with her master and owner, General Wang. Not that it was really a relationship. Or at least so she had thought. She had conceived his view of her as no more than a fuck animal. The urgency with which thy coupled a week ago, the day of the battle, had revealed to her otherwise. She imagined what it had cost the callous man to expose his vulnerability to her and understood why he now hesitated to call her to him. What would it be like? Did she dare show some recognition of his passion for her? She knew that it would be risking his wrath, now that life in his little kingdom had returned to normal.

He was like that creature of Greek myth that Jason fought, who regained his strength every time he touched the ground. Now that he was again sure of his throne, all of his weaknesses were concealed, his vulnerability dissipated. He might whip her just to prove to her that their afternoon of love, if that's what it was, was over and their relationship as master and slave restored. Zhu, the head chaperone, often threatened Violet with the prospect of sending her over to the general's whorehouse to be fucked by twenty men a day. Perhaps that would be her fate so she would be where he could see and measure her daily suffering, and still make use of her when the whim struck him.

Or would love flower between them? It was hard to see how such a relationship would fit in with his very carnal appetites. One thing was for sure was that it would not involve any sexual fidelity. It was difficult to imagine him giving up his two wives and his three other sex slaves, not to mention the maids he fucked as the whim struck him, or the whores who serviced him at his bordello. No, their relationship would not be a conventional, Western one. But might he give her just a little more freedom?

Already he had gifted her a piano, something she had dreadfully missed in her two years of embondment. She rather thought though, that it was the eunuch's idea and he had gone along with it. Nonetheless, he had approved it and she was supremely glad that he had. She spent every day since it had been presented to her playing for an hour and a half or more, alone in the general's salon on the second floor of the castle, one floor below the seraglio. Alone that is, except for the chaperone who accompanied her there, Yanyu, the same one who had taught her to play the liuqin, the Chinese mandolin, and to sing the beautiful songs with the words she barely understood. The chaperone sat and smiled as Violet played this piece or that, from Mozart to Bach to Chopin and more. She remembered some of the shorter pieces from her prior life, and there had been a treasure trove of music under the piano seat when she had looked there. There were even some popular numbers that she was able to play for the amusement of the sole member of her audience.

Having the piano was a godsend, but her heart yearned for more. Many times she had spent kneeling on a large, comfortable cushion in the warlord's library while he read from his rather extensive collection. She had seen volumes of Dickens, Austin, Thackeray, Brönte and many others. There were some American authors, Poe, Melville, Hawthorne, Whitman and Emerson. He even received two month old editions of Vanity Fair magazine. She would watch him read them jealously, knowing that an unwarranted intrusion into his attention was a punishable offense. The only recognition she received that she was even there was when he tired of his reading and wanted a nice relaxing orgasm. She would dutifully kneel between his legs and mouth him off or kneel over her cushion, her thighs tightly together while he penetrated her small rear opening from behind. When he was done with her, she would be sent back to the seraglio without comment or thanks.

And then there were the Chinese editions. She very much wanted to learn to read and write Chinese and to read the editions of poetry, philosophy and history she knew were there. It was odd to have lived in China for so long, and among the Chinese at that, and to have learned so little about the country and its inhabitants. She had learned about the various holidays and certain of their religious ceremonies from her many, prolonged conver-sations with her Chinese sister concubines, but not the heart of China itself. The seraglio might just as well be on another planet or in another dimension, that's how isolated it was.

The only real contact with the outside world she had was when her former fiancé, Robert, Lord Preston now, came to visit his partner in the opium business three or four times a year. When he was here she was always assigned to him for a few days and, between his violations of her body, he would taunt her with details of his resplendent life back in Shanghai with his beautiful, young, wealthy wife. For some reason she found hard to fathom, he believed that she had betrayed him, not the other way around. Yes, she had broken off their engagement, but only after finding him ensconced with a whore in what was to have been their marital home. No respectable woman would have done otherwise. And now that she knew how cruel he was (he often whipped her), she was glad she had thrown him over despite the horrible consequences she had suffered.

Violet shifted slightly on the bed, trying to find a more comfortable position. It was almost impossible for her to turn over on her other side. The posture of having her arms bound behind her put an uncomfortable pressure on her shoulder even though she lay atop a number of soft, giving pillows. Her maids alternated her from one side to the other every other night so that she would not develop a chronic shoulder ache. Even so, they always had to massage her shoulder and back in the morning to relieve the cramps and aches. It was still warm in the early fall in Hunan Province, now the Republic of Northern Hunan, so she was not covered with anything more than a light, satin sheet. It was a problem when her coverings came off in the night since she had no way of restoring them. Her maids were supposed to stay awake to watch over her, but sitting for six hours or so in a dimly lit room was too much for anyone to take. Even now she could hear the light snoring of Junjing. She knew that if she called, her maid would awaken immediately and see to her needs.

One of the most difficult things about being locked in a room with no windows is that she never knew how close to daylight they were. She wouldn't know whether she had slept for minutes or hours. The lighting was always the same. And unlike her former room, where although bound she could at least hear the beginnings of the morning activity in the seraglio through the paper thin walls, her room was virtually soundproof. She missed, in the spring, summer and fall, hearing the birds chirping their morning or evening songs. On some days you could hear the sound of a horn from one of the freighters or barges passing up or down the Yangtze River, not more than a mile from the castle.

During the day, you could see the Yangtze from the balcony of the seraglio and the bustling town that served as the warlord's port. Before the invasion of the seraglio she had spent hours some days standing and absorbing the vast panorama. Now, the balcony was covered with a heavy, wooden latticework. The lieutenant who had come to claim her had gained access through it and this was never to be permitted again. The view from the balcony now was whatever you could see through the small, 4" square, checkerboard openings. If she could talk to her lord and master, one of the things she would beg of him would be to restore the view.

Violet took a deep breath and tied to clear her mind. She knew that if she didn't get back to sleep, she would have an awful, long night. She closed her eyes and thought of her piano, her pretty maids, Iris, the sweet American girl who had become her lover. It was better to think about what she had than what she did not. After a few minutes, her breathing became regular. She felt her body soften and she was asleep.

* * * * * * * * * * * * *

In fact, the warlord did not call for Violet to serve him that next morning. She was awoken, as usual, just at sunrise by one of the chaperones after she had unlocked the door and handed Junjing the keys to her chains. After she performed her morning ablutions, she was led into the common area of the seraglio for her breakfast. The other concubines were already up and kneeling around the polished, gold inlaid table in the dining area. Violet knelt down at the table, resting on her haunches and placed her hands behind her back so that Junjing could bind them with a white, silken cord, as was mandated for the concubines at mealtimes. Breakfast consisted of a steaming hot porridge and fruit accompanied by strong, pungent tea. This morning there were apricots cut from their pits and slices of fresh, juicy oranges.

Iris and Hu were engaged in a heated conversation while being fed spoonfuls of porridge by their maids.

"*Someday I will have you at the end of a whip,*" Iris was saying, "*and then you will see.*"

Hu laughed. "*I look forward to that day with great pleasure, Whore Number Three,*" she responded, using the formal appellation for the American which denoted her status in the seraglio. Hu had the honor of being assigned the name Whore Number Two. Shu, her sister, was Whore Number One. "*I promise you I will not cry and wail and beg for mercy as you do,*" she added.

Iris turned to Violet. "*Good morning loved one,*" she said, using one of the many terms of endearment they had for each other. "*The master had Whore Number Two whip me again last night. Someday I hope he will allow me to whip her.*"

There were no remnants of her torment on her body, the redness having faded overnight. Violet could see though that she was still suffering its emotional aftereffects.

"*I'm sorry for you, little one,*" Violet proffered. "*I'm sure Whore Number Two did only what the master ordered,*" Although they knew each other's names, it was a whipping offense to be heard referring to each other other than by the appellations that denoted their status and rank.

"*As Whore Number Four says,*" Hu interjected, "*if I had refused, the master would have whipped me instead, and he wouldn't have used the flogger, but one of his other whips. Besides, I made it up you when I fucked you with his prick and then mouthed your pretty little pussy. You seemed to enjoy it. You should have heard her moan and scream with pleasure, Whore Number Four. She doesn't like to admit it, but being whipped brings her passions to a boil.*"

"*Please don't argue,*" Shu said as she swallowed a mouthful of porridge her maid had served her. "*We must do as the master says.*"

"*Then maybe she can whip you next time,*" Iris spat out.

"*She has whipped me many times,*" Shu answered. "*She has always been a bully. Even as a child.*"

Hu laughed again. "*Be careful, sister. Maybe he'll have me whip you tonight. I'll make sure I do a very good job.*"

Violet was chewing a piece of apricot that her maid had served her. Junjing picked up the blue and white, hand painted, porcelain cup that held her tea and proffered it to Violet's lips. After she swallowed it, she said to Iris, "*I'll make it up to you later, my love. I promise to kiss every place the whip touched you.*"

Iris smiled. "*And I'll kiss you,*" she replied.

Zhu, the dreaded head chaperone was kneeling nearby. Her face was boney and cruel. She was dressed in the bluish grey uniform of the chaperones. It draped loosely over her wiry, ancient body. She had been chatting with another of the chaperones and broke off their conversation to speak to her charges. "*Less talking and more eating or you will all feel the whip this morning. And I will decide if you will get to kiss Whore Number Three's flesh today,*" she said to Violet.

No one answered back to the domineering headmistress. Iris and Violet exchanged unhappy looks. The concubines finished their breakfast in silence.

After breakfast was their obligatory session of sexual stimulation with the eunuch. Even after more than two years, Violet had never gotten use to the ease with which she succumbed to the cold hearted man's ministrations. He performed his tasks without passion, for he had none, but nonetheless was able to draw out of the young women exhibitions of deep lust that always ended with loud, explosive declarations of pleasure as their pussies convulsed and throbbed almost painfully.

Violet watched while the eunuch stroked her three sisters to fiery conclusions. He used his hand on Hu and Iris, lying next to them, their legs splayed wide, their maids holding their writhing hands still above them, but placed his mouth between the embarrassed Shu's thighs and made her scream after tantalizing her for more than fifteen minutes.

When it was Violet's turn, she spread her thighs so that the eunuch could unlock her pussy's bindings and remove the ever present hollows balls from within her. Xifang, the eunuch who had, over the course of four days of exquisite torment, energized her sex, had instructed Li Pao that it should be kept well exercised to maintain its fine edge of sensitivity. So each morning since then, a full six months ago, the eunuch had plowed her furrow with the simulacrum of her master's cock until she groaned and her body shuddered as a result of her climax.

This morning, after a ritual shaving of her loins, rather than lying atop her, he ordered to her hands and knees. He had already stripped and armed himself with the iconic image of the warlord's cock. When she was in position, her thighs spread wide, her rear raised, her forehead resting on the backs of her hands, he began to stroke her thighs and her rear haunches lightly. It did not take long for him to wrest a sigh from the obedient concubine. He spread her thighs wider and lowered his head so that he could trace his tongue along her hairless nether lips and tickle the little bud at its apex, drawing a soft moan from her.

Violet was facing her sisters in bondage and was conscious of their eyes upon her. It did not seem to matter that they had been subject to similar acts of lusts. The fact that the cold hearted eunuch was forcing her to pleasure, that she could be so easily daily driven to passion, was a source of deep humiliation to her. It was made worse by the use of the wooden image of their master's prick, something the other women rarely suffered, and doubly worse by the extreme reactions she had to the use of her love tunnel, reactions that seemed appropriate to only the most lasciv-ious of slatterns.

Li Pao waited until he sensed the whore's hips moving in rhythm to his attentions to her slit, until the passionate organ had dilated and was gushing with her juices before leaning back and preparing to penetrate her. He rose himself up on his knees so he could obtain the proper angle and slid the cool tip of the wooden instrument that jutted from his otherwise lifeless loins across the woman's labial divide, coating it with her fluids. Her body shuddered when the dark object made contact with her and in anticipation of its insertion into her now needy tunnel. The eunuch leaned back so that the head of the wooden cock was probing at the concubine's gate and then pushed it slowly forward.

Violet moaned woefully as the finely polished, faux member gently abraded her pussy's walls. Her hands clenched into fists. She pressed her hips backwards to receive it. When the eunuch's motions began, a steady, agonizingly slow sawing motion, she groaned loudly.

He kept her on boil for a long time. Although he drew no physical satisfaction from the act, he appreciated its esthetic qualities immensely and the power he exercised over all the whores' lusts. He was a master of sexual technique, having supervised many whores over the years. He had started out as an apprentice in the Emperor's harem many years ago until he and several hundred other eunuchs were discharged in an economy move. After that, he spent time in several high priced bordellos tending to the whores as he had been taught, until twenty years ago when he had entered the warlord's employ.

The impassioned concubine groaned and sighed and thrust back at the wooden appendage yearning, despite her shame, for her completion. Sensing her urgency, the eunuch slowed his efforts, drawing out her need until, overcome by her desires, the English slut moaned deeply and begged for relief.

"*Please, master, please!*" she entreated him.

Lately, he had devised a little game for her.

"*What is your name?*" he asked her, as he continued his long, slow, patient thrusts, his voice harsh and demanding.

"*Whore Number Four, master!*" Violet replied frantically.

"*And who do you serve?*"

"*Lord Wang! Lord Wang!*"

"*And who owns your slutty pussy?*"

"*Lord Wang, master! Lord Wang owns my pussy! Please!*"

"*And no one else?*"

"*No, master! No! Please master! Let me come, master! Please!*"

The eunuch took hold of Violet's hips and thrust the stiff, thick wooden penis deep into her chasm. He began to pump at it furiously. The concubine's body began to shiver and quake. She called out her lust at each, deep, fervent thrust. "Oh! Oh! Oh! Oh!" As she rose to the summit of pleasure, she pushed her hips back madly against each thrust. "Ohhhhhhhhh!" she moaned. "Ohhhhhhhhh!"

Finally, her passion crested. Her electrified tunnel squeezed hard against the stiff pole that tormented her. She groaned again deeply. Her body shook as the convulsions of her fevered crevasse tore through her. Her head rose and her mouth opened wide. "Ugh!" she called out at each contraction of her pussy's walls, "Ugh! Ugh! Ugh!"

She was breathing deeply, her naked body covered with a sheen of sweat when the ecstasy driving sensations began to ebb. The eunuch slowed his efforts, guiding her to a soft, pleasurable finish. When he saw that she had reached her end, her body slumping, her voice stilled, he slowly slid the wooden member from her sheath. He gave her a moment to recover while he unstrapped the faux cock's harness from around his waist and redonned his blue and silver sheath. He issued a brisk order for her to turn over and lie on her back. Violet obeyed slowly, overcome by the aftereffects of her pleasure. When she was on her back, her legs spread wide, the eunuch reinstalled her hollow, gel filled, silver balls into her slippery channel and then bound it up again with the shiny, steel cables. He ran the ends of the cable into the heavy lock embossed with the golden ideograms denoting her pussy's ownership and pulled the lock tight until her pussy lips were jammed together tightly.

Violet was still woozy with post orgasmic bliss when the eunuch administered to her and her sisters a cupful of the potion that made them docile and sexually ripe for most of the day. She hated its effects and had once rebelled against taking it. She had been caught on the third day, betrayed by one of her maids and had been taught a severe lesson as a result. Since then she resignedly succumbed to necessity.

There was one more indignity Violet suffered each morning since the seraglio invasion. She no longer waited to be told. As soon as the eunuch had left, she crawled to the middle of the seraglio common room and bent over on her knees. During the invasion, the then head chaperone, Qiao, had been killed by the lieutenant, her throat slit from ear to ear. She had been Zhu's friend and the new head chaperone blamed Violet for her death. Since then, each morning, she suffered five sharp blows on her naked buttocks from the whippy stick, the three foot long, flexible bamboo rod that each of the chaperones carried.

Zhu approached her right away, eager to give her her due. She always accompanied the demeaning and painful strokes with her caustic taunts. Today was no different.

"You put on quite a display this morning, Whore Number Four," she told her as she tapped on her exposed rear end with the tip of the whippy stick. *"You are such a dirty slut. It's no wonder the master doesn't want you in his bed anymore. Soon you will be sold off to a whorehouse where you belong. Then I will have all my friends come and fuck you and make you suck their pricks. I might even pay a few coppers so I can give you a proper whipping, not the easy strokes I give you here. Believe me when I tell you that some day this will come true."*

Violet never responded to the gray haired chaperone's taunts. But her poisonous comments struck deep. Yes, one day she would probably find herself in a whorehouse serving ten or twenty men a day. Yes, they would whip her for their pleasure. Yes, she had become no more than a lowly slut.

The first blow of the whippy stick caused Violet's body to tense up tightly and she uttered a low whine. It stung like the blazes but its red mark would fade quickly. The second and third stung just as badly and she whined and stiffened as each one bit into her tender rear. Zhu saved her strength for the fourth and fifth strokes which she wielded so harshly she gave out a loud grunt as she delivered them. Violet tried not to, but she released an anguished cry as each one landed, "Ohhhhhhhhhh! Ohhhhhhhhhh!" Her eyes filled with tears. Her lips trembled both from the pain and the ignominious treatment that she endured. She had done nothing to encourage the passion mad lieutenant. It wasn't her fault that Qiao was killed. But she had to suffer nonetheless.

After that, Zhu usually left Violet to her own devices. This morning, her threat to banish her from the enjoyment of the American whore's flesh came to naught and, after her bath, it was Iris who suckled her until her breasts had released their morning's offerings. Afterwards, while all the other women watched, (the concubines were permitted to pleasure each other only in the common area of the seraglio, never in the privacy of their rooms) she and Violet embraced and kissed, driven by the lust inducing potion they had been given, bringing each other to orgasm several times.

There was not much else to do in the seraglio except to stay ready for the master's command to come serve him, which might come at any time. They played cards, talked about nothing, lay about and caressed each other. Some times they exchanged stories about their native lands. Violet often entertained the others by generalized recitations of Shakespeare's plays. Romeo and Juliet was everybody's favorite. At eleven, Violet had her mandolin lesson. She had become, if not expert, quite proficient at it and the other concubines and the women who served and/or mastered them would lay back and enjoy her playing. At noon they had lunch, usually fish and rice with a piquant sauce and then retired to their rooms for a nap and more sexual exercise with their maids. After lunch, in the afternoons around 3 o'clock, was

Violet's favorite part of the day for that's when she was permitted to go and practice her piano.

* * * * * * * * * * * * * *

That afternoon, a little after 3, Li Pao stood outside the door to the general's second floor salon and listened to the melodious tones emanating from within. The British concubine was right. He had engineered the warlord's decision to purchase the piano. He was of the old school. A concubine should be something more than a fuck animal. In the Emperor's seraglio, the concubines sang, recited poetry, danced, played musical instruments in a fierce competition for their master's eye. Li realized that General Wang was no emperor, but he hoped to continue to lead him down a path of more refinement, especially now that he had proclaimed nation status for his little kingdom.

Li was under no illusions. The Republic of Northern Hunan, which they had formally named their new state, was no match for the immense power of the national government. If the Kuomintang took it into their heads to deal with General Wang once and for all, there would be hell to pay. So far, they were too occupied with pacifying the provinces to the north to direct their full attention to the warlord. It was a dangerous game they were playing, a gamble. The next round of negotiations with the Kuomin-tang representative would be conducted nation to nation, if he had his way. When the time came to give in to the central government's pressures, they would be in a much better bargaining position.

Not that the declaration of independence was merely a negotiating ploy. It was often said that acorns produced mighty oaks and more than one dynasty in China had emerged from humble beginnings. He had already sent out feelers to some of the neighboring warlords to see how they were reacting to Wang's great victory. The coming of so called democracy was a danger to them all. It was unwieldy for such a large country such as China and would never work. At most it was a passing fad. Someone would eventually reunite China under one banner and rule it with an iron fist. Why not General Wang?

That was not what was on the eunuch's mind as he listened to the concubine's heavenly playing. He too had taken notice of the warlord's rejection of her since the day of the great battle. He knew that if he didn't do something to reunite them soon, he might tire of her and sell her off. That would destroy all the work he had been doing with her over the last two years. It was he who had encouraged the other concubines to teach her Chinese, he who had ordered the chaperone Yanyu to instruct her in the playing of the Chinese mandolin. He knew that the British whore was more than a mere beauty. She had a strong, noble soul and was capable of drawing out the warlord's purer emotions. Every great leader needed a great love. There were difficult times ahead and he needed somewhere to find peace and tranquility amidst strife.

But how to bring them back together? That was the question.

Li tore himself away from the beautiful music and went in search of his master. The general was inspecting the port facility today and the new pier construction. It was going according to schedule and it was expected that ships would be able to begin docking there by the end of the summer. It didn't hurt though for the engineer and foremen to know that they were working directly under the warlord's eye. There was always a great deal of graft in such construction, padded payrolls, substandard supplies, shoddy workman-ship. Li knew of one contractor who was planning on delivering inferior wood for the pilings. When he made the delivery, Li would have him arrested and then hung and his family sold into slavery. He had a quite beautiful daughter who would bring a very good price. It would be a good lesson to everyone else to keep their graft within reasonable bounds.

Li was waiting at the top of the stairs to the second floor of the castle when the general returned. He was wearing his khaki uniform and tall black boots. He carried a copy of the plans for the construction under his arm. He seemed happy, which was a good thing.

"*Good afternoon, my lord,*" Li greeted him when he stepped onto the landing. "*Is everything as it should be?*"

"*Very good! Very good!*" Wang replied. "*They will be finished with the third and fourth pylons this week. All the soil tests from the river bottom have been excellent, a good mix of mud and stone. Just like cement!*"

"*Excellent, my lord,*" Li replied. "*I have ordered some tea and cakes for you in the small dining room. If it pleases you, I have some minor matters to discuss with you.*"

"*Yes, yes,*" Wang replied. He knew that the eunuch never bothered to discuss minor things with him. He took care of them himself. Li Pao had his hand in every aspect of the governance of his duchy and his advice had carried him a long way. It would be foolish not to give hem what-ever time he needed.

The general handed the pier plans off to his eunuch and proceeded down the hall to the little dining room. It was where he and his wives ate their daily meals as opposed to formal occasions when they ate in the larger, more commodious room in the north wing. Li in turn handed the plans off to a servant who had been hovering nearby. He was Chu, the eunuch's private secretary. He would make sure that the plans were filed away properly.

The eunuch followed his master down the hall. On the way to their destination, they passed by the general's salon. The music from within could be hear faintly as they passed. Li noticed the warlord's head turn slightly toward the sound and a momentary hesitation in his step. Then he moved on.

The small dining room was not small in the sense of tiny. It was only small as compared to the larger one. An eight foot long table sat in the middle, set high in the Western style, with real chairs. A pretty maid was standing by a sideboard on which stood an urn with boiling water. As soon as she saw the warlord enter, she tossed three spoonfuls of the heavy tea that the warlord liked into a brightly decorated teapot with red, blue and yellow song-birds painted on it and then filled it from the boiling urn. Graciously, she set the teapot down on a silver tray on which several small cakes had already been placed. She picked up the tray and brought it to where the warlord sat, at the head of the table.

Another maid, from the other side of the long serving table had a bowl of warm, soapy water and a soft, white, cotton towel. While the tea was brewing, she proffered the bowl and the towel to her master.

Wang had removed his cap and placed it on the table and unbuttoned the top three buttons of his tunic. He turned to the second maid and dipped his hands into the water, rubbing the dust and grime from his hands away. He scooped some up and washed his face as well. When done, his eyes closed, he reached out his hand and the towel was placed into it.

While the warlord was refreshing himself, Li stood expectantly near the corner of the table. Even though he had served him for twenty years, and was fully familiar with all his habits and customs, he would never have ventured to take a seat at his table uninvited. He watched while the warlord finished wiping his face and handed the towel back to the maid.

"*Please sit down, Li Pao,*" Wang told him. Li nodded and took a chair to his master's right. His secretary, who had followed them into the room, handed Li a sheaf of papers. Li set them down before himself on the table and waited patiently for permission to speak. The maids and Chu found inconspicuous places to stand, awaiting a command from the masters.

Wang bent down and opened the lid to the decorous teapot and put his nose to the opening. He drew in the pungent aroma deeply and swirled the pot around a few times to encourage it to brew faster. When he had returned the lid to the pot, he turned to his eunuch.

"*So what is so important?*" he asked.

"*In my effort to be ever vigilant in my duty to serve you, my lord, I conducted an inventory of our rice warehouses this week. I regret to inform you that Warehouse Number Three is missing 1000 bales of rice.*"

"*Missing? How could they be missing? Is there some mistake?*"

"*There is no mistake, my lord. The figures have been checked several times. And all outgoing shipments have been accounted for.*"

"*Who is in charge of Warehouse Number Three?*" Wang asked.

"*It is Huan Fo, my lord. He is Wife Number Two's cousin.*"

"*Her cousin? How could this happen?*"

"*The warehouses are maintained by your lordship in case of a poor rice harvest to avoid famine. It is purchased at a price set by me when the harvests come in. They are sold when it appears that the next harvest will be adequate. In the winter months, while the price of rice in your territories is strictly regulated, the price normally rises high in the cities, Nanking and Shanghai. I am afraid that many of the warehouse managers sell off rice during the winter at a high price and replace it in harvest season when the price is low, thereby making a nice profit.*"

"*And Huan Fo is guilty of this?*"

"*I'm afraid he is, your lordship, as well as the managers of the other rice warehouses. I usually tolerate some speculation by the managers as a supplement to their salaries, but never 1000 bales. When the price of rice failed to fall this spring due to an unusually dry season, Huan was unable to replace the bales he stole.*"

"*What can I do? Wife Number Two will be very upset if I hang her cousin.*"

"*I have taken this into consideration, my lord and your dilemma fits in well with another topic I wished to discuss with you.*"

"*And that is?*"

"*Now that you have declared your independence, it is important that you be seen as ruling by operation of law rather than by fiat. The first step in this is the creation of a judicial system.*"

"*A judicial system? What do I need a judicial system for? Someone commits a crime, their head should roll. It's as simple as that.*"

"*Yes, my lord, but you have neither the time nor the energy to handle all of the cases. Our dungeon is always full of miscreants and many more languish in filthy huts in the larger villages awaiting judgment. Some are there for petty offenses and wait a long time until they are eventually either pardoned by you or hung. We have to feed them and guard them at a great expense. If justice was dealt out to them swiftly, they could pay a fine or, if they were unable to pay a fine, work off their sentence on one of your construction crews. More serious offenders could receive long terms at hard labor, which you will receive free of charge.*"

Wang leaned back in his chair. "The eunuch may have a point," he thought. There was much work to be done. The engineers for the road to the copper mines at Pingjang had calculated that the work would entail approximately 200,000 man days of labor. He would have to conscript 1000 men to have the work done before the late fall when the snows came. And he had to pay all of those men wages, although nothing near what he would pay a free labor pool.

"*How many judges would I have to appoint and what would it cost me?*" Wang asked.

"*I think one judge for now, my lord.*"

"*And who do you have in mind?*"

"Qin Guoliang, my lord. He is currently serving as your senior tax official. You will recall his efforts in betraying the former tax clerk, Zhou Xiaojian, who was fomenting rebellion. You seized his house and enslaved his wife and daughters. The daughters are still serving in your house of pleasure, the Golden Swan."

The sweet bodies of the three young girls came swiftly to Wang's mind, especially the younger one, Jia, who he still loved to torment. Qin had done him quite a service. But who would collect the taxes?

"I have a suitable replacement for Qin, my lord," Li Pao said as if reading his master's mind. *"He has been working as Qin's assistant. Do not worry, taxes will still be collected very efficiently."*

"But what am I to pay Qin?"

"Nothing, my lord. He will take a salary out of the fines he imposes and property confiscated. The rest will go into your treasury."

The idea was brilliant. A whole new source of revenue and free labor. And, Wang was sure, Qin would not be letting too many miscreants off the hook; there was no profit in that. Making them pay fines was much better than having them languish in jails. For serious crimes, like embezzling rice from his warehouses, they could still be hung and their whole immediate family would be enslaved and sold off.

"If you appointed Qin now, his first case would be that of the thief Huan Fo. Although Qin will, I am sure, look to you for guidance for the appropriate sentence, in the eyes of the country, and more importantly Wife Number Two, the verdict and sentence will be completely out of your hands."

Wang was stunned. As usual, his eunuch had come up with the appropriate solution for a very thorny problem. And how he hated spending time judging peasants for petty thefts, breaches of the peace and other minor offenses. That is one reason they spent so much time locked up. The people would see that justice is being done and that his declaration of independence meant more than just a new flag to them. Once in a while, he could pardon someone or commute their sentence to show how merciful and wise he was.

"*Let it be done,*" Wang said enthusiastically. "*This Huan, is he already in our dungeon?*"

"*Just this morning, my lord, together with his wife, his two concubines, his son and three daughters.*"

"*I expect I will hear something about it at dinner time. You have given me the perfect answer. His fate is out of my hands.*" Wang laughed heartily.

He leaned over and inspected the tea once more. It had brewed up nicely. He took hold of the teapot and poured himself a cup. He turned to the eunuch. "*Would you like some tea, Li Pao?*" he asked.

"*No thank you, my lord,*" he answered.

As Wang sipped his tea, into which he had dripped a large spoon of honey, and ate several of the sweetened cakes that had been left out for him, Li Pao went over other items of less significance. When he was done and received approval and/or suggestions on several matters, he remained sitting at the table while General Wang finished his tea.

After Wang drained his second cup, he noticed the eunuch still sitting there. He had thought they were done. "*What?*" he asked.

"*Your lordship seems a bit tense to me, if you don't mind my saying so.*"

"*Tense?*"

"*You have many worries and many hard tasks to perform. It is my humble opinion, should you deign to receive it, lord, that you need more relaxation.*"

"*Yes, relaxation. That is a good thing. But how to achieve it? Lately I have too much on my mind it seems even for reading. My mind keeps wandering off.*"

"*Yes, my lord. That is not a good thing. You need something that will take your mind away to a more pleasant place.*"

"*And you have an idea as to how I might do this?*" Wang asked, not without some humor. He knew the eunuch well enough to know that he rarely raised a problem without having an answer.

"*As it is, I do, your lordship. There is a place filled with peace and harmony not more than 100 feet away from where you sit every day.*"

Wang looked surprised. "*Where?*" he asked.

"*In your salon, lord. As we speak, Whore Number Four is playing the piano that you in your wisdom graciously deigned that she should have. She plays beautifully to an empty room. She should be playing for you.*"

This struck the warlord right between the eyes. When he had passed down the hallway earlier and heard the music coming from the room, he had almost stopped and gone in. But that would have meant confronting the demon that was tormenting him: how to deal with the English whore. Now his eunuch was giving him the perfect opportunity to go and see her. He didn't have to do anything else. He could listen to her play and then leave. The eunuch might think something was wrong if he didn't avail himself of this opportunity.

"*She plays well?*" he asked the eunuch.

"*Very well, lord. She was a little rusty at first, but it has all come back to her swiftly.*"

"*I don't know,*" the warlord said. "*I will need to change into my kimono if I truly want to relax.*"

"*That is not a problem, lord,*" Li answered. He clapped his hands and two more maids emerged out a darkened corner of the dining room. One was carrying his red and yellow silk kimono and the other his slippers. They bowed and awaited further instruction.

To the maid who had brought the tea, Li said, "*Come here, slut and take off your master's boots.*"

The dark haired maid scurried forward and, after kneeling at the warlord's feet, lifted his right foot and began to remove the tall, black boot. She had it off quickly and then removed the other one. She then removed the light cotton socks he wore.

At this, the general rose to his feet and loosened his trousers. There was no difficulty in being naked in front of the maids, he had fucked them all at one time or another anyway. Besides, there was no need of privacy before people of such low station.

When his trousers and tunic were removed, one of the maids held out his kimono and opened it so that he could slide it on his body. The general was clad in only his black, silken boxer shorts, an affectation he had adopted when a student at the British school in Shanghai in his youth. He slipped them off and donned his kimono, relishing the cool feel of its soft silk against his skin. He then slid his feet into his red and brown embroidered slippers.

Li Pao had stood while his master changed his clothes. He admired his fit and trim body. When he saw that he was done changing, he clapped his hands again and all the maids scurried away. "*Enjoy yourself, lord,*" he said and then he and his assistant melted away as well.

Wang took his cup from the table and tossed the remnants of the tea down his throat. He took a deep breath. He knew he was committed to going to listen to the English whore play, but he was still hesitant. "Can I contain my desire for her?" he asked himself. Well, he had to see her sooner or later. Time would tell.

* * * * * * * * * * * * * *

Violet did not look up when the door opened to the salon. She hardly noticed it. She was in the midst of a particularly difficult portion of a Mendelssohn prelude she had been learning. It was one of the pieces of sheet music she had found in the piano bench. She almost had it down pat, except for this complicated turn. It involved crossing her hands several times and she was garbling the last few notes.

When he entered the room, General Wang saw the English concubine intent at her piano. The woman did not turn to see who had entered. Yanyu, the chaperone who was minding her, did and she immediately rose from her chair to fall to her knees. He signaled her to sit back down. She complied hesitatingly.

He sat himself down on one of the padded armchairs facing the piano. The room was about 50' by 20', not small by any measure, but it was outfitted in a manner so as to make it seem cozy. There was a number of couches and easy chairs, all covered with dark green, beige or brown fabric. The walls were painted a dark cream color and there were numerous ancient, beautiful Chinese paintings mounted on the walls. It was one of the rooms that had received electricity and several electric lamps were distri-buted around the room shedding soft light. The windows were treated with blood red curtains and the soft, thick rug was colored a somewhat lighter shade of red.

The piano was set in the northeast corner of the room, pointed in towards the wall. The concubine's side was presented to him. Her taut, silken robe pulled tight at her hips revealing her delicious curves. Her long brown hair, joined at the back of her head with a blue bow, ran otherwise freely down her back. Her head was bent slightly as if in concentration and Wang could see her shoulders move as she delicately let her fingers glide over the long expanse of black and white keys.

The music from the piano filled the room. Wang quickly lost himself in the elegant, floating melody. The English's whore's countenance reflected her intensity as she concentrated on her playing. He could just see the side of her face. Her eyes never left the score mounted on the piano. The chaperone was seated nearby and stayed poised to turn the page at the opportune moment when Violet signaled her.

"*Now,*" he heard the concubine whisper intently and the frightened, gray haired chaperone, looking as if she were committing some crime by not falling to the floor, quickly jumped up and turned the page. The Englishwoman did not miss a note and a smile of satisfaction crossed her face as she continued to play.

Wang felt himself falling under the music's spell. As usual, the eunuch had been right. It was relaxing to hear and watch her play. It's a pity he did not think of getting her a piano sooner, he thought. There was a decanter of brandy on the small table next to him and he poured himself a small glassful which he sipped as he took in the rich, deep tones of the piano and the delightful and intricate procession of notes.

Three times the chaperone leapt at her ward's command to turn the page of the score. Each time Violet continued on without missing a beat. She was getting near the finale now. There was a rather complicated flourish at the end of the piece and she had been working on it all afternoon. Wang watched her face record her concentration. The tempo of the music quickened as it headed for its conclusion. Violet crossed her hands several times, hitting true on every note, and then finished off with three strong chords.

For a moment, she was stock still. The she exclaimed, "*Yanyu, I did it! Did you hear! It was almost perfect!*"

She looked up from the piano for the first time. When her eyes caught the warlord's a shadow fell across her face. She slipped from the piano bench quickly and threw herself to the floor.

The grand finale of the piece still reverberated throughout the room. Wang felt a pang of guilt that he had disturbed her obvious pleasure. She was kneeling with her head to the floor, as she had been taught, her hands extended to her sides. The chaperone had joined her.

Wang took a few moments to savor the concubine's supine figure. She was wearing a colorful kimono designed like a beautiful garden, with orange, blue and yellow flowers strewn about a background of green ferns. On its back, a peacock spread its wings, revealing its delicate, light blue array of feathers. The concubine's long, silky, chestnut hair had slid off of her back and was resting on the floor next to her. Her fine breasts were crushed against her knees.

Violet had shivered with fear when she saw that the warlord had been watching her for who knew how long. It was certainly a whipping offense to fail to pay him the proper obeisance. As she knelt before him, some twenty feet away, she said a little prayer that she might be spared the rod, especially as it was wielded by him.

For about thirty seconds there was no sound in the room. The silence felt odd after the crescendo of sound that had just filled it. Wang took a sip from his snifter of brandy and placed the glass back down on the table. He wanted to hear more.

"*Up!*" he commanded in a deep, rough voice.

Violet raised her head fearfully and then struggled to her feet. She kept her face lowered, her eyes to the floor. The chaperone had stood up too and was a foot behind her and to her right. They both awaited their master's judgment.

Wang very rarely spoke to his concubines except to give them orders to pleasure him, to arrange their bodies as he desired, to spread their legs or to open their mouths to receive him. So when he spoke, Violet had to think carefully so that she could be sure she understood what he said. Her Chinese was getting good, but it was still a foreign language and at moments of crisis her ability to understand it sometimes faltered.

Wang carefully chose his words. He wanted to hear her play more for him. He knew that he could compel her to play until her fingers bled and she fell from the piano bench from exhaustion, but he didn't want to disturb the joy and exuberance she had displayed while she had been oblivious to his presence. It was as if he had discovered a delicate bird right here in his salon. If he was too harsh to it, it might fly away and never return. If she was to play freely for him, to exhibit the same enthusiasm and dedication to her playing whenever in the future he came to hear her, he would have to strike the right tone. "*You have given me much pleasure by your playing, Whore Number Four,*" he told her finally. "*Please play something else for me.*"

Violet was stunned. He had said 'please'. She was sure it was an imperative 'please' and would brook no refusal. Nonetheless, the tone of the order and the form that it took was beyond anything she had ever experienced with him.

"*As you desire, lord,*" she replied meekly. She stepped quickly back to the piano, careful not to turn her back to the general, an act he might interpret as disrespect.

She sat down on the bench, not knowing what to play. Her hands were sweating and her stomach was roiling. The situation was fraught with danger. What if she, in her nervousness, faltered at the piece? What if his anticipated pleasure at her playing was spoiled? The score for the Mendelssohn piece was still on the piano. Her mind raced for a suitable replacement. She should play something she knew from memory, she thought. She would never be able to keep her eyes concentrated on a score while the man who held the power of life or death over her was watching. But what? It would have to be a piece she knew so well that her hands would virtually move of their own accord.

And then it came to her. She would play the Listz piece, *Liebesträum No. 3*, The Lover's Dream. It was the first extended piece she had ever learned by heart. She remembered playing it for her father, so proud, so full of love for him. She could play it in her dreams.

Violet took a deep breath. She poised her hands over the keys. She looked at her master, her owner. What was going through his mind? What did he want from her? She knew that there was no little irony that she would be playing music which celebrated love and happiness as her first command performance for the man who had kid-napped her and reduced her to the status of a sexual chattel. How she had hated him for it! And yet now, since the other day when he had lain in her arms not too much unlike the lover she had always dreamed of, her hatred for him had attenuated somewhat. She was almost ready to concede his human side, to find in him some small bit of grace.

Wang too was wondering what was going through her mind. He saw her eyes darting over to him as her hands hung in the air ready to obey his command. "Does she know?" he wondered. "Does she know what her mere presence does to me?"

And then her hands descended and began to coax out the delicate, fragile melody intended for the ears of lovers, composed almost a hundred ago.

For the first few bars, Violet's hands were nervous, tentative. She closed her eyes and brought her mind to that flower strewn music room in her home so many years and miles away. She saw her father standing there, handsome, pleased, warm and loving. She smelled the flowers whose fragrant perfume filled the air. She thought of all the beautiful dreams she had had of love, companionship, fulfillment. In an instant, she was gone, back there, and any thought of the presence of her lord and master, the owner of her very flesh, faded away.

Wang watched as the concubine's face melted into bliss. The light, harmonious notes flowed over him like a gentle bath. He knew this piece. He had heard it once before back at the British school. It had awed him then, uplifted him into a realm of beauty. It had stayed with him all of these years. He closed his eyes and let his mind drift away to a simpler, less tension filled time.

Violet played on as if her hands were guided by heaven itself. Her eyes began to tear as her heart was filled with warmth and pleasure. She wanted the song to go on forever. As long as she could play, as long as the notes sprung happily from the beautiful, shiny, black instrument beneath her hands, she was miles away from her fate. She imagined herself floating high above the castle that was her prison, dipping and soaring amidst the clouds, the bright, yellow sun warming her body, cool, wonderful tasting air filling her lungs.

When she finished, her heart was beating wildly and she was short of breath. The room seemed to be spinning around her. She looked over at her master. His face was as she had never seen it before. It was perfectly at rest, soft, unfocused. His lips were upturned in a nascent smile. His hands were hanging loose over the ends of the arms of the chair

His eyes opened and their gazes met. In an instant, he was on his feet. He strode quickly over to where she still sat, too overwhelmed to move. He grabbed her by the arms and pulled her to her feet. Taking her in his arms, he pressed his lips against hers. She opened her mouth and, breathless, overcome by the same passion that had seized him, accepted his tongue, placed her arms around him and kissed him back.

In a moment, the two lovers were on the floor. Their hands and mouths explored each other frantically. Wang ripped her kimono open and began suckling on her milk filled breasts, drinking her in, as if he could consume all of her then and there. Her hand flowed over his tight, firm belly and seized his thick cock, stroking it needfully.

The sonorous melody that had filled the room was replaced by the lovers' grunts and moans of lust. The warlord's hand floated over Violet's belly and down below, finding the steel lock that held her loins prisoner. The key was in his pocket. He had transferred it automatically from his pants when he had changed. He always kept it with him as if it were a talisman of the flesh that had bewitched him. Rising from their embrace, he pulled the key from his pocket. Knowing what he was about to do, Violet lay back on the soft, thick rug and spread her legs wantonly.

In his excitement he fumbled with the key. He cursed himself and, with a mighty effort, calmed himself long enough to slide the key into the lock and turn it. When it had clicked open, he pulled it free and then gently drew the long, thin supple, shiny steel cable from his concubine's loins. His fingers pushed aside her enflamed love lips, making her moan, and he pulled delicately on the string that connected the hollow balls within her, easing them out. Violet's eyes rolled back and her hands flowed over her belly down to her loins as the sensation of the round objects traversing the walls of her steamy cleft sent her a wave of pleasure.

Once they were free of her crevasse, and the pathway to her inner person free to be plundered, their eyes met. It was like the day of the battle all over again. The air about them was heavy with moment, like a caldron ready to boil or a room filled with a volatile gas, ready to explode. Wang's kimono was loose about him. He shrugged it off of his shoulders and tossed it aside. He crept between Violet's expectant thighs and poised himself to enter her. She brashly took hold of his rampant, steel filled wand, caressing its length. She placed its head at the entrance to her womb and slid it up and down between her distended, swollen love lips, coating it with her moisture. Then, her eyes brazen, placing the rock hard cock's tip within her, she closed her ankles around her master's thighs and drew him in.

Wang issued a deep, satisfied sigh of pleasure as he felt the warm, smooth wetness envelop him. He let his body fall slowly upon hers as his manhood slowly sank deep into her welcoming well. She sighed too, her pussy's walls energized and sensitive. When he was in her to the hilt, she wrapped her arms around him and drew him close.

Oblivious to the startled chaperone, their bodies began a rhythmic beat against each other's. Their mouths rejoined and they both groaned with pleasure. Wang started slowly, letting his cock plow back and forth the full length of her reverberating cavern, but quickly, overcome with need and desire, he began to thrust hard and fast. His grunts of pleasure as his lusts mounted were met with equally impassioned moans from below. He could feel her thighs pressed against his back, urging him onwards. Their tongues writhed madly together.

Violet screamed into his mouth when her pussy began its first wild convulsions. Its walls tightened against him with each delirious contraction. Wang's body tensed as he felt his juices rising to boil. He began to pound his hips into hers. Violet met each thrust desperately, urging her cunt on to a second and a third outburst of virulent throbs.

Wang wanted this moment of other worldly lust to continue forever, but his passions demanded completion. When his cock began to throb and spurt his essence within her, he grimaced as if in pain, his body tensed and he gave out a deep, throaty groan.

The pair lay clutched together, out of breath from their endeavors for a few, long, comforting moments. Suddenly, Wang realized what had just happened. He had shown the English whore his passion for her, and in the presence of the chaperone to boot. He felt a well of panic rise up in him.

Wang pushed himself off of the supine concubine and rose to his feet. She looked up at him, her luscious body displayed, legs and arms akimbo, her love slit gaping wide. "She knows," he thought. "I'm doomed."

He stepped away from the still panting woman and grabbed his kimono. He left her there, lying on the floor. He didn't even stop to return her now soggy cleft to captivity.

It was the eunuch who did that later, when he entered the room. He had been carefully watching the door to the salon, awaiting his master's exit. He had not been surprised when he saw him leave, his hair disheveled, his face flushed from his passion.

The British whore was still lying on the floor when he entered the salon. It was clear to everyone that music lessons were done for the day. Once he had restored her pussy to its imprisonment, he ordered the still over-whelmed concubine to her feet. The chaperone adorned her with her kimono and then Li tied her hands behind her back with a white silken cord. He fastened the traveling chains to her ankles and led her back to the seraglio.

He had her go directly to her room. Once she had stripped naked at his command, he presented to her mouth one of the opium laced leather balls he used when he needed to keep the concubines sedated. The dazed woman obediently accepted it and stood still while he wrapped a white cloth around her head, imprisoning the leather ball in her mouth. Obediently, she lay down on the bed as he ordered and he rebound her wrists behind her back with the white cord. After he had similarly bound her feet, he doused the lamp and left the room, closing the door behind him.

He instructed Zhu, the head chaperone, to release her from her room at dinnertime. He wanted to give the whore a long time to contemplate her duties to her lord and master and to relive her recent experience with him. The opium would leave her groggy and senseless. He didn't want her to dissect mentally what had happened. On the contrary, structured thought was inimical to her role as a provider of pleasure. Instead, he wanted her mind floating on a sea of physical and mental rapture, as if her copulation with the warlord had caused it rather than the drug itself.

Violet felt a rush of sensation as the first wave of pleasure from the opium struck her. Shortly, her mind became blank. Her body felt sluggish and heavy, but at the same time, paradoxically, light and airy. She thought for a moment she was going to float right off the bed.

The eunuch had been right. The only thoughts that could pierce her bedrugged fog were of her recent experience with her owner, her lord. She hadn't the mental strength to analyze it, yet the sense of something special forming between them was unmistakable. She relived the wondrous feeling that had run through her when he pierced her with his cock. Her pussy seemed to trill in remem-brance. Although she was bound, she could still rotate her hips and the act of recalling their bout of coitus triggered the subconscious rotating of her hips, allowing the little, gel filled balls in her crevasse to collide and reverberate, sending murmurs of pleasure through her body. Her mind seemed to detach from her cranial cavity. It descended down through her throat and chest to her stomach and then centered itself around the precious organ whose adornment declared it to be the property of her master.

She groaned and squeezed her thighs tight. She rolled from her belly to her side. Her eyes were open, but she could see only black. She lay in virtual absolute darkness. There was no world other than her little room and the sensated, glowing sexual organ which pulsed in the middle of it.

军阀 外家
CHAPTER FOUR

The mid-day summer sun beat down harshly on the resplendent garden appurtenant to General Wang's 13th century castle. Gaily colored midsummer blooms, peonies, lilies, chrysanthemums, marigolds and more, graced the graveled pathways. Fine, delicate fruit trees, pears, apricots and peaches, offered their shade. The well tended, well watered lawn was a deep, welcoming green. The women from the seraglio, dressed in their brilliantly decorated kimonos splashed with fine decorations of silver, gold, green, blue and yellow, in a rare treat, had been allowed to come outside and enjoy its magnificence for an hour or so.

It was almost a year since that afternoon in the warlord's salon. That day was a watershed in the relations between the English concubine and her master. Every afternoon that he could, he came to listen to her play. Each time, afterwards, they made love on the thick rug. When they were done, and the warlord gone off to return to his duties, the eunuch would lock Violet up in her room for an hour or more, entranced by a ball of opium, to reexperience that afternoon's delight.

Slowly, but surely, Violet's life improved. A month after their rendezvous began, the eunuch came into the seraglio and announced to her one morning that she was to be permitted to read for an hour each day. It was shortly after that that her lessons in calligraphy began, taught, ironically, by a nun from the French orphanage in Yeuyang, Sister Therese. The woman had spent forty years in China. She was a young girl of eighteen when she arrived, and from day one had deeply immersed herself in Chinese culture. They spoke French together, English was still banned, and Violet's understanding of Chinese grew exponentially as a result.

The real treat came when Violet was permitted a journal. Every day, she wrote out her thoughts. She began to write poetry mimicking the Chinese style. Sister Therese would help her to translate her verses into Chinese and soon Violet began putting them to music which she accompanied with the Chinese mandolin she had learned to play.

It was only in the afternoons, after she had played for him, that the warlord made love to her. At nights, or at other times of the day when the need struck him, he made use of the other concubines or one of the maids. It was like she and the love besotted warlord had created a little world for themselves that only existed at certain times and in a special place. They never talked of their passion. Violet was, in fact, as embarrassed at it as was the general. She could not reconcile having fallen in love with a man who had kidnapped and raped her and kept her prisoner for all of these years.

Did she still yearn for freedom? Very much so. Yet there was much about her life now that was eminently satisfying. Her love for Iris had grown exponentially and they made love as often as they could. When it had been the American girl's turn to be in milk, Violet made sure that she suckled her at least once each day.

Life in the seraglio had taken a turn for the better as well. Whether it was the feeling of confidence she had discovered since her relationship with her master had blossomed, or just that a person could only be pushed so far and no further, her conflict with Zhu, the head chaperone, finally came to a head

One morning, after all the concubines had been bathed, Zhu had ordered the diminutive Chinese concubine, Shu, and Iris to perform for the group in the middle of the common room. Shu was in an unhappy mood. The night before, she had been loaned out to one of the general's guests and he had been particularly abusive to her. She was covered from neck to knees with angry red stripes from her beating. When Zhu ordered her to make love to Iris, she began to cry.

"*Please, mistress, please let me rest today,*" she asked. "*My pussy is sore and I don't feel that well.*"

Zhu, who had been kneeling imperiously on a large, comfortable pillow, immediately rose to her feet.

"*You slut!*" she yelled. "*You will do as I say and not complain! You are a worthless whore! For that you will get ten lashes of my whippy stick! Bend over and show me your ass!*"

Shu burst into tears. Obediently, she crawled to the center of the room and bent over on her knees exposing her rear cheeks to the head chaperone's depredations. She was naked but for the leather collar around her neck with the gold embossed ideograms denoting her as "*Concubine of General Wang*". The angry red trails across her flesh made her chalk white skin seem even paler. Her long, black hair was tied into a ponytail. Her usually pleasant face was distorted by sorrow and fear. As she bent over, her full but dainty breasts pressed into her sensuous thighs.

Zhu immediately reared back with the supple instrument and laid a blow across her already striped rear mounds. Shu gave out a terrible shriek. The man who had beat her last night was especially cruel and the welts and lacerations he had left there were as sensitive as a bad tooth. "Ohhhhhhhhhh!" she cried.

"*Be quiet!*" Zhu yelled. "*If you make any more noise, I'll make it twenty!*"

The rest of the subjects of the seraglio, except for Zhu's callous lieutenants, shrank back in fear and horror at the harshness of the head chaperone's tone. Violet was watching too and her heart went out to the simple, pleasant girl. Shu was the one of them mostly out of place in a seraglio. She was constantly shamed by the voracious sexual need the daily potion she was required to drink produced in her. Unlike her sister, Hu, she trembled at the thought of her use by the warlord, her master and owner, not to mention the strange men he loaned her out to. And she was the least able of them all to take a whip.

Violet had grown somewhat inured to her whippings. Well, if not inured, then at least had developed a higher tolerance for them than she had before. The fact that she started every day for the last year and some months with five sharp blows from the head chaperone's whippy stick, had something to do with that.

Zhu reached back and delivered another blow to the young woman's proffered posterior. The 'crack!' resounded through the room. Shu's body tensed and she emitted a long, high pitched, piteous whine. Her forehead was on the floor and her hands were to either side of her head. They scrunched up into little fists as the pain from the blow coursed through her.

Shu had barely enough time to recover from the blow when another one succeeded it. This time her whine grew a little louder. She started to sob. Her knuckles were turning white and her body was shaking. She had compressed her lips together in an effort to suppress her exclamations of pain. Zhu reached back with the long, supple bamboo stick. A wry, demonic grin spread across her face. Violet knew that the cruel woman was going to put all her strength into this stroke. She knew that Shu would not be able to withstand it. She drew in her breath as she helplessly watched the stick whistle through the air.

Shu let out an agonized screech. It echoed through the room. Then, realizing that she had earned ten more blows, she began to blubber and sob. "*Oh, please, mistress! Please don't beat me! I'll be good! I'll do what you say! Please!*"

"*You are a worthless slut, Whore Number One!*" Zhu shouted. "*I should give you a hundred strokes of the whip! Now I will have to do something to silence that dirty mouth of yours!*"

Zhu ordered one of the other chaperones to bring her a leather gag and a length of white, silken rope. When the grey haired woman had complied, Zhu told her, "*Put it in the little pig's mouth and tie it off tight. Then tie her hands behind her back. I'm going to whip this slut until her ass is bright red!*"

Muffled pleas for mercy and forbearance emerged from Shu's gagged mouth as the chaperone fixed her wrists together behind her back. Her face was awash with tears. When the chaperone who had bound her stepped away, Zhu stepped forward once again, the whippy stick at the ready.

"*Here it comes, whore!*" she yelled. "*And when I'm done, I'm going to fuck you with the master's prick!*"

Sweat had broken out over Zhu's face. Shu's body was gleaming from fear induced perspiration. The poor girl uttered a plaintive, muffled. "*No!*" as the whip descended. It landed athwart her wounds from the night before, leaving a long, angry red mark of its own. "Mmmmmmmmmmpf! Mmmmmmmmmmpf!" Shu screamed as it struck her flesh.

"*That's only five, whore!*" Zhu screamed. "*You've got fifteen more to go!*" When she brought back her arm, the fold of her bluish gray robe got in her way. "*Damn!*" she uttered. She quickly undid the thick, coarse cord that bound the robe to her body and shrugged it off of her shoulders. Now she was naked, her bony, wrinkled body bare for all to see. Her wispy, gray streaked hair fluffed out wildly. Somehow her nakedness made her seem all the more demonic, like some witch arisen from hell intent on the deliverance of torment.

"*That's much better, whore,*" she snarled. "*Now I can hit you much harder!*"

She brought the whip back and delivered a stroke that virtually lifted her off of her feet. Shu let out an anguished wail. The sound of the whip striking flesh was like a firecracker had gone off.

"*Six!*" Zhu yelled.

She struck her again with all her might.

"*Seven!*" she called out. Then "*Eight!*" and then "*Nine!*"

Violet was watching with horror. Zhu had always been cruel and temperamental, but she had never seen her like this. It was as if something had snapped inside her. Violet's heart went out to her the sweet, young victim. Shu was blubbering and moaning uncontrollably.

Finally, Violet had had enough. As the scrawny, naked chaperone reared the whip back once more, Violet, overcome with revulsion, leapt into action. Springing to her feet, she grabbed the whippy stick out of Zhu's hand. Zhu turned to her, surprise and disbelief flashing across her face. Without hesitation, Violet let the whip fly and struck the woman across her withered breasts.

"Ohhhhhhhhhhhhh!" Zhu cried out. "*What are you doing?*"

Violet paid the old woman no heed. She brought her arm back and struck the woman again, this time across her back.

"Owwwwwwwww!" Owwwwwwwwwwww!" Zhu cried out.

If Violet was beyond control when she stood up, the satisfying effect of striking the woman who had tormented her cruelly for almost two years raised a fury in her. Like a fierce tornado, her naked breasts jumping this way and that, her long, pinioned hair flying, she rained blow after blow across the fiendish chaperone's flesh. Zhu cried out at each one. She tried to back away, but Violet pursued her. She found herself in a corner with nowhere to go.

"*Pleeeeeeeese stop! Pleeeeeeeeeese! Help!*" she yelled. She raised her arms and fell into a crouch to protect herself. Violet kept pouring on one stroke after another until the old woman was scrunched into a little ball on the floor crying and sobbing.

"Take that, you old hag!" Violet screamed in English. "I've had enough of your bullying! How do you like the whip, eh? Do you like it? Well, here's some more!" She raised her arm to deliver another fierce blow to the defenseless woman's flesh when she felt someone grab the whippy stick from behind her.

When Violet had risen to save Shu from further torment, the other women in the seraglio, even the other chaperones, were aghast. It happened so quickly that none of them had the opportunity to react. The two ancient, grey haired chaperones who were on duty that day along with Zhu watched while their mistress was beaten back into a corner crying and begging for mercy. Then, as if it had finally registered to them what was happening, they rose to their feet and advanced on the furious Englishwoman.

One of them grabbed the whippy stick while the other wrestled Violet to the floor. Violet rolled about, struggling with her. While Zhu remained sobbing in the corner, the other chaperone entered the fray. Between the two of them, they were able to subdue the English whore. They held her down on the floor. Violet was still screaming invective after invective at the old woman in the corner, against all of the chaperones. She knew that she had breeched a serious barrier, gone way past the demarcation of what would be tolerated from one of the warlord's sex slaves, and she was going to get all of her hatred, anger and resentment out at the same time while she could. She knew that she had earned a terrible punishment, and was using the occasion to get everything off of her chest.

"You filthy hags! Let go of me! I hate you all! I'll kill her! Let go of me you ugly bitches! I'll scratch your eyes out!"

Zhu had recovered from her panic. Seeing that the English whore was now helpless, she got to her feet. *"You are going to the dungeon for that, you whore! But first I'm going to flail you until you are a mass of bloody wounds!"*

Violet knew that the cruel woman meant what she said. She desperately tried to free herself. *"Help me!"* she called out. *"Junjing! Help me!"*

Junjing was the only one of her maids on duty at the time. The poor girl was torn between her fear of the head chaperone and her love for her mistress. Violet screamed again as the two chaperones tried to flip her to her belly so that they could tie her hands behind her back. *"Help me, Junjing! Help me!"* Violet called out again.

That was all Junjing could take. She rushed to her mistress's aid. She leapt at one of the chaperones, dragging her to the floor. Her action was like a spark that set off an explosion. All the other women in the room, Hu, Iris and their maids rushed to Violet's aid. The chaperones were overwhelmed. They had them all, Zhu included, on the floor in an instant. Violet scrambled to her feet. She rushed off to the closet where the tools of subjugation were kept and returned quickly with three silken strands of rope.

"Here! Tie them up! Quickly! Tie them up!" she called out. Within a few moments the three chaperones had their hands bound behind their backs. They were screeching and yelling, uttering dire threats to the rebellious women, but it failed to dampen the revolt. Hu ran off to the cabinet and came back with three gags. The chaperones were swiftly and efficiently silenced.

Once all the gags were in, the rebels sat back and took in what they had done. A wave of elation went through them. They laughed and laughed until they began to cry. Shu's maid remembered her mistress and unbound her wrists and removed the gag from her mouth.

"Ohhhhhhh, Whore Number Four," Shu moaned fretfully. *"What have you done?"*

Violet rushed to her and hugged her. *"Something I should have done long ago,"* she said.

"But we'll be punished!" Shu protested.

Hu had come over to her sister. *"Yes, we'll be punished, but it was worth it. I can't believe the look on old Zhu's face when*

Whore Number Four grabbed the whip from her hands. It was worth a hundred strokes of the whip."

Iris joined them. *"What do we do now?"* she asked.

Violet looked over at the sputtering, enraged chaperones. *"I don't know,"* she answered. *"There's not much we can do. The eunuch will be up here sooner or later and then there'll be hell to pay."*

The women looked at each other. The four maids who had helped subdue the chaperones looked particularly forlorn. It was all well and good for the concubines to rebel. They might face the eunuch's whip, but they were much too valuable to be truly harmed. This was not the case for the maids whose lives were worth less than that of an old horse.

Violet realized at once the gravity of what had happened. She looked at Junjing. *"I'm sorry, sweet one,"* she told her. *"I've gotten you into a real mess."*

"Not to worry, mistress," Junjing replied. *"I'll take whatever punishment that comes. I was glad to help you. I can't stand it when Zhu whips you. Finally, I did something about it."*

Violet reached out and hugged the young girl. Just then, they heard the sound of a key in the lock to the seraglio door. Fear passed through them like a bolt of lightning. The door opened slowly. It was the eunuch.

Li Pao hadn't planned to come to the seraglio that afternoon until it was time for the English whore to go to the salon and play the piano. He was passing by the stairs to the third floor of the castle when something made him think of the women on the floor above him. It was the American slut's turn to service the master in his study should he choose to go there this afternoon and he wanted to make sure that she would be ready. He sensed something was wrong immediately as the door opened.

The concubines and maids had all fallen to their knees and bent over, their foreheads to the floor. His eyes went from them to the three chaperones bound and gagged. Zhu was naked! What was going on?

Li knew that order had to be restored right away. "*Up!*" he yelled as he clapped his hands sharply several times. The maids and concubines rose from the floor in an instant. "*To your rooms!*" he yelled. And to the maids he yelled, "*Tie them up! Hands and feet!*"

The concubines all dashed to their rooms. Junjing started to cry as she bound Violet's hands behind her back with a silk chord. "*I'm sorry, mistress. I have to do this. I'm sorry.*"

"*I know, sweet one,*" Violet told her. "*It's all right. I know you love me.*"

When he was alone with the chagrined chaperones, Li paused for a moment to think. Whatever had happened, the authority of these three chaperones was irremediably broken. Zhu was a fool. He would have removed her long ago but for the fact that she had seniority over the other chaperones and it was her right to take upon herself the leadership role. If he had chastised her for her iron fisted rule, she would have lost much face and probably taken it out on her charges. But now she had given him the excuse to relieve her.

"*Stand!*" he told the three unhappy, old women. He led them straight from the seraglio out into the main hallway of the castle. They still had their hands bound behind them and their mouths gagged. Zhu was still naked.

He paraded them down the stairs, past the gawking guards, right down to the dungeon. He would let then stew there for a few days until he decided what to do with them. Whatever wrongs the other women had done them, they were responsible for keeping peace and harmony in the seraglio and they had failed at their task. He would punish them and then cast them out of the castle.

Before he left the dungeon, at the point of a whip, he received Zhu's version of what had happened. He was not surprised that the English whore had finally revolted against her treatment. She would have to be punished, as would the other women. But this was the opportunity to make the seraglio a more peaceful place. Yanyu, the chaperone who had taught Violet the mandolin and who accompanied her every day when she went to play the piano was next in seniority. She would now get her chance to rule.

As it turned out, Yanyu was an excellent choice. She had a firm but gentle hand. The whippings stopped for the most part. The concubines were given permission to wear clothes again while in the seraglio. And although she made sure that the embonded women were kept in a state of heightened sexuality and continued the practice of compelling them to make love to each other in the seraglio commons, she was understanding when, from time to time, one of them begged off due to harsh treatment the night before.

But first the concubines and maids had to pay the price for their rebellion. Li made them all line up that afternoon. There was much wailing and sobbing. Iris and Hu each received ten strokes of his whippy stick. Receiving strokes from Zhu was one thing, but receiving them from the eunuch was something else indeed. Even Hu, who often bore the master's whip in silent suffering, begged and pleaded for mercy by the time it was over. The four maids received ten also and were all sent to the dungeon for a week. Shu received only five strokes since she was tied up at the time. But what to do with the English whore was the question. He could give her ten strokes, as he had Whore Number Two and Whore Number Three. But she had been the ringleader and should suffer more than the others. On the other hand, he didn't want to break her spirit.

His verdict was that she would receive the same ten strokes as Iris and Hu, but she would also spend ten days in isolation in her room. She would have only her two maids, Ting and Wen, for company. And no piano for a month.

The one who received the worst of it was poor Junjing. The demons who ruled the dungeon had been waiting their chance to get their hands on her ever since she had insulted them the last time Violet was confined there. She was morose and unhappy for a long time after she returned. Violet blamed herself for what had happened and did her best to cheer the unhappy maid up. Eventually, she put it behind her.

That was many months ago now. Since then, life in the seraglio was much improved. Yanyu made sure that the women obeyed all of the eunuch's rules to the letter, but she was usually so pleasant about it that the women didn't mind.

A little picnic had been arranged in the garden and Violet knelt on a plump cushion, her hands bound behind her back as her diminutive maid, Wen, fed her little tidbits and gave her to drink the cool tea. Ting, the lanky one, was holding a parasol over her head so that she did not suffer from the direct rays of the sun. It would not due to have her pallid skin marred by sunburn. The other concubines were kneeling around the other three sides of the colorful, cotton cloth that had been laid out for them.

The warlord's garden was inside the fifteen foot high inner wall that ran around the castle. Beyond that was a taller, more formidable wall, over thirty feet high and separated from the inner wall by a wide pathway. Violet had often stared at the two walls from her perch on the balcony to the seraglio. They were formidable obstacles to freedom.

But Violet was not thinking about that now. She was enjoying their little sojourn too much.

When the meal was finished, the concubines' wrists were unbound and they were permitted to walk along the gravel pathways that intermingled with the lush fruit trees, flowers and plants. She walked hand in hand with Iris, their maids scurrying behind them, desperate to keep the parasols over their heads.

They were both dressed in gaily colored, silk kimonos which hugged their torsos tightly. On their feet were delicate brocade covered slippers. Their hair was tied off behind their heads, flowing long down their backs. They walked slowly, taking in the beauty that surrounded them, enjoying the pleasant fragrances. Although permitted to walk around the garden, security measures were in full force. An 18" long chain connected their ankles, making it impossible for them to do more than take tiny, little, measured steps. Morose looking guards, trying hard not to stare too lustfully at their master's beautiful prisoners, patrolled the garden's perimeter.

"A penny for your thoughts," Violet said to her blond haired companion in Chinese.

Iris gave her friend and lover a smile. *"I was thinking how lonely this place would be without you,"* she replied.

Violet squeezed her hand. *"I feel the same way,"* she returned. *"I sometimes feel guilty about it. I'm sorry that you were kidnapped and made one of the master's whores, but, on the other hand, I don't know what I would do without you."*

Iris squeezed Violet's hand back. *"It's terrible enough to have been made into a whore,"* she said. *"But to know that someday I will be sold and probably forced to live in a brothel is too much to bear."*

"I worry about it all the time," Violet replied as they turned a corner in the garden. *"I think often about poor Tatiana and wonder what terrible fate awaited her after she was sold. I can't bear the thought of it and I can't bear the thought of it happening to you, or me for that matter."*

"Surely, you don't have to worry," Iris said. *"The master loves you. He would never sell you."*

"Oh, I'm not so sure," Violet replied. *"I don't know if you would call whatever feeling he has for me love. It's a form of passion, but I don't think it's love."*

"Whatever it is, he treats you so specially. He must feel something."

"*Yes, I suspect he does. And I am glad that he doesn't force me to fuck his friends anymore. Only, I'm sorry every time he makes you or Whore Number One or Two do it. I feel so guilty.*"

"*Don't, my love,*" Iris protested. "*We've benefited too from his love for you. He hasn't whipped any of us for months and he seems to have become more gentle. And it's all because of you.*"

"*I'm glad that he treats you better. I just wish I had the power to convince him to free you.*"

"*He'll never do that. If the American government found out that he had held me in sexual slavery, they would send a gunboat up the river and blow his castle into smithereens.*"

Violet stopped and turned to her lover. She placed her hands on her face and caressed it. "*I don't know what the American government would do. I'm sure that the eunuch would figure some way out of it. But let's not talk of things that can't be. Give me a kiss to show me you love me.*"

Iris closed her arms around Violet's body and drew her close. Their lips met and their mouths opened. Ting and the other maid giggled and lowered the parasols they were carrying to shelter the kissing women from the view of the warlord's soldiers who were standing sentry. The kiss was long and passionate.

Violet took Iris's hand in hers again and they resumed their walk.

"*Do you ever think of running away?*" Iris asked her.

Violet smiled. "*Every day,*" she answered. "*But how could I ever get past the guards never mind out of the seraglio? And then there are the two walls.*"

Iris moved her body closer to Violet and went to kiss her again. Except she did not kiss her but, rather, began to whisper in her ear in English so if the maids heard they would not understand.

"Do you see that tree over by the inner wall near the chrysanthemum bushes?"

Violet was startled to hear English spoken. "Yes," she answered, looking over to where Iris had indicated.

"If you climbed that tree and then jumped, you could get over the inner wall."

Violet looked closer at the tree. She saw just what Iris had pointed out. A little thrill went through her body. "But then you'd have to get by the outer wall," she whispered.

"There has to be some way," Iris said lowly. "There has to be a place to climb. I've seen soldiers walking on it."

"But the stairway would be guarded. How would you get past them?"

"Believe me, if I could figure out a way to get out of the fortress and over the inner wall, I'd figure a way over the outer one too."

Violet's maid, Ting, suspicious, having heard the women's whispers but not understanding their content, made to separate them.

"*No talking in English,*" she said sternly. "*You know it is the master's rule.*"

Violet tried to make light of it. "*I was just telling Whore Number Three how much I loved her. There's nothing wrong with that. Is there?*"

"*No, mistress, but if the master ever found out that I let you speak English to Whore Number Three, I would be beaten. Please don't make me report you. You would be whipped too.*"

Violet leaned forward and gave Ting a little kiss. "*Don't worry, little one. I would never do anything to hurt you. To prove it, when we get back to the seraglio, I will take you to my room and make love to you. Would you like that?*"

Ting blushed. "*Yes, mistress,*" she said.

Just then, Yanyu, the head chaperone, stood up from where she had been kneeling and gossiping with the other chaperones. She clapped her hands loudly. "*Time to go back inside,*" she announced. Shu and Hu had also gone for a walk and they were on the other side of the garden. Once all the concubines and maids were assembled together, they formed themselves into a little parade. As they were turning the corner to go back to the side gate they had come out of, Violet looked back one more time at the tree Iris had pointed out. She etched it into her memory.

* * * * * * * * * * * * * *

As the concubines were being escorted back into the castle, Li Pao was making arrangements for that night's banquet. It was a very special occasion. As part of his efforts to assemble a sort of self defense league amongst the neighboring warlords, he had convinced General Wang to invite General Chi, from Chengdu, a major city some 50 miles to the south, for a few days to discuss a possible alliance. While the Nationalists would have to fight their way through Wang's kingdom in order to get to him, it would be plain to anyone who looked at a map that once General Wang was gone, he would be next.

Violet's piano had been brought to the main dining room for the occasion. One of the servants, who Li had had trained in such arts, was busy tuning it so that its pitch would be perfect for the guests. Besides General Chi, a number of local merchants were invited. It would be good for them to see the warlord hobnobbing with his fellow potentate. And there were some commercial agreements Li was seeking to work out with General Chi while he was here.

Maids and male servants were scurrying about cleaning, dusting, arranging flowers around the room. The table was being set with the general's best silver and china. General Chi was due to arrive around five o'clock. He would be coming by automobile over the narrow, dusty roads and would undoubtedly bathe before dinner. Li had instructed the cook to be ready to serve at 7.

Li left the dining room to go up to the seraglio. He had already instructed Yanyu to make sure that the concubines all bathed and were dressed in their fine, silken gowns. They were to be present at dinner. Undoubtedly, General Chi would select one of them to be his bed companion. They had to all be looking their best and brightest so not to bring shame upon their master.

He arrived there just as the concubines were being admitted to the seraglio wing. A guard was ever present at the doorway to the enclosure and the door could only be unlocked from the outside. Inside the doorway was the outer seraglio. It contained several private rooms and the cavernous bathroom where the concubines bathed. It also led to the door to the inner seraglio. That door was always locked as well from the outside. Thus, a fleeing concubine would have to get past two locked doors plus the guard to escape.

Li followed the concubines into the inner seraglio common room. When he entered, the women all fell to their knees and bowed to him.

"Tonight your master has a much honored guest", he told them. *"You are all to be on your best behavior. Whore Number Four will play the piano for him. One of the others will serve him tonight. When he looks at you, he should see smiles and pleasant faces. If I see anything else, you will be beaten."*

The women remained silent. There was no need to respond. There was no need to elaborate. Obedience to the eunuch's orders was always assumed to be immediate and absolute.

When the eunuch left, Yanyu stood. *"Whore Number Two will take the first bath. The rest of you should go to your rooms."*

Violet and Ting went immediately to Violet's room. Once Ting had lit the lantern and shut the door, Violet shucked off her brightly colored kimono. Ting happily drew off her clothes. They joined each other on the bed.

* * * * * * * * * * * * * *

Later that afternoon, General Wang was in his luxurious bedroom dressing for the day's festivities. He had taken a hot bath, tended to by one of the youthful maids embonded to him. A thin, graceful girl of about twenty, with long, black hair tied behind her head in a ponytail, and wearing the standard maid's uniform of tight, white pants and a light green blouse, was scurrying back and forth, bringing the general his clothes.

It was a night for his best uniform: dark green with bright red stripes down the legs of his pants. There was gold braid sewn into the collar and bright gold buttons that the maid had dutifully polished. His boots, with which he had not yet adorned himself, were knee high and had been shined to a brilliant gloss.

The warlord was a little on edge. He wanted to make a good impression on General Chi and his advisors. An alliance with him could bring great dividends. Some of the other neighboring warlords had given favorable reception to the idea of an alliance amongst them to withstand the inevitable onslaught of the Kuomintang forces. None of them, however, had committed themselves. If General Chi fell into place, the others might follow.

Wang, still in his stockinged feet, his tunic not yet buttoned, strolled over to one of the side tables in his room and poured himself an inch or two of brandy into a wide, delicate snifter. There would be a lot of drinking tonight and he didn't want to get too much of a head start on the festivities, but he needed to cool his nerves. He took a sip of the honey colored liquor and sighed as he felt its heat pass down his throat and into his belly.

The problem was that if Chi didn't agree to become an ally, he could very well pose a significant threat. Already he chafed at the tolls and fees charged to goods from his duchy as they made their way through Wang's on their way to Nanking, Shanghai and the sea. If Chi made a deal with the

Kuomintang, one that would leave him in place as governor of Hunan Province, his own territories would be surrounded by hostile forces. Wang had to convince him that his long term interests were better protected by an alliance with him. Like Wang, he was absolute ruler over his domain and answered to no one. If the Kuomintang obtained his fealty, it was only a matter of time before the central government would try and exercise dominion over General Chi's affairs. He would have to share a part of his tax revenue with the Nationalists. He would have to commit soldiers to their army. And, if the winds changed in Nanking, he might find himself pushed aside in favor of someone more amenable to the government's control.

On the other hand, if no deal was made, and the Kuomintang forces were victorious in overthrowing him, he would be left with little, perhaps, if he was lucky, with his life.

The same logic, of course, pertained to Wang and his territory. Once a deal was made with the Nationalist forces, it could never be unmade. And once they had overrun his defenses, he would have nothing to bargain with.

The liquor was not having its usual calming effect. He needed something else to take the edge off of his tension. He turned and saw the pretty maid kneeling on the floor, his boots in her hands, waiting for a signal to help him step into them. Here was just the thing he needed.

The warlord gave the humble looking girl a signal to approach him. She rose to her feet, her eyes downcast, and stepped over to where the warlord stood, her steps small and measured, her shoulders hunched. Wang snapped his fingers and she fell to her knees in front of him.

Easing his prick from his pants, he spread his legs for balance and awaited the girl's commencement of her duty. She looked up at him shyly, a wave of unhappiness flitting briefly across her face. Then, without further hesitation, she took his soft, thick, dangling tool into her mouth.

The girl worked slowly and skillfully to bring her master's prick to hardness. It did not take long. She washed the head with her tongue as she held her pursed lips firmly against his pole. Her dainty, almost fragile fingers surrounded his tool, holding him steady and in place while she rendered adoration to his cock.

The warmth of the girl's mouth sent a relaxing wave of pleasure through him. He closed his eyes and placed his right hand lightly on the girl's bobbing head. The snifter was in his left and he took an occasional sip as the girl bent to her task. His thoughts drifted to his English concubine. He never used her English name in his thoughts and, since his liaison with her had begun to blossom, tried to avoid thinking of her as Whore Number Four, which was technically her name now. Using any name for her would only serve to diminish her. She was a paragon to him, a symbol of more than mere beauty. She had a complexity to her, a depth of soul, that rendered her almost mythic. He had met with her yesterday in the salon. She had played for him, a wondrous sonata. Afterwards, they had made love. She had mouthed his cock to explosion and then he had plowed her hot channel, making her call out with pleasure. As the maid continued to suckle and stroke his prick with her mouth, he began to fantasize that it was her mouth, her lips, her tongue that was pleasuring him.

His need was slowly rising. He gave out a sigh of approval for the girl's efforts. She was making faint, little whining sounds as if in protest to his callous use of her. He would have to remember to tell the eunuch to have her whipped later.

As his passion rose, he decided to take command. He grabbed her ponytail in his right fist and pushed her head down as far as it would go against his loins. He felt the head of his cock poke into her esophagus. She gave out a squeal of unhappiness. Holding her hair fast in his grip, he began to pump her head back and forth on his cock, thrusting his hips out to meet it on each downward stroke.

His thrusts were becoming more violent. The girl released a gagging sound each time he struck the back of her throat. Her whining was becoming more pronounced. Her hands were pressed against his thighs in an effort to assuage the force of his downward thrust of her head.

He stopped in mid stoke. Her lips were firmly pressed against his pole. Her chest was rising and falling rapidly. He let himself lie there in her mouth for a moment, allowing her to catch her breath. *"Hands behind back,"* he ordered her briskly. With a faint whine, she complied, crossing her wrists behind her. Now there would be no resistance to his efforts.

Wang recommenced his thrusts of the girl's pretty head against his loins. He took a large sip from the snifter in his right hand, leaning his head back and finishing it off. His mind then concentrated on the mouth that encompassed him.

Back and forth, again and again, he drove the girl's head while he pumped his hips. She was crying now. "She must be new," he thought. "She will learn better."

When he felt his juices building towards a flow, he accelerated his efforts. He felt a surge of pleasure run through him. He groaned as he tottered over the edge. His cock began to pulse and throb. He groaned again and sought the back of the girl's throat. She coughed and gurgled, trying desperately to free her head while obediently leaving her useless hands in place behind her. Her movements and the sensation of holding her prisoner to his lust accelerated his passions. His cum jetted out of him in mighty spurts. His knees buckled. He threw back his head. "Ohhhhhhhhhh!" he exclaimed. "Ohhhhhh-hhhhhh! Ohhhhhhhhhhhhhh!"

He waited until his cock had stopped dancing to withdraw it from the girl's mouth. She took in a deep breath of air. He looked down and saw that her face was covered with tears. Her look of misery enhanced her not inconsiderable beauty. He gave out a great sigh. "Now, that feels better," he thought.

After the girl had assisted him in mounting his boots, he ordered her to strip. He brought out a leather thong from his cabinet of toys and bound her wrists together in front of her. She was sobbing quietly and her face displayed her obvious fear. She had a beautiful body, soft and smooth, nice, heavy breasts and a round, plump derriere. He tied off her bound wrists to one of the posts at the foot of his bed. There would be a break in the proceedings after he greeted General Chi and his guest went off to refresh himself. "I'll whip her myself," he decided, "when I come back. And then I'll fuck her."

军阀 外家
CHAPTER FIVE

Three hours later, Wang was kneeling on a plump, soft cushion at the head of the long and wide table in his main dining room. General Chi knelt next to him. The food and the rice wine had flowed non stop for the last hour. They had moved onto the brandy and Wang, a man of not insubstantial appetites, was beginning to feel the effects of so much booze.

General Chi was kneeling next to him. Chi was very tall, over 6', and wide of shoulder. While Wang was a fit specimen at 53, Chi had let himself go to pot. He had a big belly and jowls that descended from his cheeks. His face had a sallow look, although a deep, dark intelligence clearly lurked there. His eyes were yellowish and red rimmed, probably due to the opium he smoked regularly. He was wearing a dark brown uniform which was bedecked with bejeweled medals. His shoulder boards were covered with gold braid as was the military cap that he wore. On his hands were rings of ruby, diamond and emerald. Like Wang, he was nearing his mid fifties.

Unlike Wang, he was of noble stock. His family had held positions of authority under the Ming Dynasty for two hundred years. When the Ming's had fallen, it was natural for Chi, as the oldest son of the Imperial Governor of the province, to assume control. He had, in fact, laid claim to the territory which included Wang's little duchy. It had been wrest from him by Wang's predecessor, a colonel in charge of one of Chi's regiments. Wang had supplanted him some ten years later.

The hall was festooned with lively yellow and white banners on which were written the slogans of Wang's republic. A large flag, yellow and white with a red dragon emblazoned on it, draped the wall behind them. Wang's second in command, Major Won, sat to Wang's right and Chi's number two man sat to his left. The rest of the table was populated by the important citizens from Yeuyang, a banker, one of the leading traders, the owner of the textile mill, the engineer in charge of the electric company. Their wives, including Wang's two wives, Li Hua and Yu Jie, were interspersed among them, dressed in their best finery. Chi had not brought either of his wives on this trip as he was counting on partaking of General Wang's well known hospitality.

Several courses had been served, duck, pheasant, chicken and pork. There was a plethora of crisp, fresh fruits and vegetables. Dancers from the Bamboo Tea Room had been hired and put on a salacious but tasteful show. Wang's private orchestra was at its best.

The warlord's concubines knelt along the end of the table opposite the two generals. They were dressed in their finest gowns, slinky, white silk sheaths covered by colorful, flowing robes decorated with bright, blooming flowers. The robes left the upper parts of their chests bare, exposing the rise of their breasts. Their faces had been expertly painted, light green eye shadow, dark kohl around their eyes, ruby painted, plush lips, white powder applied to their cheeks, making their already pale faces appear almost ghost like. Their hair was raised upon their heads, held fast by long, golden pins, revealing their delicate necks. As usual for when the concubines were permitted to be seen in public, their wrists were tied to their waists by white, silken cords and their ankles were joined by bright, silvery chains that allowed them to be spread no more than 18" apart. Their maids, bedecked for this special occasion in light green sheath dresses, knelt by their sides and were feeding them small portions of the splendid repast.

The concubines had been taught to be demure in public and their gazes were, mostly, directed downwards at the brilliantly set table in front of them. From time to time, Violet let her eyes wander upwards to take in the somewhat rambunctious crowd and the uniformed men at the other end of the table. When she did, she often found General Chi staring back at her, a lascivious mien to his face. His attentions produced a great anxiety in her. From what the eunuch had said earlier in the seraglio, she did not have to worry about being subject to the man's sexual attentions this night. That role was delegated to her sisters in embondment. The man's perfidious appearance made her uneasy nonetheless.

Many times during the festivities one or another of Wang's guests called out a toast to either General Wang or General Chi, or to them both, and all glasses went bottom up. Wang toasted his guest several times and Chi responded suitably.

When the last dish was cleared away before dessert, General Wang got up and made a little speech. His words were slightly slurred and he was a little unsteady on his feet. He raised a glass of brandy in the air.

"*For many years,*" he said to the crowd, "*General Chi and I have been neighbors. During that time, he has earned much glory for himself as the peaceful ruler of some 750,000 souls. His subjects sing out his praises for his wisdom and foresight. Because of him, Chengdu is wealthy and prosperous.*

"*But there are clouds on the horizon. The same forces which seek to absorb and despoil our new nation, threaten the peace and tranquility of Chengdu. The so called Nationalists in Nanking seek to establish their hegemony over all of China. But they do not have the people's best interests at heart. They seek only to line their pockets and steal from us what we have earned by the sweat of our brow.*

"*And they are the tools of the white devil foreigners. They serve at the beck and call of their British masters and the other European powers. They would take away our traditions, make good little Europeans out of all of us, despoil our temples in the name of their white, Christian god."*

Wang turned from the crowd and looked directly at Chi. *"But General Chi will not let that happen to the people of Chengdu!"* he pronounced. *"I have invited him to join forces so that the Kuomintang devil invaders can be repelled. Together, we can protect our way of life, our families, our property. General Chi, I salute you!"*

He raised his arm in toast to his guest. The men and women in the room stood and raised their glasses as well. Wang tossed the glass of brandy down his throat and his guests followed suit. A great cheer erupted in the dining hall.

General Chi smiled and accepted the accolades of General Wang and the crowd. His smile was not so much smug as self satisfied. He was a man used to hearing panegyrics in his name; his staff was primarily manned by sycophants. And to say that the people he ruled were happy and prosperous was a stretch to say the least. Sure, there was prosperity, for those in General Chi's inner circle. But all wealth was held at the pleasure of the general and could be taken away at his slightest whim. The people were heavily taxed to pay for Chi's two lavish palaces, one in the city and one in the nearby lake district.

While in Wang's domain Wang's word was law, he kept a reign on his baser instincts and made his men toe the line. No so with Chi. Chi's men ran rampant over his territories and no businessman, farmer or merchant was safe. Not to mention their daughters. Chi was notoriously venal and maintained a seraglio of twenty beauties. He used them up rapidly due to his cruelties and then sent them to serve in his officers' brothel or in the many whorehouses in Chengdu, replacing them with new alluring young women stolen from their families. His lieutenants were not much better. The only thing that ever stopped them from claiming a young beauty was if the general wanted the girl for himself.

Chi raised himself to his feet, needing to press his fat hand on the table in order to get his bulk vertical. The crowd was still clapping and cheering as he waved his jewel encrusted hand until they finally silenced themselves. When the revelers were silent he raised his glass.

"I am honored to be spoken of so highly by a man for whom I have so much respect," he said, his voice deep, authoritative, used to instant obedience. *"When General Wang said those kind words about me, he was really speaking about himself. I have traveled all over China and I have never met a man of such vision as he. His glorious army serves as a bulwark against the oppressors from Nanking. His marvelous victory against those dark forces has ensured continued liberty for all of his neighbors."* Chi raised his glass a little higher.

"I give you the savior of Hunan, the President of the Republic of Northern Hunan, my friend, General Wang Ku!"

Waiters had scurried about filling the glasses of the other guests while Chi spoke and everyone was prepared to join in his toast. Chi brought his glass to his fat lips and drained it. Once everyone else had done the same, there was a repetition of the crowd's enthusiastic cheers and applause.

General Chi waited for it to die down. He waived the audience to silence.

"In testimony to General Wang's great victory over the Kuomintang forces, I have brought him a humble gift," Chi said. He waived to a member of his retinue who was standing by the door to the dining hall. The officer nodded and stepped outside. When he returned, he was holding something under a large yellow and white cloth. The officer scurried to the head of the table and handed the cloaked object to his general. Chi waited a moment so that the crowd could hold its breath in anticipation of learning the nature of his bequest. Then,

smiling, he withdrew the yellow and white cloth, letting it fall to the floor.

In General Chi's hands was a long, shiny, jewel en-crustted sword. The golden scabbard was covered with glittering rubies, diamonds and sapphires. It was inlaid with hand tooled silver. The golden hilt was covered with jewels as well. Chi proffered the priceless instrument to Wang.

"*To the Conqueror of Northern Hunan!*" Chi exclaimed.

The notables and their wives erupted into cheers. Wang was set aback. He had expected nothing like this. The sword was worth a fortune. Dazzled by its beauty, dazed by the unexpected nature of the gift, the general's appellation, and the surfeit of alcohol he had consumed, Wang rose to his feet. He took hold of he proffered hilt of the glittering sword and drew the blade out slowly. The shiny, well oiled, steel blade emerged easily. The electric lights of the dining hall glinted off of it, making it sparkle. When it was fully free, Wang swung it back and forth gently a few times. It was perfectly balanced, an expertly honed instrument.

General Wang gave Chi a nod of thanks and respect and then handed the sword over to a servant who was standing behind him. The servant, somewhat taken aback at being in possession of such a fine instrument, looked to the eunuch, Li Pao, for instructions. Li made a motion for him to walk around the table and exhibit it to the master's guests so that they could appreciate the fine gift. There was much ooing and ahhing as the brilliantly decorated weapon was shown to them. When he was done, the servant resumed his place behind the warlord holding the sword in presentation position so that it's magnificence could be displayed for the rest of the evening.

When Wang knelt back down on his cushion, another toast was in order, this time to the generosity of General Chi. Another toast followed that, called out by one of the guests, in honor of the friendship between the two warlords. Another one followed that.

Li Pao, seeing that the drinking was about to get out of hand, ordered that the entertainment begin again. The lights were dimmed. Several of the maids had been working on their dancing skills. They emerged from a side room, outfitted in long, glittery dresses, their hair stacked upon their heads, delicate rice paper fans in their hands. The orchestra played a traditional Chinese folk song and the four maids conducted a slow, seductive dance before the guests.

While the dance was going on, the servants distributed desserts and tea. Nobody paid the tea much mind, but the cakes and fruit were quickly consumed.

Violet watched the youthful maids step back and forth graciously in time with the music, swaying their hips, hiding their faces with the fans, and then fluttering them about their bodies, giving out warm, welcoming smiles. They were a big hit and received long, appreciative applause when they were finished.

Next came Yanyu, the head chaperone. She was dressed in a dark green and silver robe with wide sleeves that covered her almost to her feet. Yanyu was an expert with the liuqin, the Chinese mandolin. She had taught Violet to play, but Violet was far away from being able to duplicate the chaperone's skills.

Yanyu knelt on a cushion, stroked the luiqin several times to loosen her fingers and then began to play.

Her fingers drifted nimbly over the four strings. She had a soft, mellifluous voice. She sang of lost loves, distant homelands, the beauty of the earth. The room was stock silent except for the harmonic echoes of the strings and the sweet, sultry voice.

Many eyes became wet with tears as the concubine sang. Many glasses of brandy were emptied and refilled. General Chi made sure that his and Wang's glass was always brimming. Wang was no slouch when it came to drinking, but he was impressed with Chi's ability to consume alcohol. The huge man seemed to have a hollow leg. For himself, he wished that the river of intoxicating liquid would slow a bit, but he dared not allow the fellow warlord to get the better of him before his guests. When Yanyu finished her final song, Chi and Wang toasted again, this time to the woman's angelic singing.

Now it was time for Violet's performance. She often played for the warlord's guests, but was always shunted off back to the seraglio before the occasions degenerated into drunken revelry. Her sister concubines were not so fortunate, and they were often paraded around half naked and made available for the guests' pleasures, as she had been before the blossoming of her relationship with her master.

The piano had been brought down to the dining room earlier and placed in a corner. Several of the servants wheeled it out now. Li Pao came over to where the concubine knelt and instructed her to rise. Little Wan, Violet's diminutive, third maid, had been given the honor of attending her tonight and she immediately, but discretely, untied from behind her the silken cord that had bound her mistress's wrists close in to her hips during the festivities. The eunuch crouched by her feet and released the chain that bound her ankles.

Violet had a sense of foreboding as she stood, waiting to be freed. She raised her eyes briefly and saw the repulsive looking general at her master's side leering at her lasciviously. She also saw that Wang was very drunk. He had a tendency to weave slowly from side to side when he was in his cups. She had seen it many times.

Li Pao saw it too. It was now when he was usually sent off the English concubine to the seraglio, since, once the warlord was deep in his cups his banquets started to get out of hand. Li had worked hard at developing the relationship between the English whore and his master, and he didn't want a moment's drunken foolishness to destroy the bond that had developed between them. He knew that it was a delicate and fragile and that if, in his drunkenness, the warlord treated her before his guests like the whore that she was, it would set his work back perhaps irretrievably. Li chided himself for not taking into account General Chi's legendary thirst by having the concubine entertain the guests earlier in the evening.

Violet made and obsequious bow to the warlord and his guests and slowly, gracefully, taking tiny steps as she had been taught over the years, moved over to the piano. When she reached it, she made another bow, as if begging for permission to be seated. Her eyes caught the warlord's and he gave her a brief nod.

General Wang was watching her every move. He was proud of her abilities with the piano. He liked to show her off. She was the most precious jewel of all his possessions. His blood rose as he had watched her drift off to the piano from where she had knelt, her hips swaying slightly. Her long, chestnut colored hair was piled up on her head, exposing her long, gracious, seductive neck. Her breasts, full and plump, shimmered as she walked. She was a pleasure to behold and he knew that every male eye in the dining hall was wishing they were him right now.

When she sat down on the piano bench, Violet drew back the sleeves of her fine silk gown, exposing her slender, pale arms and her delicate, fragile looking fingers. Her nails had been kept trimmed somewhat shorter than he liked ever since she had been playing the piano. Nonetheless, they had been covered with bright red polish to match her full, painted lips. When she looked at him with her sultry, grayish green eyes, expertly outlined in black, her eyebrows trimmed and blackened, Wang felt his cock rise. He had not spent time with her today, or yesterday either. He had been too busy. He made a vow that he would make sure that he visited her in the salon tomorrow afternoon while she played and that he would make long, passionate love to her there on the plush carpet when she was done.

Violet clasped her hands together, stretching her fingers, limbering them. She placed her feet on the pedals, pressing them, as was her habit, as if making sure that they were operational. She paused for a moment, her fingers poised above the glittering black and white, polished keys. She waited until she had the attention of everyone in the room and the sound of their raucous laughter and conversations died down. All the lights were dimmed except for the one over the piano. She took a deep breath. And he she began.

She had chosen a Beethoven sonata. Her hands flowed gracefully over the keys. She had no need for sheet music; she knew the piece well. She often played it for the warlord when he came to visit her. She closed her eyes and let the gentle, tranquil sounds reverberate all through her.

The guests were all silent, mesmerized by the spleen-diferous sounds. Even the coarse General Chi was moved by her playing. The notes, in perfect combination and harmony, spoke of beauty, love, passion. Some of the guests had heard her perform before and had been waiting anxiously for the moment when she would deliver them into the magical world that she created for them. The others had heard of her skills, and her beauty, and con-sidered themselves blessed that they would finally be able to see and hear the legendary concubine play.

There had been many rumors passing around in Yueyang that the warlord had become besotted with her. They all knew the story of how he had saved her from beheading at the last minute more than a year and a half ago. Some of them had been there personally to witness it. She had been naked then. She had proudly walked to the blood covered dais where the others had gone before her, ready to greet eternity. They had had glimpses of her since, for instance at the parade when they had celebrated the warlord's great victory and the founding of their new state. But to see her up close and to hear her play, that was something they would lord over all of their jealous friends for years.

Wang let the gentle music flow over him. He closed his eyes to better appreciate it. When he did, he felt himself sway and he had the sensation of the room spinning around him. He was disturbed that he let himself get so drunk. Soon the banquet would be over, though. The English concubine's playing would end the night. The maid who had dressed him was still in his room, tied to the bed. She had been a delight when he had fucked her earlier and he had promised himself that he would go back for more. He just hoped he wasn't so drunk he would pass out instead.

When the song was ended, Violet paused again. Playing the piano always brought her to a special place, a place of comfort and peace. She breathed deeply, reveling in it.

She was brought out of her reverie by the sound of excited, appreciative applause all through out the room. She turned to acknowledge it and then stood up from the piano and bowed.

Wang opened his eyes and took in her beauteous form. "Tomorrow," he thought.

General Chi disturbed his enjoyment of the song's aftermath by tugging his sleeve and proffering another toast. *"The jewels that I gave you tonight pale in comparison to this, most precious one. I give you a toast to her beauty and her heavenly skills."*

It was a toast that Wang could not refuse. He lifted his glass and brought it to his lips. When the fiery liquid poured down his throat, he had to close his eyes again to stop his head from spinning.

Li Pao ushered Violet quickly back to the table where, after her wrists and ankles had been confined again, he had her kneel. He ordered the other concubines to stand up and he led them, shuffling, to the head of the table where their master and the other warlord knelt.

"*General Chi,*" Li Pao said, his voice unctuous and subservient, "*my master begs you to honor him by selecting one of his unworthy concubines to grace your bed for the evening. May I present them to you?*"

Chi gave out a throaty laugh. "*Of course,*" he replied. "*General Wang's hospitality is legendary. I have been watching his beauties all night trying to decide which one I want. Please show them to me.*"

Li bowed and brought the trembling women forward. None of them wanted to be the one selected to entertain the debauched looking man. He had a mien of cruelty that bespoke an evening of torment ahead for whoever he selected. But they feared the eunuch more, who could bring a world of torment to them that would last for days and days. To dishonor their master would be one of the worst sins they could commit.

"*This is Whore Number One,*" Li said as he took hold of Shu's arm and made her step closer to the leering general. "*She is the shyest of all the general's whores, but she will bring you great delight with her mouth. She has been well trained. And she begs and cries deliciously when whipped.*"

"*Very nice,*" Chi answered. He reached his hand out and took hold of her cheeks, pressing them together harshly. "*She has a pretty face that I am sure looks prettier in anguish.*"

Shu uttered a little whine and her eyes watered. A chill of fear ran through her body. "Not me! Please, not me!" she thought desperately.

Li pulled the unhappy woman back and brought her sister Hu forward. Hu was a bit taller and a bit more filled out than her older sister. Normally, she had no qualms about fucking the warlord's guests. Being turned into a whore had been a liberating experience for her and she gave in to her carnal desires whenever she had the opportunity. But this man inspired fear even in her. She tensed involuntarily as she was brought near him.

"*This whore is a tiger in the bedroom,*" Li said. "*She has beauteous curves and her pussy is always hungry.*" Li turned Hu around so as to demonstrate to the general the fullness of her posterior. He lifted her robe so that the general could see her ass which was tightly wrapped by her long, sheath dress underneath.

General Chi leaned over and rubbed his meaty paw over the woman's rear inviting rear mounds. He had an appreciative grin on his face. "*Nice,*" he said. "*She seems particularly suited for the use of a cane.*"

"*She can take much punishment,*" Li proffered.

He brought Hu back and then took hold of Iris's arm. She recoiled, her revulsion at the thought of serving the general overwhelming her for a brief moment. Li tightened his grip on her arm and she obediently shuffled forward as he led her closer to the dreaded General Chi.

"*This is General Wang's American whore,*" Li told Chi. "*Her skin is tender and smooth and as pale as alabaster. And she has breasts just made for the whip. And she is in milk too! Her product is as sweet as nectar!*" Li took a position behind the young, blond headed American and pulled her robe and sheath dress off of her shoulders. He tugged them down until her ample, pale breasts were revealed. Iris gave out a moan of protest, but otherwise did not resist.

Chi took hold of her plump mounds with both his hands and gave them a mighty squeeze. Iris cringed in pain and tried to pull back, but her breasts were too firmly in his grip.

"*I see what you mean,*" Chi said, grinning. "*Once, in Shanghai, the captain of an American gunboat insulted me. It would be fun to make this whore pay for his rudeness. And we get so few European sluts in Chengdu that it would be a refreshing change to fuck her.*"

"*Her pussy waters easily, lord,*" Li said. "*And bruises come up nicely on her tender skin.*"

Tears had begun to form in Iris's eyes. She was sure from the general's comments and the eunuch's laudatory references to her suitability for use that she would be chosen. Her hands tugged at the bindings on her wrists.

The crowd of guests were enjoying the display of General Wang's concubines. A few of them had had the pleasure of partaking in their flesh from time to time and they knew what delights the well trained females were capable of delivering. In the corner of all of the male minds in the room was the hope that one of the whores would be doled out to them that night.

Wang looked down at his proffered property with satisfaction. He knew that Chi had a well populated seraglio, but he doubted that any of his women were as beautiful or well trained as his whores, especially the American. He looked at his fellow warlord, awaiting his decision.

"*It is so hard to decide,*" Chi said. "*They are all so alluring. But there is one whose charms I have yet had the chance to peruse.*" He looked down the table at Violet who was still kneeling there in place.

"*The General's English whore would not be to your satisfaction, lord,*" Li said quickly. "*She is older and lacks the passion of General Wang's other concubines.*"

"*She doesn't look too old to me,*" Chi responded. "*Don't I get at least the chance to see her up close?*"

Li looked anxiously at his master. This was precisely the situation he wanted to avoid.

General Wang felt a stab of unease at the mention of his English concubine. He realized that he should have sent her away long before this. He was about to, as politely as he could, indicate that the English whore was reserved to him when General Chi spoke to him.

"*As I said when she was finished playing, she is a true jewel of a possession. I was wondering how she would appear standing next to the beautiful sword you honored me by accepting. Let me see how her brilliance compares to its jewels.*"

The mention of the sword made Wang squirm. He didn't want to appear to be impolite. The sword was a great gift. He had given the general nothing in return. If he was rude to Chi, it would seriously diminish his chances of working out an alliance.

"*Bring her here,*" Wang blurted out to his eunuch.

Li Pao looked back at him sternly. "Don't do this, master," he thought. "Let me handle it."

Despite his consternation at the order, Li was bound to obey. He left the other women in place and quickly walked to where Violet was kneeling. "*Up!*" he ordered her briskly.

Violet had watched while her sisters were displayed to her master's guest. She had heard the comments that were made. A pit formed in her belly. To disobey was unthink-able, although every part of her wanted to run from the room. Obediently, with the help of her maid, she rose to her feet. She docilely allowed herself to be led to the head of the table. She kept her eyes downcast, not wanting the repulsive general to see her fully in the face, and so that she did not have to see his.

When she was next to General Chi, the eunuch presented her.

"*You see my lord,*" he said, lifting Violet's chin with his hand, "*she is old, probably soon destined for a brothel. Only her piano playing is beautiful.*"

"Ahhhhh," Chi replied, "*I'm not so sure. She has a pretty face, one that is truly ageless. Bring me the sword and have her stand next to it.*"

Li ordered the servant who was displaying the jewel encrusted object to come forward. Nervously, he approached the two generals, holding the sword out from his body.

"*You see,*" General Chi said. "*She outshines its beauty. A man would sell his soul to spend the night with her.*"

Wang, hearing this, decided to put his foot down, alliance or no alliance. The English whore was his and no man had the right to claim her, not even this pig from Chengdu.

"*She is not available,*" Wang said. He tried to make his comment authoritative, but, due to his inebriation, it came out more like, "*She issh na abailable.*"

Chi laughed. "*I have heard the stories about General Wang's infatuation with the English whore,*" he said. "*But I told my men that it was untrue. No respectable Chinese man would fall in love with a Western devil, and a whore to boot. Tell me that I am right, dear General Wang,*" he asked pointedly. There was a devilish grin on his face.

Violet heard the man's comments. She looked at the warlord directly. Neither of them had ever spoken about their passions. He had never declared love for her. She had never truly decided whether she loved him or not. But this was the moment of truth. If he loved her, he would not whore him out to his friends.

"*But General Chi,*" Li Pao spoke out, "*my master would never dishonor you with this lowly whore's flesh. She is tired and worn. She could never give you the delights that the others could give you. Take all three if you like. They will bring you great pleasure.*"

Chi paused. He was a man used to getting what he wanted. He looked at his fellow warlord. "*She does not look old and worn to me. She has a beauty that age cannot destroy. I can understand General Wang's reluctance to share her. She is truly a valuable possession. But if I'm not mistaken, General Wang is a gambling man. Why don't we let fate decide? I'll put up twenty gold pieces against my use of her tonight. Surely a man as daring as General Wang would not refuse such a bold wager.*"

General Wang felt the door to a pit of doom open up before him. All of the most prominent members of local society were present in the room. If he refused the wager, he would lose great face. It would show that he was afraid of the judgments of the gods. He would lose the respect of everyone. To be known as a man who had lost his heart to a foreigner and, as General Chi had said, a whore at that, would be a disgrace. It was one thing to gratify his private, secret longings for the woman, another thing entirely for the whole world to know it.

Seeing Wang's hesitation, Chi spoke again. *"I'll make it fifty gold pieces. But if I win, you must give me the key to the whore's heavenly gate. I have heard how her pussy is all bound up. If I win, I want the use of all of her."*

The room seemed to be spinning around Wang's head. He could not refuse fifty gold pieces. It was enough to supply a battalion of his troops for a year! People would say he was a fool to lose the chance to win it all because he refused to let a distinguished guest partake of the hospitality of one of his concubines. And not the first one, either. She was ranked fourth in his seraglio, and he had already offered up one through three. And she had been made available to many men in the past, countless men. To refuse a bet because he couldn't part with her for one night was unthinkable!

The warlord straightened himself up, trying to shake off the torpor induced by so much alcohol. He wished he could think more clearly. In the end, he had no choice. *"It's a bet,"* he said finally. *"Bring us a deck of cards."*

Muttering under his breath a prayer to his ancestors, Li Pao ordered one of the servants to go get a deck of cards. He was back in about thirty seconds. During the wait, the crowd buzzed with excitement. Li looked at the face of the English whore. Her face was pale, but there was anger in her eyes. He looked at his master's face and saw his fear. Had the damage already been done? Was the bond broken? If only Wang could win the bet, maybe something could be done. But if he lost, there would be no going back.

The servant handed the deck of card to the eunuch. It was a brand new pack, its seal unbroken. Li stepped forward and placed it on the table between the two men. Chi picked it up and inspected it.

"*Very good,*" he said. "*Let your number one officer, Major Won, shuffle the deck. As the guest, I shall pick first.*"

Major Won looked at his master. He knew what was at stake. Everyone knew how the general had fallen in love with the English whore. If he shuffled the cards and his master lost, the blame might be put on him. Nonetheless, he couldn't refuse.

Won picked up the deck and broke the seal. He withdrew the pack of cards and peeled the joker away from it. He divided the pack into two stacks and then shuffled it. The crowd was silent and the click of the cards as they beat against each other could be clearly heard. He shuffled it three more times. He presented it to General Chi, placing it in front of him.

"*My number one officer, Major Li, will cut the deck,*" Chi announced.

Chi's major, a slender, debauched looking man, smiled. He was enjoying his master's game. It was fun to watch the upstart warlord, General Wang, squirm. He leaned forward and, without uncovering a card, split the deck. He put the top layer down on the table and then covered it with the bottom half. He leaned back and grinned.

General Chi was grinning too. Fifty gold pieces meant nothing to him. There were any one of a hundred merchants he could shake it out of to replenish his coffers if need be. It was worth it just to watch General Wang's discomfiture. On the other hand, a night with the beautiful and legendary English whore would be something.

Chi picked up his glass of brandy and poured it into his mouth. Placing the glass back down on the table, he brought his fat, jewel covered hand down to the stack of cards. He let his thumb slide down the deck until he was about one third of the way down. He looked about at the crowd. Whatever happened tonight, the crowd would carry home with it his willingness to part with fifty piece of gold for the chance at one night with a beauteous whore. The thought made him happy.

He gave the spellbound crowd a polite nod and the uncovered a card. It was the seven of spades. Inwardly he seethed at the unkindness of the fates, but outwardly he looked calm and collected. "*It's your turn, General,*" he said.

General Wang's heart leapt. A seven! All he had to do was beat a seven! Surely the gods were smiling on him. He had almost a sixty per cent chance of winning the bet. He stretched out his hand, trying not to let it shake. It was if all his chances at happiness rested on this one turn of a card. His fingers drifted down the pack. He tried with al his might to gain some intuition as to where to cut. Near the top? The middle? The bottom? Where were all the high cards? Would the gods guide him?

He decided to cut the deck about ten cards from the top. He lifted the small stack up. He was afraid to turn it over. He took a deep breath and flipped the cards.

His heart stopped. A great gasp arose from the crowd. It was the five of hearts. He had lost.

Violet felt a surge of nausea flow through her. She looked over at General Chi. He was leering at her hungrily. Her knees went week and if weren't for the perspica-ciousness of the warlord's eunuch, she would have fallen to the floor.

Wang too felt a wave of nausea rise up within him. He had never meant for this to happen. If he hadn't been so drunk it wouldn't have. He looked into the eyes of his concubine and saw her fear and revulsion of what he had done to her. Something had just broken between them, he knew that. For the first time in the longest while, he actually felt sorrow well up in him.

But it wasn't just sorrow for the concubine. It was sorrow for himself. And not just for the wondrous relationship he had just destroyed. No, it was much more than that. Wang was a great believer in luck. The gods bestowed it or they took it away. Losing to General Chi in front of the cream of Yeuyang society was bad joss indeed. It could be the sign that the heavens had withdrawn their munificence from him. All kinds of bad things could happen now. He could lose everything.

Wang's sorrowful reverie was interrupted by Chi's deep, grating voice.

"Tonight the gods seem to be smiling on me, General Wang," he said as he patted Wang on the shoulder in mock commiseration. He picked up his glass of brandy and rose to his feet. He raised his arm.

"Here's to my courageous host who has shown himself to be also a great sportsman. I salute you General Wang."

Wang turned to the audience and smiled weakly. A great cheer of agreement arose from them and dozens of glasses were upended. Wang nodded to them all the while gripping the edge of the table in frustration and self recrimination.

When Chi put down his glass, he announced that he was ready to retire for the night. *"I will enjoy sampling your treasure, General Wang,"* he said. He held out his hand. *"The key,"* he said.

General Wang looked at the distended, fat, glittering paw. He would rather take hold of his new sword and run the man through. But not only would that be a gross breach of hospitality, he would immediately be immersed in a war with the general's survivor and heir. Any hopes that the other warlords would cast their lot in with him would be lost. The tale of his brutal betrayal of his guest would run like wildfire throughout China. No, the only way out was to appear gracious in defeat. Tomorrow he would have to try and regroup.

Wang wore the key to Violet's loins on a chain around his neck. He unbuttoned the first button on his tunic and pulled the chain free. He unclasped the chain and let the little, silver key fall into his hand. He looked at it for a moment and then begrudgingly handed it over to Chi.

"*Thank you, general,*" Chi said. "*I will give you my appraisal of your concubine's skills tomorrow morning.*"

Li Pao was, as usual, ready to rise to the occasion. Inwardly he agreed with his master. This was a disaster of the first magnitude. But his job now was to ensure that no further damage occurred. The concubine must go with the devilish warlord from Chengdu, and she would have to perform for him as dutifully as she would for the master himself.

"*With your permission, lord, I will prepare the slut for your pleasure. I will bring her to you in about ten minutes. This will give you time to perform your ablutions and make yourself ready to enjoy her flesh.*"

Chi nodded. He knew that the eunuch was about to pass on last minute instructions to the concubine and, undoubtedly, remind her of the abuse he could rain on her should fail in her duties. He didn't mind. He needed to piss anyway.

Violet watched forlornly as the sallow mountain of a man stepped down from the platform on which he and General Wang had knelt and exited the room. His number two, Major Li, went with him.

When the men had exited, Li Pao clapped his hands, calling several of the servants to him. "*Take these other sluts back to the seraglio,*" he told them. "*Have them wait for me. They will each receive five strokes of my cane for failure to please our guest.*"

Iris, Shu and Hu quailed at the announcement of their punishment. Their lips trembled as the servants affixed chains to their collars so they could be led away. To be flailed by the eunuch's four foot long whippy stick was one thing. The cane was something else entirely.

As they left, shuffling along, their ankles confined by the 18" chains that connected them, they all cast commiserating glances at their sister. No one wanted to be selected by the cruel looking warlord from Chengdu, but all of them had sympathy for the one that was.

军阀 外家
CHAPTER SIX

Violet watched her sisters in bondage go, her heart heavy. When the eunuch attached a chain to her collar, she realized that her whole body was shaking. Without ceremony, he tugged at the leash and led her away. As she was leaving the expansive dining room, passing through the double doors that guarded it, she cast a last, desperate, fear filled look at her master.

When they entered the cavernous hallway outside, she began to sob. "How could he do this? How could he do this?" she exclaimed in her mind as she glumly followed the eunuch's lead. She cursed herself for her foolishness in thinking that her life had changed. The last ten months or so of her life had seemed almost idyllic compared to what had gone on before. She had thought that things had changed for her, that maybe, someday, the warlord would free her from her chains. That he loved her. But if he loved her, he would never have done this to her. He had proved himself once more as a dissolute, callous, evil monster. Her hatred of him, dormant for so long, sprang up within her. She vowed never to be fooled by him again. Somehow, someway, she would get away from him. Even if it meant her life.

The eunuch brought Violet to a little room down the corridor from the dining room. When they entered, he brusquely ordered the concubine to kneel. She hesitated for a moment, a venomous look in her eyes. But then she obeyed, slowly lowering herself to her knees.

Li had set up the room earlier knowing that one of the concubines would be chosen to serve General Chi this night, although not which one. On a table near the door was a shiny silver pitcher containing the love potion which was administered to the concubines daily and whenever they had be selected to serve the warlord or one of his guests. He poured a cupful into the beautifully hand decorated porcelain cup next to it and then presented it to Violet. "*Drink*," he ordered.

Violet took a look at the cup. She knew what it was and what it did to her when she drank it. She would be helpless to prevent her passions rising when General Chi made use of her. She gritted her teeth in revulsion at the thought. She looked down at the table from which the eunuch had taken the cup. There, lying next to it, was a riding crop. Its finely polished leather glistened. She knew that if she refused the drink, she would be beaten. And that that would just be the beginning of her travails.

Every part of her wanted to revolt, wanted to, once and for all, cast aside her submissiveness, her obedience. There was a time that she been a woman and not a slave. She had been free. She had dignity and honor. That had all been taken away from her. She had undergone brutal torture, shameful use, countless humiliations. Was there any of that woman left? Could she summon up the same bravery which had filled her the day she had been officially inducted as the warlord's sex slave, giving her the courage to defy him, only to have it dashed when she learned of the foul betrayal by her erstwhile fiancé, Richard, who had delivered her into his hands?

Li peered down at the kneeling concubine. He saw the courage and stout heartedness rising up within her. He too remembered that fateful day. It was then that he had realized that she bore an exceptional soul. All of his work over the last three years to mold her into the valuable gem she had become was now dashed. He knew that. But he also knew that if she refused him now, if she disobeyed, rose in revolt, a punishment would begin that would only terminate in her death. Once she had crossed the line, she would never give up. He knew that he had to convince her to obey or else she was doomed.

He drew the hand back containing the porcelain cup. He knew that a mere repetition of his order would have no effect, might even push her over the edge. A new approach was called for. She needed to know what rebellion would mean.

"*Do you want to live?*" he asked her.

Violet was taken aback. The eunuch had never spoken to her this way. From his mouth she only heard orders, commands. He had never in the three years that she had been subject to him asked her a question. She was so shocked that, for a moment, all that had gone on in the last hour was washed away. He was treating her like a person for the first time that she had known him.

And then the question sunk into her mind. Did she want to live? Her refusal to cooperate in her rape by General Chi would be disobedience of the first order, would bring shame upon her master. In her mind's eye, she had a vision of herself down in the dungeon basement of the fortress, kneeling abjectly on the floor. The warlord would watch while the eunuch slowly strangled her. Her body would be burned and her ashes cast to the winds. And before that, she would indubitably undergo the most fiendish torture.

Whatever torment the devilish General Chi had in store for her, she knew that she would survive the night. As long as she was alive, there was hope that she could escape somehow. There just had to be a way. And then she remembered the soldier who had invaded the seraglio that night so long ago. He had made her promise to live. To live and remember their night of bliss. He had given everything to be with her. She had never known a night of passion like that. Foolishly, she had let the warlord, her master and owner, lead her astray from her pledge.

Violet looked up at the man who had been her jailer for so long. She hadn't thought that it would matter to him whether she lived or died. She saw a depth to the man that she had never seen before. She had always thought of him as an enemy. He had been the one who had broken her to her slavery, molded her as a sexual instrument, brought her to orgasm against her will every morning since she had been a prisoner here, whipped her many times.

And then it struck her. He had been molding her all this time to be much more than the warlord's sexual slave. He had arranged for her to learn to play the mandolin, to learn Chinese, had undoubtedly arranged for the piano that had brought her so much joy during the last year. He had brought the French nun to teach her to read and to learn Chinese poetry. And now, all his work had come to naught. She would never serve the warlord as a lover again. Never! And yet he still wanted to protect her. Not from the devilish man who waited for her down the hall in one of the warlord's guestrooms. But from herself. He wanted her to live.

"All right," she said to herself. "I'll live. Who can tell what the future may hold." She straightened her back, kneeling up straight. A band of fear ran through her, fear of whatever torment faced her this night. Her mouth was dry and she could not speak. She nodded in assent.

Since her hands were still affixed to her waist, the eunuch brought the cup containing the passion producing elixir to her lips. She tilted her head back and received it. As usual, almost instantly the opiate that was its base began to have an effect. Her head began to cloud and she felt a tingle go through her body. The eunuch poured a second cup and she drank that one down too.

Li Pao watched the concubine consume the potion and he noticed the tell tale signs of its effect. As long as the English whore was alive, there was still hope. As long as she remained obedient, she might yet prove to be the vehicle for the blossoming of his master's soul.

When the second cup had been consumed, the eunuch placed it back on the table. He turned back to the concubine. "*Up!*" he ordered. She rose unsteadily to her feet. He took the leash that still dangled from her neck and led her from the room.

The dining hall was in the north wing of the second floor of the general's castle. The guest bedrooms were in the south wing. Violet followed the eunuch down the hall. Their pace was slow, almost ceremonial, as she took the tiny steps permitted to her by the chain that connected her ankles. Despite the calming effect of the opiate, her heart was racing from fear. Her palms were sweaty and a vast trough had opened up in her belly. She kept her head bowed, her eyes on the plush carpet putting off for as long as possible her view of the doorway that would lead to her night of torment. And then they were there.

The eunuch did not bother to knock on the door. He turned the handle and pushed it open. The room was large; General Chi had been allotted the best guestroom, of course. A vast four poster bed dominated the room. Well polished mahogany furniture graced the walls. The one, large window was adorned with lavish red curtains into which elegant scenery had been woven with strands of golden yellow. The carpet was soft and thick. A delicate, crystal chandelier hung from the ceiling, filling the room with soft, electric light. Beautiful, ancient Chinese paintings decorated the walls.

Violet had seen this room many times, had lain with seemingly countless men in it. She was familiar with its princely attributes. But what met her eyes was not its lavish furnishings, but the chain that dangled from the ceiling in the corner of the room, the whips that were mounted on the wall and the small steel cage in which she had heretofore spent so much time..

Chi was just emerging from the bathroom appurtenant to the chamber. He had shed his uniform and was dressed in an elegant silk robe splashed with presentations of colorful, languid orchids. His feet were bare. He grinned when he saw her.

"*Ahhhh, my little prize at last,*" he said. The eunuch had brought Violet to a halt when they entered the room. Chi stepped up to them and took the leash that led to Violet's collar from his hand.

"*Thank you, Li Pao,*" Chi told him. "*I don't think I'll have need of your services for the rest of the night. This little whore is going to keep me well entertained.*"

The eunuch bowed to the general. Before he left, he gave Violet what she thought was a sympathetic look.

When the door closed behind her, Violet's heart turned to lead. A shiver went through her. Her eyes began to water, but she quickly fought off the urge to cry.

Chi pulled her to the center of the room. He removed the chain from her collar and tossed it aside. He took hold of her cheeks with an iron like grip with his right hand and squeezed them hard until Violet involuntarily let out a low whimper.

"*So this is the famous English concubine that has stolen General Wang's heart,*" he said. "*I've wanted to meet you for so long. Tales of your beauty and passion have reached as far as Chengdu. I have to say that seeing you in the flesh, I know that the rumors are more than justified. I'm going to enjoy playing with you.*"

Chi's reddish eyes glared at her. They appeared to Violet more like the eyes of a beast than of a man. A demon lived behind them.

Chi released her face and stepped back. He slowly began to walk around her. Despite his bulk, he had a cat-like grace and his movements gave Violet the sense of being stalked.

"*Yes,*" he continued to say, "*the whore who stole General Wang's heart. But General Wang's greed is greater than his passion for you, isn't it. He gambled you away easily enough. So you see, no matter what you might have thought you were to him, you're just another commodity, a whore to be let out for profit."*

Violet trembled at the man's cruel words. But she could not deny the truth of them. Her lips trembled, her eyes watered.

He had come around again to her front. *"I admire your grace and beauty, my little whore,"* he said. *"But I think its time to see a little bit more of you."*

Chi took hold of the belt that held her robe and loosened it. He spread it wide and then, taking the edges of her elegant silk gown, pulled them down sharply from her shoulders, revealing her pale, plump breasts.

"Ahhhhhh! Delightful!" Chi said churlishly. He took hold of her delicate mounds, squeezing them harshly. Violet moaned as the pain went through her. Her hands, balled into little fists, strained at her bindings.

Chi continued his assault on her breasts. He took hold of her long, thick nipples, rigid with fear, and pinched them harder and harder until Violet gave out a squeal of pain. Smiling, he pulled the two bruised darts upwards, higher and higher until Violet was forced to stand on her toes in a vain attempt to relieve the harsh pressure.

"Why don't we start off with a nice whipping?" Chi said. *"Your breasts are just begging for it."*

Pulling on her nipples, Chi dragged the frantic Violet over to the corner of the room where the chain dangled from the ceiling. Releasing her burning points, he took the chain and hooked it to the ring on the front of her collar. He then pulled the chain taut until Violet could barely touch the floor with the tips of her elegantly brocaded slippers. Her neck strained and she was forced to tilt her head backwards to ease it.

So far, she had said nothing in response to the man's taunts. She closed her lips tightly, suppressing her urge to beg for mercy. She knew that nothing would forestall the man's intent to gain his pleasure by harming her. It would only serve to stoke the flames of his passion.

Chi went to the wall and removed a tasseled whip from its mounting. It had stiff, knotted tips that had been soaked in vinegar and left to dry. He stepped up to his unhappy victim and dragged the tassels slowly over her breasts. Violet suppressed a moan of fear as she felt the coarse leather irritate the soft, delicious skin. She closed her eyes and steeled herself for the pain that would shortly ensue.

The potion she had been forced to drink was making her mind woozy and, despite her frightful predicament, was beginning to draw out her body's lustful needs. She tried to fight them, wanting to deny the man her excitement and so not to lead him to believe that his treatment of her had sparked her lusts. She could feel her breasts becoming firm and her nipples tightening. A low burning had commenced in her loins. "Oh, god, help me," she prayed desperately.

Chi brought the whip down by his side. He used his free hand to massage her breasts, squeezing and mashing them against her chest. "*I think I'll have a little taste of these fine beauties before I whip them,*" he said. His voice was low and there was a tremble in it evidencing the development of his own passion. He leaned over and took the nipple of Violet's right breast in his mouth while massaging the other with his left hand. Violet gave a little jump as she felt the moist heat envelope the tip of her breast. He had sucked in the nipple and all the surrounding areola into his mouth.

The pull of the suction from his mouth in combination with its heat sent a tremor through her and her pussy tingled with unwanted excitement. When he took the other breast in his mouth, Violet gave out a moan of enforced pleasure. She cursed the man inwardly, cursed the warlord, her master. Maybe she should have fought him, she thought desperately. She knew that he would have had his way with her nonetheless, but at least she would have had her pride. As it was, she felt like the abject whore the man had described, a conspirator in her own violation.

Chi moaned with pleasure as he suckled Violet's teats. His hand circled her free breast, squeezing it along its base. Violet's pleasure at his oral ministrations was mingled with the pain brought on by his hand. She cursed herself again as she swayed in her chains, her toes barely able to anchor her to the floor.

Having had enough, Chi stepped back. He took a moment to savor the view of his tempting targets. Violet was naked from the waist up, the folds of her elegant, bright green and silver gown serving as an elegant contrast to her pale white skin. The only adornment above her waist was the black, leather collar around her neck with the gold, embossed ideograms declaring her as General Wang's concubine. It pressed harshly against her chin, forced up by the chain that held her aloft. Just the toes of her elegant slippers touched the floor giving the impression that she was dancing on her tippy toes.

"That was delicious," Chi told her. *"But I think it's time for your whipping to commence. I can't wait to see your twin beauties reddened with the effects of the whip's kiss and hear your screams of pain. Call out all you want. It will be music to my ears."*

He brought the whip back and then forwards quickly. The coarse tassels and stiff endings collided with her pale, soft, tender mounds. They made a sharp slapping sound as they landed. Violet's body stiffened as the pain shot through her. It was like a dragon had drawn its claws across her mammaries.

With all the effort she could command, Violet suppressed the violent moan which arose from deep within her. She compressed her lips together tightly and jammed her eyes closed tight. She could not see her tormentor; her eyes were directed to the ceiling above. But she could feel the heat of his body, sense his malevolence inches away from her.

"*I gave you just a little taste, my little English whore,*" Chi told her. "*Just to get you warmed up. I'll stop when your cries of pain are sufficiently exquisite so I know that you are truly at the edge of what you can endure.*"

Chi stepped back from her once more and let the whip fly. It struck with measurably more force than the first blow. Violet's breasts burned as if a fire had been alit on them. She could feel them jerk with the impact of the whip. Tears had begun to flow down her cheeks. Despite her frantic efforts, a high pitched whine escaped her lips. Her hands tugged fruitlessly at the bindings that kept them tight to her waist. The force of the blow caused her body to turn, forcing her to shuffle on the tips of her toes.

"*That's a little better, my sweet,*" Chi said. His voice was tremulous with his excitement. "*Here's another,*" he taunted.

The first two blows had gone from right to left. The third one went in the opposite direction, proving that the general had a very creditable back hand swing. While the first blows had forced Violet to turn towards her right, this one forced her body, in reaction to the savage blow, to turn back to her left.

Violet's whine this time lasted longer and was more heart rendering than the first. But the general had no heart to be rent. He smiled as he watched Violet's body twitch and spasm as the results of his cruel blow went through her.

Violet's breasts were already reddened by the effects of the whip's rough tassels. Angry, blood red marks had arisen where the stiff, knotted tips had struck her. The pain coursed through her, driving out all other sensations. She knew another blow was coming. She tried to steel herself against it. Her pledge to deny the cruel man the benefit of her wails and laments was weakening. She felt words of desperate supplication welling up within her.

The fourth blow came quickly, again left to right. It was the harshest yet and felt like the man had plunged a thousand knives into her proffered, defenseless mounds. The sounds emerged from her lips before she even knew it. "Ohhhhhhhhhhh!" she moaned. "Ohhhhhhhhh!"

"That's more like it, my little whore," Chi said. The exertion of administering the blows was telling on his corpulent, bloated frame and his words sounded rushed. Administering whippings to his wives and concubines was about the only physical work, besides fucking, that the jaded general ever engaged in and the effort of putting his back into the blows had made him almost breathless.

Violet heard him take in a deep breath, his lungs wheezing. Then he spoke again.

"That was much better, whore!" he told her. *"But I think you can do better still!"*

When the next blow fell, the dam burst within her. *"Ohhhhhhhhhh! Please stop! Pleeeeeeease! Pleeeeeeease!"* she called out desperately. Violet had acquired a quite sophisticated mastery of the Chinese language by this time, but that mastery escaped her now as she frantically yelled, *"No hurt. Pleeeeeease, no hurt more! No hurt, pleeeeeease!"*

Chi paid her supplications no heed. He struck her again. And again. And again. He alternated from right to left and left to right. All pretense of stoically receiving his ferocious assault had fled. "Stop! Stop! For god's sake, please stop!" she begged in English. "I'll do whatever you want! Let me serve you! Pleeeeeeeease stop! Pleeeease!"

Violet's distended body twisted and turned in reaction to the blows. She tried to turn her body away by dragging her toes on the thick carpet below her, but each time she tried to shy away, a blow came from the opposite direction, forcing her body back. Her collar cut harshly into her neck as the chain kept it remorselessly held taught against her chin.

It was only when Violet had turned into a blubbering, frantic, abject being that the rapacious general stopped. The sounds of her sobs filled the cavernous room. Satisfied at the misery he had induced, Chi tossed the whip aside. He stepped to the wall and began to lower the chain that had held his victim erect. Slowly, Violet's body sagged. Her legs were too weakened by her ordeal to hold her up. When she had sunk to her knees, Chi tied off the chain once more.

"*Now that we understand each other,*" he told her, "*it's time for you to go to work.*" His rigid, thick cock was jutting from the confines of his robe like a spear pointed at Violet's head. "*Open your mouth and suck my cock, whore,*" he told her churlishly. "*And if you don't make a good job of it, I'll have you back on your feet to receive another lesson from the whip!*"

Violet was sobbing and moaning, but the warlord's threat pierced the fog of her distress. "*No more, no more,*" she said in Chinese. The chain was just slack enough so that she could turn her head and open her mouth to receive the fierce man's weapon. He took hold of her head with both his hands and plunged it in.

The salty, rigid, inflamed instrument filled her mouth. A wave of revulsion flowed through her, but the unhappy, miserable concubine leapt quickly to her repulsive chore. She surrounded the thick shaft with her swollen lips and began to suckle the iron hard snake that had pierced her. Guided by his fat, meaty hands, she began to bring her head back and forth, lavishing the remorseless prick with her tongue. She was desperate to avoid another session with the whip. Her breasts burned as if they had been inundated with acid, but she did not let them distract her from her odious task.

"Ahhhhhhhh! Ahhhhhhhh!" Chi moaned as he sawed himself back in forth in rhythm with the Englishwoman's efforts. "*Good! Good! That's good, my little whore!*" he exclaimed. "*I see that General Wang has taught you your duties well! You're a good whore after all! Do all Englishwomen suck cock as good as you or is it your special talent, eh, my little whore? Ahhhhhhhh! Ahhhhhhhh!*"

The cruel taunts filled Violet's heart with hatred and shame. "Yes, I am a whore," she thought miserably as the thick, hot meat traversed her oral cavity. Chi was thrusting harder and harder and the head of his foul protuberance was striking at the edge of her throat. His hands were clasped tightly on the sides of her head, forcing her to obey his whims. His groans of pleasure were getting louder, his grip tighter.

"*Here it comes, whore!*" Chi exclaimed. "*Drink down every drop of my cum like the whore that you are!*"

Violet felt the man's hips press forward. She gagged as the tip of his cock plunged into her throat. Her face was mashed against the evil man's fat belly. She felt his cock commence its dance within her. She had taken her master's cock down her throat many times and had become quite adept at it, but the suddenness of the man's thrust had caught her off guard and she began to choke and gasp for air. Her hands were clutched into tight little fists and she strained to free them from her waist so she could push the man's corpulent thighs back, freeing her air passage. "Mmmmmmmmmm! Mmmmmmmmmmmm!" she moaned frantically. Chi ignored her desperate protests. He kept he face buried tightly against his belly as he emptied himself within her.

"*Ahh! Ahh! Ahh!*" he exclaimed as his cock jumped and throbbed. "*That's good! That's good! Ahhhhhhhhh!*"

When his cock had finished its pulses, he kept her face pressed against his belly as he enjoyed the moist heat that encompassed his softening pole. Violet was desperate for air and she tried with all her might to pull her head back to free her air passageway. Her mind was swimming and her lungs were heaving. It was only when his cock had diminished to its dormant state that he withdrew.

Violet took in a deep, frantic breath. Her chest rose and fell mightily and she tried to bring more oxygen to her brain. Her body was weak and ravaged. It slumped, forcing her collar more tightly against her neck. A wave of misery flooded her and she began to sob again.

Chi stepped back from her. He was huffing and puffing too. He staggered over to a hutch against the wall and poured himself a brandy from a delicate, etched decanter into a wide mouthed crystal goblet. He downed it quickly and then looked back at the miserable form of the woman he had just violated.

Violet was still trying to catch her breath. Her plump, wounded breasts swayed back and forth, shimmering with her efforts. Her hair, which had been piled on top of her head, had become undone and loose strands fell wildly across her shoulders. Her fine robe and dress was down around her arms revealing her bare upper torso. She was a refined, yet abject victim. Chi paused for a moment to take in what he had wrought.

"*Let me know when you've caught your breath my little whore,*" he told her. "*We've just gotten started.*"

Violet looked up at him in misery. She knew that the cruel man was not bluffing. When he finally came towards her, she flinched and a void opened up in her belly.

"*Stand up!*" he ordered her harshly.

Filled with dreadful anticipation of the man's next depredation, Violet struggled to her feet. It would be much worse to disobey him, to give him an excuse to worsen her ordeal. When she had reached her feet, he ordered her to turn around. He reached under her robe and untied the belt that had held her hands prisoner. When her hands were free, Violet let them dangle at her sides. Although she now had the use of them, she doubted very much whether they would be of any aid in ameliorating his upcoming assault.

He undid the chain that still connected her ankles. "*Take off your rags,*" he ordered. "*I want to see the rest of you.*"

Slowly, as if in a trance, Violet discarded her raiment. Her beautiful silken robe fell the floor at her feet. Her dress was already at her waist and she was able to shimmy it off with a few movements of her hips. She stepped out of her slippers and turned to meet her assailant.

"*Very pretty, my little whore,*" he said. "*If I owned you, you would remain naked all the time. Your charms are too magnificent to hide.*" He stepped up next to her, to her side, and placing one hand in the small of her back ran his other over her taut belly.

"*So smooth and delicate,*" he intoned. He moved his hand lower. He towered over the young woman and that, together with his bulk, made Violet as if she were being stroked by a monster. His hand reached the shiny, silver lock that imprisoned her loins. "*And this is the famous lock I've heard so much about. You must be quite a slattern for your master to have to lock away your intimacies that way. I've heard the story of how the lieutenant stole into the seraglio and had his way with you. If you had been my whore, I would have boiled you in oil for that. Have you ever seen anyone boiled in oil? The oil is kept just below boiling, actually, so that you body poaches from the inside. And then when you were at the point of death and the oil had soaked into your skin, I would tie you to a stake and set you alight. I've done it many times. It's quite a spectacle.*"

Violet's body quailed at the thought of the man's cruelty. Her hands were free and she resisted the urge to push his meaty paws away from her. It filled her with revulsion to feel him touch her.

He took the heavy lock that guarded her portal in his hand and gave it a harsh tub, making her squeal. "*Should I unlock it, or just rip it from your loins?*" he asked her. For a moment, she was filled with terror that he would do it. She knew he was capable of the most extreme forms of cruelty. She took small comfort though from the fact that this time at least he had to return her to master all in one piece.

Chi abandoned her steely adornment for the moment and ran his other hand up and down her back and then over her beckoning rear mounds. "*Very nice,*" he cooed. "*Your ass was made for the whip. Before we say goodbye I'll make sure I mark it up nicely. But that's for later. Right now I want you to turn around and look at me.*"

Quivering, Violet turned until she was facing the man. Her eyes were downcast and he took hold of her chin, gripping it tightly and raised her head. "*What's the matter, my little whore, am I too ugly to look at? You're not afraid of me are you?*" He gave a great belly laugh at his joke. "*You're right to be afraid, my little whore. I'm the demon from your worst nightmare.*" He laughed again. The he turned serious.

"*Put your hands in front of you,*" he ordered. Violet moved quickly to obey. He reached down to the floor and picked up the silken rope that had confined her wrists to her belly until a few moments ago. "*Cross your wrists,*" he spat. Violet hesitatingly complied, knowing full well that he could only have some nefarious purpose in making such a demand.

The cord was about six feet long. He placed the middle of it across her wrists and tied it off, crisscrossing it between them and using two strong knots. "*Put your hands behind your head,*" he instructed her. All of his false charm was gone and he was intent on his purposes once again.

When Violet moved her hands behind her head, Chi took the ends of the cord and wrapped them around her neck several times. The he passed the ends through the ring of her collar and tied it off tightly. Her hands were now pinioned in place behind her neck. The ends of the cord dangled between her delicate, if marred, breasts.

He took hold of her elbow and marched her over to the bed. He pushed her down on it and instructed her to lay down on her back. When she was in position, he went to the foot of the bed and, taking hold of her ankles, dragged her so that he heels were resting on its edge.

"*Stay there,*" he ordered. He stepped over to the cabinet on the far side of the room and opened it. He brought out two three foot long leather thongs and returned to the bed. Taking hold of her ankles, one by one, he tied them off to rings near the middle of the six foot high posts on each corner.

Violet lay there with her legs spread wide and lifted up. Her rear end was raised a few inches off the bed. She suppressed a sob, knowing that her most sensitive place was now subject to his cruelties.

When he came over to the side of the bed, Violet saw that he had also retrieved a leather gag from the cabinet that held the various sex toys used and useful in tormenting helpless females. He presented it to her mouth. "*Open up, wench,*" he told her. "*I've no use for your mouth for the time being and I've heard enough of your wailing.*"

Violet obeyed, her lips trembling, and he jammed the leather prong between her lips, filling her mouth. He then tied the straps tightly behind her head. "*Feel free to cry and plead all you want now, my little slut.*"

Chi stood up and went over to the hutch were the brandy was kept and poured himself another glass full. He took a mighty swig, his "Ahhhhhhh!" announcing his enjoyment of it. He placed the glass back down and returned to the bed. Next to the bed, resting on a chair, was his uniform pants. He dipped a hand into one of its pockets and produced a silver object on a chain. It was the key to the lock that had for more than a year protected her velvet passageway from being violated by anyone except her lord.

Dangling the chain from his hand, Chi floated over to where Violet lay on the bed. He stepped between her legs and swung the key back and forth, grinning lasciviously at her. "*You see what I have here, my little whore?*" he asked her tauntingly. "*It's the key to your master's prize possession. I'm going to see if your pussy is as sweet as everyone says it is. I'll bet that before you had it locked up, a hundred men have tasted your honey pot. So for you it should be nothing special. But I'll see if I can make it interesting nonetheless.*"

He knelt down by the foot of the bed, his face level with her loins. Violet involuntarily tugged at the bindings that held her ankles high and at the tie that held her wrists pinned to the back of her neck. Just the thought of having her pussy put to use, despite her revulsion for the man, was making it tingle. While she was being whipped the lust induced by the double dose of potion given to her by the eunuch had been submerged in her consciousness. Being whipped had the tendency to erase all other thoughts and sensations. But now that the burning on her breasts had subsided somewhat, the need for sexual relief was growing in her. The prospect of its immanency accelerated it.

Chi ran a hand up and down the insides of her exposed, sensitive thighs. *"Your thighs are as smooth as silk, my little whore. The eunuch takes good care of you. They're like a baby's bottom."*

The heat from the man's bear sized hands sent a tremor through her. She squirmed her hips and bit her lip. She knew the display that she would shortly be putting on for the callous, cruel warlord. It shamed her to think of it. She closed her eyes and tried to take her mind to a different place.

She felt a sharp tug on the lock that held her pussy prisoner. Her eyes opened and took in the face of the leering general between her thighs.

"Look at me slut," he told her. *"I want you watching everything I do. I just know you're going to enjoy it."*

Violet suppressed a moan of misery. Although she knew that the man had undoubtedly not yet expended all of his inclinations to cause her pain, she knew that defying him would make the whippings that were sure still to come that much worse. She obeyed, all the time trying to drive the picture of the man's evil, flaccid face from her mind.

Chi lifted the lock from Violet's loins. *"Belonging of General Wang,"* he read from its inscription. *"The general has locked up the most important thing about you, my sweet. The rest of you is just a delivery service for it,*" he said grinning. "*Well let's see what all this fuss is about.*"

He inserted the key into the lock and turned it. It slid off of the ends of the thin, glittering steel cable that bound her love lips together. He tossed it aside carelessly. The pulling on the cable caused Violet's pussy to trill. She felt the muscles on her thighs quiver. When he began to slide the cable through the holes on her outer labia she had to steel herself to suppress a moan.

Chi took notice of the effect on the helpless woman. He laughed. "*You are a slut!*" he announced. "*I'll bet you spend the whole day trying to figure out how to get your pussy stuffed. And, poor thing, it's usually all locked up. Well, tonight I'll try and make up for lost time.*"

When the cable was finally pulled free, Chi tossed it aside. Although, as the general had said, many men had penetrated her there, she had never felt so exposed as now. It was an unusual sensation to feel her pussy lips come free. Her inner self had been made so sensitive, that she could feel the air flowing over it. Frantically unhappy at her predicament, she shifted her hips and pulled at her bindings. A low pitched whine escaped from behind her gag.

Next came the three, gel filled steel balls that served as violet's constant companions, swaying and jostling as she walked, echoing he slightest movements of her hips. They kept her in a continual state of near arousal. Chi merrily pulled on the string that emerged from the nearest ball. Slowly, exquisitely slowly as far as Violet was concerned, he pulled them out.

The movements of the balls, scraping the inner lining of her already excited pussy sent a wave of lust through the unfortunate concubine. She shuddered as they moved slowly along her passage, giving out a moan of passion only when they were fully removed.

Chi carelessly tossed the balls aside and then placed his hands on either side of her love channel and spread her love lips apart. He looked Violet in the eye, grinning and then lowered his mouth to her loins.

Violet's body came alert as she felt the hot tongue run the length of her labial divide. When she felt the tip flick at her already engorged love button, her body twitched. When the man's lips descended on it and began a soft, leisurely suckle, she could not prevent a moan from escaping her.

Chi was well experienced when it came to cunts. His concubines' pussies were all well licked. It did not take long for him to have Violet writhing and moaning on the bed.

"Ohhhhhhhhhhh!" Violet moaned as the tongue enflamed her. Despite Chi's prior warning, she closed her eyes. She bit down harshly on the leather prong in her mouth. Her hips writhed, her thighs twitched. She could feel her blood rising higher and higher. The witch's brew she had consumed was accelerating her lusts. She could feel herself climbing the mountain. Despite her shame, all of her being was enwrapped in the pleasurable sensations. Her passions were near to burst. She needed release like she needed air to breathe. She felt like she would die without it.

Then, just as she was approaching the pinnacle of passion, about to erupt into a wrenching orgasm, the lips and tongue stopped. She opened her eyes and saw the warlord grinning at her. *"You didn't think it was going to be that easy, did you?"* he teased her. *"You'll come when I say so."*

Chi waited until Violet's need had subsided, rubbing his hands up and down her tender thighs, before starting again. He had a long, agile tongue and practiced lips. He teased the nubbin at the apex to her loins, flicking it with his tongue, gently biting it with his teeth. He plunged his tongue deep within her, tickling the spot on the roof of her crevasse where her orgasms originated. Violet's body twisted and turned. She moaned loudly, tried to beg the monster who supped at her hot, oozing chasm for relief. All that emerged were anguished, muffled sounds.

Three times the callous general drove her to the brink of ecstasy, denying her each time. "*Please! Pleeease! Pleeeee-eease!*" Violet moaned. The sounds she made did not emerge as words. That didn't matter. Chi knew what she was saying. It thrilled him to hear her in the depths of desperation. From time to time, he lifted his head from his task to watch her body writhe in place, to see the anguish in her eyes as she stared back at him. Finally, he deigned to give her release. He tickled the tip of her stiffened love button until she screamed with need and then he subsumed it into his mouth, suckling it, running his tongue back and forth over it.

Violet's orgasm seized her as if it were a demon possessing her. Her thighs shook and quaked. Her hips thrust madly at the face that was tormenting her. "Uuuuuug! Uuuuuuuugh! Uuuuuuuugh!" she moaned violently. The contractions of her pussy's walls continued on and on in a relentless, *rapidimento* rhythm. Chi had circled her thighs with his arms and buried his face in her steaming, vibrating quim. His tongue was plunged deeply inside her, lapping at the special spot at the roof of her canal. Ruthlessly, each time that her throbs of pleasure started to wane, he drove her once more up the steep slope of desire, forcing her to plunge once more into the abyss of ecstasy.

When he was satisfied, Chi withdrew his mouth from Violet's organ. Violet's body still shuddered with the aftershocks of her ordeal. Sweat covered her in a fine sheen. Her chest was reddened and the tips of her breasts were as hard as steel. Her chest rose and fell rapidly causing her scarlet breasts to sway and shimmer. To Chi it was a heavenly sight.

He left the exhausted woman softly moaning on the bed and went to get himself another brandy. He was still wearing his colorful kimono, but it was untied and his huge belly extruded like a huge loaf of rising bread. His cock was at attention, rampant and ready. He stroked it while he drank his brandy, his mind debating whether it was time to fuck her or not.

Due to his dissolute lifestyle, General Chi, despite all the potions his herbalists could muster, rarely could make it more than twice a night. So he had to conserve his resources. He decided that more torment was due the unfortunate concubine before he became sated. He would wait to fuck her.

He went to the wall to examine the array of punishing instruments. He espied what was called for right away. He took down a long, thin, leather switch. He ran his hand down it, appreciating its form and utility. He swished it a couple of times through the air to test its resilience.

Violet heard the tell tale sound of the whip passing through the air. She looked over and a chill went through her. There was no pretense of maintaining a stoic demeanor now. Her emotions were at their height. The terror of being at the warlord's mercy was telling on her. She moaned as her body began to shake. She watched the evil man step towards her, the whip in his hand. He was casually flicking it against his thigh.

"*Look what I have for you, my little whore,*" he said. "*Our evening was starting to become dull, but I have just the right thing to liven it up a bit.*"

He stood between Violet's splayed legs, smiling. Violet tried to beg him not to harm her, but her pleas emerged from behind her gag only as garbled sounds. Instinctively, she pulled on her bound ankles, strained to work her pinioned wrists free. The general just stood there and watched her, enjoying her acute distress, her powerlessness to avoid what he had determined to mete out.

When the general finally moved, it was like a flash. In one swift motion, he brought the long, supple length of leather up over his head in a wide arc and brought it down on the crux of

Violet's thighs. The instrument struck her directly along the crevasse between her love lips.

Violet's whole body jumped. She had been hoping for a warning before the blow was delivered so that she could prepare herself for it, but it came so fast that she had no time to react. She howled with pain. Her body twisted and turned in her confinements. She closed her eyes and bit down harshly on the gag in her mouth. The pain was unbearable, yet had to be borne all the same. Tears were flowing down her face.

When the first wave of brutal pain had passed, Violet opened her eyes and looked up again at her tormentor. Her pussy burned as if it were afire. She saw his amused face. It was slightly off balance as if it reflecting his warped soul. His kimono was open and Violet could see from the hardness of his cock the delight he was taking from her distress. She saw him raise the whip again. She could not help the loud, anguished whine that escaped her lips. She shifted her hips as if there were some possible way to draw her sex out of danger. She was just in the midst of uttering a piteous plea for mercy when, lightning like, the man's arm moved again, describing a wide arc and the whip came hurtling towards her loins.

"Ahhhhhhhhhhhiiiiiie!" she screamed as the pain flowed through her. He had struck her again in the center of her being, ravaging the tender tissue. Her back arched, her legs shook. Her chest heaved.

She was bitterly sobbing now. Chi took in her abject dismay with satisfaction. His cock was rock hard and throbbing. He often whipped his whores, but knowing that he was tormenting the heart's desire of General Wang, the upstart, the peasant who dared to presume he was on an equal footing with him whose family had ruled for generations, that was satisfaction indeed. Tomorrow, or the next day, or the day after that, for if he could he intended to keep the whore to himself for his entire three day stay, Wang would see the evidence of his brutality on her person. He only wished that he could be there in person to see his humiliation.

Violet was squirming and moaning on the bed. Chi's thoughts about the parvenu warlord, his enemy, had triggered an awful rage. This very castle had once been his. Wang's predecessor had stolen it and Wang had stolen it from him. Someday it would be his again, or it would be rendered into crumbled stone!

Before she knew what he was doing, Chi let the whip fly once more. It struck the same target as before, causing the miserable concubine to screech with pain once again. But, unlike before, he did not pause to take in her dismay. He brought the whip back up and then down again. He struck the tender skin of her upper left thigh. He struck her again, this time on the right. And then again and again and again. He worked his way up both distended, helpless legs to the knees and then back down again. When he reached the angry red honey pot, he gave it one more, harsh blow and he stopped.

Violet was driven to hysterics by the whirlwind of blows. One after the other they came, without pause, without amelioration. She had no conscious thoughts about what was happening, the pain drove all such thoughts right from her head. She was reacting purely on a primal level as her body twisted and turned, her screams, high pitched and frantic, escaped her gag, filling the room.

Outside the door to General Wang's best guest room, a diminutive figure, dressed in unaccustomed finery, knelt weeping. It was Violet's youngest, child-like, maid, Wen. She had snuck up here, desperate to know her mistress's fate. She could hear her anguished wails even through the heavy door. She knew she was powerless to help her. Her heart ached with sorrow and pity. She would gladly have exchanged places, done anything, even given her life to absolve Violet from her miseries.

A tall, dark figure came walking down the hallway. It was the eunuch. He too had come to witness the concubine's travails. He too knew that there was nothing he could do about it. Although he had no heart in the real sense of the word, he could not help but feel some sorrow for the English whore. Chi was well known as a rough customer. It was a pity.

When he saw the little maid scrunched up by the door wailing her heart out, he barked out a stern order. *"Get up! Up! What do you think you're doing here?"*

"Please master, I was only trying to find out what was happening to my mistress. Can't you do anything? Can't you stop him?" she asked miserably.

Li Pao rarely felt as powerless as he did that moment. He too wanted to run into the room and stop the torment of his charge. Because he could not, anger ran through him at the worthless maid's effrontery.

"This is none of your business!" he railed at her. *"Go to the steward and tell him to give you ten lashes with the cane! If you are ever so disobedient again, I will send you to the dungeon for a month!"*

Poor little Wen gave out an unhappy cry and jumped to obey the god-like man's command.

Li Pao watched her run down the hallway, her cries of woe echoing off of the stone walls. He turned and looked at the door. The cries of anguished pain had seemed to stop. For a moment, he tried to visualize what was happening inside. And then he paused. Thus was no business of his. What happened to whores was no business of his. She had her fate just as he had his. Who could question what the gods decreed? He turned and walked away.

Inside the chamber, General Chi was taking a rest. His heart was thumping in his chest and sweat had broken out all over his corpulent frame. He was breathing heavily. His face was red. He had had quite a workout. He poured himself another brandy. The concubine was still sobbing and moaning on the bed. This was turning out better than he had ever anticipated. His hand reached for his rampant prick and stroked it. There was just one more thing that was needed before his night would be complete. He downed the brandy, shucked off the kimono from his frame and returned to the scene of the concubine's torment.

He watched her for a while between her outstretched legs. Her eyes were closed. Her flesh gleamed with perspiration. All up and down her legs, like red painted ladder steps, were the evidence of his efforts. Her anguished moans continued to emerge from her gagged mouth. He looked down at the woman's quim and saw the enflamed tissue, red and swollen. He would have to make it ready for him.

He advanced to the woeful woman and placed his hand on her lower belly. She flinched at the touch. Her eyes leapt open and her body cringed. Her flesh was hot and slick.

"*I hope you enjoyed that, my little whore. I certainly did. And now there is something that you need to take care of for me.*" He circled his prick with his other hand. "*My cock needs someplace warm and wet and I think you have the place that will suit it well. When I fuck you, I want you to squeeze me nice and tight or I'll have to get the whip out all over again. Do I make myself clear?*"

Through her anguish, Violet was able to discern the cruel general's words. She was filled with disgust that he would now have access to her inner self, but she knew that there was nothing she could do about it. It was far better to have him fucking her than beating her. She vowed to fight through her revulsion and do her best.

Chi placed his thumb on Violet's pleasure bud and began to gently rub it. Violet cringed at the painful contact, but after the first rush of pain passed, she began to feel a tell tale tingle in her womb. The potion she had consumed was doing its work. Her need for sexual completion was driven not by her psyche, but by her body's physical reaction to the elixir. It did not fade merely because she was distraught, repelled or unhappy. Her body's reactions were chemical and, like a well oiled machine, once it received certain stimuli, its processes would commence.

Although her pussy and legs still burned, Violet closed her eyes and let the warmth of the feeling growing in her loins suffuse through her. It would not be the first time she had cause to be thankful for the workings of the potion. Many a night, coupled with a strange, repulsive man, all too aware what the consequences would be if she were to disappoint him, she had been saved by the passion inducing liquid. Tonight was no different, or, rather, different only by degree.

The general's digit kept up its callous but gentle stimulation of her nub of pleasure. It dipped between her swollen labia and coated itself with the moisture that was growing there and then returned, spreading the slick substance over it, making it slip and slide beneath. General Chi smiled. She was a well trained whore indeed. He pressed harder now, and then slid his thumb inside her slippery tunnel, caressing its walls.

When the thumb entered her chamber, Violet gasped. Ever since she had been treated by the man or witch or whatever she/he was, after the incident with the lieutenant, her pussy had been supersensitive. The eunuch kept it so by daily administration to it of his attentions and the cream that the half man, half woman had left behind. Her thighs quivered and she had an urge to close them on the hand that delved between them, trapping it in place, encouraging it to do more.

Chi did not miss the signs of the woman's arousal. He withdrew his hand and then rubbed both of his hands up and down her wounded thighs, appreciating their graceful tone, the smooth, warm skin. Violet's pussy, shaven clean as a baby's, was opening, dilating and he could see the gleam of her arousal within.

Enough was enough, he could wait no longer. He pressed himself forward, his belly extending over the foot of the bed. He leaned over, supported by just one hand on the bed next to Violet's writhing hip. He took hold of his cock, addressed the tip to the entrance of her simmering sex and then slowly eased his way in.

Violet gasped as she felt the man's steel hard rod penetrate her. A wave of pleasure flowed through her. Her mind grasped hard at it, desperate to find some consolation for her ordeal. After three years of subservience, daily immersion in physical pleasure, her body had become hypersensitive to sexual stimulation. It had become the core of her being, virtually the sole reason for existence. Its suffusion through her body was like the greeting of a warm, welcome friend come home at long last.

When he had plunged his cock into her well to its hilt, the general began a slow, patient motion. His hands were on the bed to each side of Violet's torso. His was unable, due to his girth, to lie down upon her since the size of his belly would force his cock to pop right out. As it was, his belly pressed down hard on Violet's, pushing it in, and the heat transferred thereby from her flesh accentuated the thrill of his possession of her.

Violet groaned with pleasure as the cock abraded the walls of her canal. Her assailant's posture caused his meat to drag relentlessly directly across her button of love. She reveled each time the meat passed over it, sighed deeply each time it filled her to her depths. She began to grind her hips in time with his thrusts, desperate to gain maximum benefit from his long, thick prick.

It was not long before she felt the forces of lust rising within her. Her mind focused on the growing force of her need, coaxing it, willing it to swell, urging it to overflow.

Her pussy grew seemingly hotter and hotter. The piercing stabs of pleasure became stronger and stronger. She gave out another deep groan and arched her back. Her legs began to shake and her hands twisted in their confines behind her neck. Her breasts had swollen and she could feel her heart pounding. And then it came.

Violet gave out a deep, hearty groan of pleasure as her pussy began to convulse and throb. She could feel it closing over the meat that pervaded it. Wave after wave shot through her. She bit down hard on the gag in her mouth, balled her hands into tiny fists, pressed her eyes closed, curled her toes, flexed her thighs. Her whole body celebrated. The evening's torment was, for the moment, forgotten. Only the fierce contractions of her canal and the ecstasy it produced mattered.

Her body's reactions to her orgasmic thrall was exhilarating to the decadent general. His thrusts became harder and faster. He was breathing hard, sweat pouring off of his face and chest. It had been a long time since a whore had excited him so. He blessed the fates for the beneficial turn of cards in his game with Wang. His cock could feel each spasm of the concubine's throbbing quim. He yearned to suckle on the heaving, plump breasts swaying before his eyes, but his belly was in the way. He struggled to contain himself, wanting the pleasure to last. He gritted his teeth and thrust hard in and out, again and again. His tremendous body shook, his belly quivered.

Violet's second orgasm followed directly on the first. Her assailant's increase in passion and pace accelerated her own. She moaned loudly again and again. She yearned to wrap her bound ankles around the man's thighs and pull him deeper and deeper within her. Her hips thrust madly back at him, her pussy shouting out to her, "More! More! More!"

Finally, General Chi could hold himself back no longer. His cock exploded, sending jet after jet of his hot jism deep into her womb. He groaned and shook, his knees weakened, his mind short circuited.

The throbbing of his cock and the man's exuberant, unrestrained pounding at her hips plunged Violet's pussy into another wave of almost painful contractions. "Oh god! Oh god! Ohhhhhhhhhhh!" she called out in English into her gag. "Ohhhhhhhhhhh, fuck me! Fuck me! Fuck me!" she tried to yell.

Violet's pussy was still throbbing when the general's forces exhausted themselves. As he tried to recover his breath, she continued to moan and squirm beneath him. Slowly, her spasms ebbed, her mind returned to conscious-ness. When she opened her eyes, she saw above her, the black, shark like eyes of her oppressor and his flaccid, satisfied face.

A wave of shame went through her. This grotesque hulk of a man had abused her, degraded her, tormented her and yet she had responded to his cock like it was the tool of her most passionate lover. Yes, she knew that it was the potion at work, but that did not assuage her remorse. He had been calling her a whore all night, repeating it again and again. And she had proven him right.

It was a while before the aging general could lift himself off of his victim. His cock had grown soft and slid out of her when he rose. "Now that was worth the trip!" he said to himself. He staggered over to the hutch on which the brandy was stored and poured himself another glass. He swallowed it quickly. His body was rung out. He needed rest. He was done for the night.

He returned to the bed and unsteadily untied Violet's ankles from their bindings. When he was done, he ordered Violet to her feet.

"*Come here, slut,*" he told her. Reluctantly, her body wrung out like a dishrag, Violet stepped towards him. He took hold of the ring on her collar and propelled her to the front of the room opposite the bed. The cage was there and he opened it.

"*Get in,*" he said.

Violet was hoping to be sent back to the seraglio where her maids would treat her wounds. But she had no vote in the matter. With a deep unhappiness, she fell to her knees, tears in her eyes, and crawled forward until she was inside the small enclosure. Her hands were still imprisoned behind her neck and she had to shimmy on her knees. There was just enough room for her to scrunch up her legs. Keeping her head bent over, she turned around. When she was facing her tormentor once again, he swung the cage's door shut and locked it.

He leaned over, his face inches away from hers, the merciless steel bars separating them.

"You have given me a wonderful evening, my little whore," he said. *"I will remember it for a long time. Someday, General Wang will tire of you. When he does, I will be waiting. Someday you will belong to me."* He smiled evilly. Violet released a wretched sob.

军阀 外家
CHAPTER SEVEN

General Wang watched numbly as the long, black touring car containing his guest drove away. His three day stay had been a long, drawn out source of torment for him. He had thought constantly of his English concubine and the depredations he had made her subject to. It had filled him with anguish and self hatred, a hatred he had acted out with his whip on the bodies of his other three sex slaves.

The morning after the banquet, when Chi asked casually if he could keep Violet for the duration of his stay, Wang had tried to act nonchalant as he consented. What else could he do? If he refused, all the world would know his weakness for her. And, he knew, it was too late to repair the damage he had done.

And so, during the days, he led General Chi on the tours of inspection of his troops, the viewing of the various defenses that had been constructed, the improvements he had made to various of the villages. At each site, the populace had been brought out and given little flags to wave and banners proclaiming the friendship between the two warlords. At night, and whenever they had returned to the fortress for refreshment, General Chi retreated to his bedroom to visit more abuse on the English whore.

The worst of it all was that he knew that it was all to no avail. He sensed the futility of expecting Chi to enter into an alliance with him. In fact, his worst fears had been confirmed. When the Kuomintang attacked again, and he knew it was only a matter of time before they did, he would have a serpent at his back. He would have to fight a battle on two fronts. The Nationalists would come at him from the north and General Chi would come at him from the south.

Thanks to Li Pao, they had not shown General Chi all of the defensive arrangements he had made. Both he and the Kuomintang would have some surprises in store. It would be a fight to the death and he would use all of his wiles to win it.

When General Chi's car and his accompanying entourage were out of sight, he turned and walked disconsolately back into his castle.

* * * * * * * * * * * * *

Days later, Violet was still suffering from the effects of the cruel general's torments. She had cried and cried the morning after the banquet when Li Pao and her maid Junjing came into the bedroom to take care of her. She had cried even harder when she learned that, after she had been cleaned and her wounds tended, had been allowed to relieve herself and eat, that she was to be returned to the cage to await the return of the evil man. When the eunuch had bound her as the general had left her, her wrists pinioned to the back of her neck, the gag returned to her mouth, she sobbed and sobbed and sobbed.

General Chi did not repeat the extended torment she suffered on the first night of their encounter, although he beat her one way or another at the commencement of each of their many sessions, and he did fulfill his promise to take a cane to her posterior. He gave her seven telling blows that left deep, angry red welts. Afterwards, he took advantage of her prostrate position to make use of her nether hole.

That was now two weeks behind her. During the whole time, General Wang had not called for her once. For the first few days, Violet lay about the seraglio listlessly. The eunuch allowed her to skip her daily dose of the witch's brew that accelerated her libido, but he did make her consume several balls of opium. Her maids and her sister concubines were intently solicitous of her need for solitude, although they all were sympathetic, especially Iris, who held her in her arms for several hours each day. On the fourth day, when her wounds had started to fade, the eunuch gave her a double dose of the aphrodisiac and she spent much of her day fucking.

While Violet had not been called to the warlord's service, the other concubines had. The benefit they had all enjoyed from Violet's special relationship with him was at an end. He beat them all and was particularly brutal in his use of them. Violet felt guilty that the others should suffer because of her, but that did not modify her resolve not to open herself up to him again.

On the fourth day, her sessions with the piano in the afternoons resumed, as did her language and poetry lessons with the French nun. Violet wrote some particularly dark passages in her journal during this time. When she showed them to Sister Theresa for her correction, the elderly woman wept.

Today, Violet was practicing a new piece. From time to time, new sheet music was delivered from Shanghai and this one had come in a few days ago. It was Debussy's 'Arabesque'. Its delicate beginning, languid pace and soft tones comforted her. Yanyu, the head chaperone, was with her as usual. She sat on a stool nearby the piano her eyes closed, as if the delicate sounds had mesmerized her.

Suddenly, the door opened. Both Violet and Yanyu turned as one to see who had come in. It was General Wang.

Wang had been in an almost dehabilitating funk ever since the visit of General Chi. He was angry with himself for allowing his feelings for the English concubine to get so far that the loss of her affection struck him so deeply. His anger, however, did not ameliorate his deep sense of loss. He spent hours alone in his second floor salon, drinking scotch, staring at the piano, pining for her. He knew that she was still his to command, that he could have her brought within his presence at any moment, day or night, where he could force her to submit to him, to perform for him. Yet, he could not bring himself to do it. He realized that he had betrayed her and was ashamed.

He had been walking down the hallway past the salon where Violet practiced, when he heard the light notes of the piano through the door. It made his heart ache to hear them, knowing what he had lost, remembering the paradisiacal interludes he had spent there with her.

The sound of the music rent his heart. If only things could be the way they were, he thought. His hand went out to the door handle, hesitating. "Should I go in? Will she forgive me?" he wondered fearfully. Then, steeling himself, he entered the room.

The music stopped as soon as he stepped in. He saw the doleful face of his concubine and his stomach fluttered. It was virtually inconceivable that he should be in such a state of apprehension and fear over a mere woman. He resolved not to show her any of his emotion. He sat himself down in the chair where he normally sat when she played for him and then looked at her expectantly.

Violet knew what the man had come for. She was overwhelmed by a rabid sense of unhappiness and anger. She was nothing more than a performing animal to him, she thought. Her hands were resting on her thighs. Her eyes were pointed downwards at the piano keys. The room seemed fraught with tension. Bright light poured in through the large windows. Flowers were strewn around the room in brilliant, ancient vases. The room was elegantly appointed. And yet to Violet, it seemed as dismal and miserable as the cell she had twice occupied in the warlord's dungeon.

She didn't want to play for the enjoyment of the man whom she considered little more than a beast. But she knew that if she refused, she would be whipped. That's what everything came down to: obey or be whipped. She didn't want to be whipped. That was clear. She would play, she thought. Someday soon she would be free. She had sworn it to herself. Until then, she would submit.

She would play a little Brahms piece she knew. She lifted her hands to the keys and straightened her back. She went to strike the opening chord. For some reason, her hands would not move. They seemed heavy and frozen in place. A chasm opened in her belly. She couldn't do it! She couldn't play for the man as if nothing had happened. She had undergone terrible abuse at the hands of the visiting general and he had betrayed her to him. He gave her away as if she were a whore in the lowliest brothel. She had to preserve some dignity! There had to be a line she would not cross!

The pause in Violet's playing, commencing as an aesthetic effect, had extended now for about thirty seconds. Wang became concerned. He waited. And he waited. And he waited. No sounds issued forth. Then it occurred to him. She was refusing to play for him! His astonishment at the affront quickly turned to rage. She was a slave! She had no right to deny him anything! His hands gripped the arms of his large, heavily cushioned chair. His rage was growing so intense that he had trouble speaking out. "*Play!*" he finally managed to shout, his voice deep and rough. "*Play for me!*"

Violet quailed at the sound of the fearsome voice. Her hands started to tremble. She tried to command them to press down upon the glittering black and white keys below them, but they would not move. And even if they had moved, the notes that constituted the beginning of the piece had flown right out of her head. It was like her mind was a blank wall. Some inner force had hold of her, refused to let her demean herself any further. It was if the core to her being was in revolt.

Seeing no reaction to his command, Wang repeated it. His anger rose exponentially. The room became tinged with red. "*Play! Now!*" he repeated, his voice emerging from deep in his chest. His knuckles had turned white and bile had risen from his belly. "*Play now!*" he yelled.

Violet began to cry. She knew that she was about to subject herself to a hellstorm of violence, but she had no choice. It was not within the realm of possibilities that her hands would descend upon the sparkling keyboard and commence a tune. Her shoulders were hunched and her thighs clamped tightly together.

Yanyu, the head chaperone just sat there amazed. She had never seen anyone defy the warlord before, had never even heard tales of it being done. It was a concept totally foreign to her. General Wang's command was like the word of God. She knew that there would be terrible consequences for the English concubine's actions. Despite her role as the warlord's enforcer of his discipline on his concubines, Yanyu had developed a strong affection for them all, especially Whore Number Four. She trembled when she thought of what she might face.

Violet had given up on forcing her hands into motion and she dropped them to her lap. "I can't!" she answered in English, a language forbidden to her, her voice tremulous. "I just can't!"

Seeing the woman break down into sobs, Wang caught himself. He was witnessing the harvest from his callous treatment of her. That part of his heart that still functioned broke in two. Part of him felt like running to her, falling at her feet and begging forgiveness. Then he looked at the face of the chaperone. The whole world would soon know what happened here. In that moment, his heart turned finally and irrevocably into stone.

He jumped from his seat. "*Get up! Get up!*" he shouted. His voice thundered through the room.

Violet jumped when she heard his command. Her body, as of its own volition, rose immediately from the piano stool. Her heart was beating wildly. Cold had descended down her spine. Her hands broke out into sweat.

"*Come here!*" the imperious voice commanded.

She moved instantly, her head bowed, her hands clinging to each other, writhing madly.

"*On your knees!*" Wang ordered.

She fell swiftly to the floor. Anticipating his next command, she bent over and placed her forehead and the palms of her hand on the plush rug. She knew this position well. It was the position for receiving punishment.

All sense had left the general. All he could think of was his loss of face before the world. All he had worked for these many years, destroyed by a vile Englishwoman! He looked around for a weapon. A pair of crossed whips were mounted decoratively on the wall. He rushed over to them and grabbed one. It was a four foot long, leather switch. He returned to where the concubine knelt abjectly and took a position behind her. She was wearing a green and red silken kimono. He bent over, took the hem by her feet in his hands and ripped it straight up her back, so that her naked flesh was exposed. The traces of her ordeal with General Chi were still visible. Seeing the reminder of his own weakness, his own stupidity, Wang became even more enraged. He raised the whip in his hand and brought it down in a mighty blow. The sound of the leather meeting flesh resounded through the room. It was followed by a loud, long, anguished female wail.

Later, Wang often thought back to that moment. The first blow that he struck was all that he could remember well. But he knew of course, from what he saw later, that he had commenced a terrible, vicious beating. His whip rose and fell with rapidity. Bright red lines formed wherever it met flesh. He belabored her pale, proffered rear cheeks and her back remorselessly. It was as if he were trying to destroy her, the symbol of his weakness, his defeat.

Violet screamed and sobbed as she was beaten. Although not chained, she was powerless to remove herself from the spot on which she knelt. It felt like the sky had begun to rain hot, fiery lava and her skin was being repeatedly seared by it.

She gripped her hands into little fists, pressing the tips of her fingernails into her palms. She pressed her forehead firmly to the floor, clasped her knees forcefully together. As blow followed blow in fierce, rapid succession, her conscious mind fled leaving behind only the terrorized, anguished part of her.

When the warlord finally exhausted his anger and energy, Violet's back was a mass of red wounds. She continued to issue loud, doleful sobs. A sudden wave of passion passed through him. He needed to seal his victory over her. His cock had swollen to its mighty girth and length and he fished it out of his pants, tossing the whip to the side. He fell to his knees behind the sobbing woman and placed his right hand on her hip. He guided his rampant, steel hard rod to her dainty nether hole and then, placing his left hand on her hip, pushed himself forcefully in.

Violet wailed when she felt herself pierced. There had been no chance to prepare herself, there had been no magic potion administered. The thick, hard meat abraded the delicate tissue of her anal ring, causing it to burn. Through her virulent sorrow, a wave of revulsion flowed through her as she felt his instrument fill her. She was consumed by a ravenous, soul eating hatred. She gritted her teeth, begging God to visit the most rapacious vengeance on him.

It did not take long for him to come. He was enraptured by his fury. Ten, fifteen, twenty harsh, forceful, remorseless strokes and his cock exploded. He growled like a wounded beast, his voice echoing against the walls.

And then it was over. He was breathless and weak. His mind was swimming. He rose from his weeping, disconsolate victim and stumbled from the room.

* * * * * * * * * * * * *

He gave her a week to recover from her wounds. Then he had her delivered to his bedroom fully stoked with the witch's brew that enforced her passion. He beat her again, this time with a riding crop and then, disdaining the use of her pussy, used her mouth and rear most brutally.

Violet was placed back into the usual rotation of concubines. She dreaded going to him on her assigned nights or on the nights he especially demanded her. Although he forced her repeatedly to passion through the use of her back portal, he kept her pussy locked and sealed. Sometimes, when she was accompanied by one of her sister sex slaves, he would open it and have the other fuck her with the polished, ebony carving of his prick, or mouth her to hysterical, body wrenching orgasms. He beat her often.

Li Pao was greatly disheartened by the turn of events. He kept up, as best he could, the concubine's education in poetry and music. Often, over the ensuing months, he would often see his master paused outside the door to his salon while the music she continued to play emerged from behind it. He would never go in. When he saw the eunuch watching him, he would give a disdainful look and walk away.

While General Wang had seemingly forsworn use of her pussy, his property, he had no qualms on lending it out to others. During one or another of his increasingly boisterous, drunken feats, he would make his guests role the dice to see who would get use of her while he paraded her naked around the room. More than once, he sold her use to the highest bidder, pocketing the pieces of gold or silver and handing off the key to her loins to the winner.

In the seraglio, Violet increasingly withdrew into the solitude of her poetry and music. She still engaged in the physical act of love as ravenously as before, stoked by the potion now administered to her sometimes thrice a day by the eunuch, but there was something missing.

She wept silent tears when poor Iris was sold, was indifferent when Shu was married off to one of Wang's captains and when Hu was sent to his whorehouse, the

Golden Swan. She refused to allow herself to become close to the unfortunates who replaced them, two young, bewildered Chinese girls and a big breasted, miserably unhappy Dutch girl. She had been kidnapped during a pirate raid on the steamer that was taking her from Amsterdam to Jakarta to unite with her parents.

Her only real friend was the French nun from Yeuyang who she continued to see on a weekly basis. It was the only bright moment for her. They talked in French and Chinese of love, God, fate. She enthralled the sister with the increasing sophistication and beauty of her poetry. Sister Therese gave her weekly updates on activities in the orphanage and Violet soon came to feel that she knew the children well. Twice a month, during good weather, Li Pao let the children come up from the orphanage to play in the warlord's garden while the concubines were there and Violet got to add faces to the names and even hold a wonderful, beaming, fat baby in her arms.

Months and months went by. While the other concubines took their turns in milk, Violet was now at least spared that indignity. But, on the other hand, she seemed to be the one most preferred to entertain the warlord's guests, fucking three or four, and sometimes more, men a week.

It was close to a year from the dismal turn in her status at the fortress, during the month of May, when something happened to raise Violet's hopes of escape. She had never given up on it. There were two seemingly intractable problems. The first was how to get outside the fortress. She was too heavily guarded in the seraglio and still chained in her room every night. Every time she was escorted from one part of the fortress to another, she wore a chain between her ankles. There were soldiers at attention at every exit.

The second problem was how to vault the thirty feet high outer wall. The stairways to the top of the wall were always heavily guarded. The wall was made of smooth brick so that it could not be scaled. Iris had shown her how to surmount the inner wall by using the tree at the end of the garden, but the outer wall loomed as an impenetrable barrier to freedom.

One day, while looking through the trellised windows of the seraglio, Violet realized that the answer to the second riddle had appeared. As part of the routine maintenance of the fortress, the bricks on the outer wall were being repointed. During the day a seeming hundred men would mount scaffolding piled up high against the wall and chip away at the old, crumbling cement and a fellow behind him would slosh in some new. The scaffolding went all the way up the wall to its very top. She saw the men going up and down it all day. If they could do it, so could she.

Now the first riddle needed to be solved. The final piece to the puzzle fell into place a few nights later.

There had been a particularly raucous banquet that night. Violet had been ordered to play the piano for the warlord's guests. When she was done, he ordered her to strip and she was passed around the guests. They used her mouth and rear callously, laughing at her shame. At the end of the night, General Wang held an auction. Her use for the night was won by a large, elderly, fat man who bid an ounce of gold for the privilege, far outstripping the other bidders. He was ceremoniously handed off the key to her loins. Her wrists were bound, a leash attached to her collar and she was led away to the guest room. It was not the first class room she had had her encounters with General Chi in, but one of the smaller ones that overlooked the garden.

This gentleman, if the term could be used, had considerably more stamina than would have been supposed. Li Pao had given Violet a double dose of the potion before she was delivered to him and she writhed and screamed in passion as he plowed her steaming crevasse. She was on her knees, just finishing off sucking his cock when one of the maids came in. The man had called for some refreshments and she brought a tray loaded with delicacies. Once his orgasm had finished, the man forced the maid to stay and ordered her to strip and make love to Violet while he ate. He watched them go at it for more than an hour, downing brandy and treats the whole time, giving instructions on who was to do what to whom and when.

When his cock had risen again, he gagged and bound the maid and locked her up in the small cage in the room. He ordered Violet to the bed. He groped and suckled at her for twenty minutes or so, driving her into a frenzy, and then mounted her, her back to the bed, her legs splayed wide. He made Violet come twice and then, with a loud, anguished groan, came himself. By the time his cock's throbs ceased, he was fast asleep.

When Violet had recovered from her own bout of bliss, she realized that the man had passed out. At first she was worried that she might suffocate under his vast bulk, but she eventually managed to squiggle out from under him.

She looked at the bound and gagged maid in the cage. Then she looked at her dead to the world assailant. Then she looked at the maid's discarded clothes on the floor. Then she heard a deep, teeth rattling roar of thunder outside. And then it all came together at once. This was the night.

The first thing she did was bind the man up hand and foot. She forced a gag into his flaccid mouth and fastened it behind his head. After chaining him to the bed, she pulled the sheets off of it, ripping them into two foot wide strips. She tied the strips together and then tied one end off to the poster on the foot of the bed.

The bedroom was on the second floor and was at least thirty feet above the garden. She had about fifteen feet of sheet rope. It was five feet from the bed to the window. It was just enough. She could lower herself until her feet were about twelve feet off of the ground and then she could let go.

She was working hurriedly. She did not pause to take in the demeanor of the maid until she reached for her discarded clothes. It was lucky that she was one of the taller ones. He clothes would just fit. The maid, all scrunched up in the cage had long ago figured out what Violet was up to. She was whining and moaning, shaking her head, her voice garbled by the thick gag in her mouth, trying to dissuade Violet from her purpose. It was almost certain that she would receive some terrible punishment for letting the concubine escape even though she was powerless to prevent it.

Violet felt a twinge of sorrow for the hapless maid. But she did not let it deter her from her purpose. She quickly donned the light green pants and the white blouse. She tied the girl's sandals together and hung them around her neck. Everything was done except for the window.

Since the concubines spent considerable time in them alone with guests, the windows to the bedrooms were always locked. She would have to smash through it to get out. Normally, this would have been a problem, and one she had pondered often. The peeling thunder and the heavy rain outside had provided the solution.

Grabbing a small side table, Violet stood by the window at the ready. Her heart was beating heavily in her chest and her mouth was dry with tension. There were a few light rumbles, but they were not loud enough to cover the noise of the broken window. For a while, she feared that the worst of the storm had passed and that she would have to take her chances. Then a bright light filled the room as a long bolt of lightning crackled downwards from the sky. A second later there was a deafening crash. Violet timed the blow with the table perfectly. Even she did not hear the window break.

Suffused with success and glee, Violet tossed the end of the sheet rope out of the window. It spiraled out towards the ground.

Now this was the tricky part. She had never been very athletic and had never climbed down a rope. She didn't know if she could hold her own weight for very long. But it was the only hope.

She picked off the shards of glass that remained in the window and then stepped over the sill, the sheet rope in her hand. Slowly, she lowered herself out. When she brought her other leg over the sill and took her whole weight on her hands, they slipped and she thought she was going to fall. Panicked, she gripped the sheet tightly. She held on.

Slowly then, ever slowly, she inched her way towards the ground. The rain was coming down hard and she was quickly soaked. The rainwater was making it hard to keep a tight grip on the rope. The storm made everything as black as coal outside, but once, when she was about half way down, there was another long, bright flash of lightning, brightening up the garden like it was day. She could see the guards patrolling the perimeter of the inner wall clearly. But it was only an instant and then everything was black again.

Her arms began to ache. She was tired from her night of fucking and still somewhat dazed from the dose of opiates she had been given. Slowly, slowly, slowly, her muscles screaming, she went down the rope lower and lower. She knew she was near the end when the end of the sheet came up between her legs. She looked down. There was nothing but the grass of the garden beneath her. It looked like a long drop. She could see pieces of the glass glittering between the blades of grass. She chided herself for not putting the maid's sandals on, but she had been afraid of them falling off her feet. She contemplated trying to put them on now, but knew that there was no way she could hold herself up with one hand. There was no choice. She let go.

It seemed to her more like a mile that she fell, but it was only about fifteen feet. Her knees jammed when she hit the ground and then she fell to her side, making a loud,

"Ouuuuuuuf!" Instantly, she rose to her knees and looked to see if anyone had heard her. There was no sign that anyone had. She took the sandals from around her neck and went to put them on her feet. She felt a warm stickiness on her right foot. She had cut herself. There was nothing she could do about it except hope that it wasn't too serious. She couldn't see it now.

She put the sandals on her feet and, looking carefully right and left, began a slow, crouched walk to the corner of the garden where Iris's tree grew. All of her wanted to run, but she knew that if she ran into any soldiers she was doomed. Going slowly was the only chance of seeing them before they saw her.

When she reached the tree, she paused. She remem-bered vividly the conversation she and Iris had had. She felt a sudden, deep pang of sorrow for the young girl. Who knew where she was now and what depredations she was being subjected to? She made a vow that if she made her escape she would do everything in her power to find and rescue her. And Tatiana too.

A wave of despair and sorrow flowed through her as she realized what a huge, virtually impossible task she had ahead of her. She knew only that she was hundreds of miles up river from Shanghai. There were a million obstacles to overcome, a million ways that she might be waylaid and caught. She wore around her neck the black collar that denoted her as General Wang's property. If he was as widely feared as she suspected him to be, no one in their right mind would help her. She looked back upon the castle. It appeared only as an amorphous, black mass. She had suffered so much misery there that she wished she could pound it into rubble. Just then, another lightning bolt lit up the sky. The fortress in all its evil and heartlessness became alive with light. She shuddered at the thought of its malignant spirit. "Well," she thought, "I'm going to make it no matter what you think." In a trice, she was up the tree and onto the wall.

She had never seen what was directly on the other side of the inner wall. You could not see it from the third floor seraglio window. In the darkness, it was hard to tell whether it was dirt or stone. There was another flash of lightning and she crouched down low on the wall, peering over its side. It was stone, rough looking stone. It was about 15 feet down. "At least I have the sandals on now," she thought. She lowered herself over the edge of the wall and then let go. She did not fall as far as before; her feet had only been less than 10 feet from the ground. But the lack of light made her fall unsteady and she groaned when she landed. She had twisted her ankle. The pain shot through her viciously. She moaned and crouched down to rub it. "I'm not going to make it very far at this rate," she thought.

She stood up and tried to put some weight on it. For the present, it seemed okay although she knew that it might swell up later. She looked around and seeing no one, walked swiftly and silently to the outer wall.

The scaffolding was made of thick bamboo tied together tightly. It made a natural ladder. Taking a deep breath she began to scale it. The rain was still coming down hard and she had to be careful placing her footing so that she didn't slip and fall. It took less than a minute to reach the top.

While the top of the inner wall was narrow, no wider than the breadth of two men shoulder to shoulder, the outer wall was wider, about 20 feet.. It was the first line of defense for the castle. It had a crenellated wall atop its outer edge with embrasures to shoot arrows down at any attackers. It was regularly patrolled and Violet watched carefully before she crept out onto it. So far so good, but what she hadn't solved was how to get down the outer wall on the other side.

She had hoped to see scaffolding there too, but she was disappointed when she peered down over the edge. She couldn't see any scaffolding or anything else either. It was so dark that the ground under the wall was just a dark mass. To make matters worse, the wall was built on top of a slight rise making it taller on the outside than on the in. It was at least a fifty foot drop. It would take a miracle to jump and not suffer any injury. She would probably break a leg or an ankle, or worse, her neck.

A wave of misery went through her. To have gotten so far only to be stymied at the last obstacle was too much to bear. She knew that she was in deep trouble already. Tatiana had spent a week in the dungeon for her escape attempt and she had merely tried to slip out the door. Violet had bound and gagged a guest, a direct insult to the general's hospitality. She knew she would suffer the most outrageous punishment the warlord could devise.

She peered into the darkness below the wall. If she knew that the fall would kill her, that would be one thing. If it only injured her, she would still be in the warlord's clutches. Then far off to her right, she heard something. It was the patrol. It was too late to climb back over the edge of the wall onto the scaffolding. They would see her as she darted across. She had no choice but to remain where she was. She dropped to her belly and scrunched up as close to the outer portion of the wall as she could. She froze.

Two of Wang's soldiers came stepping up the pathway. She could hear the hobnails of their boots clicking on the stone. The men were talking lowly. There seemed to be two of them. Violet moved her head slightly so that she could take a peek at them. They were wearing rain gear and carried rifles upside down on their shoulders so that water would not get into the barrels. To her dismay, they stopped very close to her.

"*I'm sure I saw something,*" the one said to the other.

"*You're just spooky because of all the thunder and lightning,*" the other said. "*You think a demon is going to come flying out of the sky and swallow you up!*" He laughed.

"*No!*" the first one said adamantly. "*I definitely saw something. It moved right across the pathway, quick, like a wild animal or something.*"

"*There's no wild animals around here,*" the other man said. "*Except for maybe cats and rats. Maybe you saw a cat chasing a rat.*"

"*No cat would be out hunting in this weather,*" the first man protested.

"*Well, there's nothing here now. Let's get walking again. It's the only way to stay warm in this damned rain.*"

"*You'll be warm enough if someone has sneaked into the castle when the general chops off your head!*" the first man said.

"*I thought you said it went this way,*" the second man said pointing to the outer portion of the wall, just above where Violet was lying.

"*I don't know,*" the first man said. "*It could have been the other way around. It happened so fast.*"

Just then a lightning bolt lit up the sky. It made the area on top of the wall as bright as day. A deep roll of thunder followed it. For a split second, Violet could see the men plainly. One was turned looking in her direction. It was a miracle that he didn't see her.

"*There,*" the second man said when the light faded. "*Did you see anything?*"

"*No....*" the first man said hesitatingly.

"*Then let's get going. Two more times around the wall and we can take our break. I have a bottle of rice wine in the guardhouse. It'll warm us up good.*"

The first man mumbled something and the men began to walk away. Violet, shaken, cold and scared, listened closely to the diminishing sound of their boots.

She waited a full minute before moving. She had to get off of the wall. She peered out over the edge through one of the embrasures. She still could see nothing. The there was another flash of lightning. It lit up the ground in front of her. There, at the bottom of the wall, was the solution to her problem.

She hadn't thought of it. Most castles were surrounded by a moat. This one was no different. She could jump off and the water would break her fall. On the other hand, she had never jumped such a long distance into water before. She had been to a pool once, back in England, when she was young. It had a high dive. Just to see what it was like, she had climbed up it. It was maybe fifteen feet high. It seemed so far to go down that it made her stomach turn over just to think of jumping.

But now she had to do it. It was that or suffer hell. She closed her eyes and whispered a little prayer. Then without opening her eyes, she climbed up on the wall and jumped.

The fall seemed to take forever. On the way down she suddenly wondered if the moat was loaded with underwater spikes or something to make it difficult to breech it. It was too late to worry about that now. A millisecond later, her feet hit the water and she plunged in.

Her body dropped like a stone. Her feet immersed themselves into a thick muck. She was holding her breath desperately. She pulled and tugged and squirmed and could not free her feet. For a moment, she panicked. If she drowned here stuck in the mud, they wouldn't find her until her feet rotted away and her body floated to the surface. The image of her lifeless form floating upright on the bottom of the moat flashed through her mind. She was losing breath. There wasn't much time left and then she would drown. She pulled and tugged her feet with all her strength, gyrating her body wildly. Then one foot came free. And then the other. She swam desperately for the surface. When she broke it, she took in a deep, wonderful breath of air.

She floated there for a moment, thanking God for his mercy. A distant rumble of thunder brought her to her senses and she swam to the bank. She pulled herself onto the solid ground.

She was exhausted. It was probably about 3 in the morning. She had been up since the break of dawn. She had had two long, exquisite sessions of lovemaking in the seraglio, one with the Dutch girl and one with her maid, Ting. The warlord had used her once in the afternoon and she had spent a prolonged session of passion with the man who had passed out, not to mention the men who had abused her mouth and ass at the party. She had climbed up and down two walls and jumped down another. Struggling to free her feet had taken a lot out of her. As she lay in the grass, all of her just wanted to stop and rest.

But no, she could not rest. She could not give in to her exhaustion. The town was about a mile away and there the river. And on the river there were boats. She had to get there and put many miles between herself and the castle before the sun rose. The eunuch would probably come to see if the man she had tied up wanted any breakfast at about 8. The rope dangling from the bedroom window would be clearly visible long before that. That gave her approximately three hours. It was not a long time so she had to get moving.

She struggled to her feet. Her body was soaked to the bone. She had lost the sandals in the mud. Her long hair, tied up in a ponytail behind her head, was heavy with water. Like the soldier said. It was cold out with the rain and all. She had been too frightened to notice it, but she noticed it now. There was no remedy but to get moving.

As she put the castle farther and farther behind her, a sense of exhilaration came over her. She had done it! She had escaped! She felt like laughing and dancing. For the first time in four years, she was free! All she had to do was to make her way down river. Maybe she would come across a patrol boat like the English general had come in about a year and a half ago. If she did, she would be saved! God would protect her, she knew it! He wouldn't raise her hopes so high and then dash them. That would just be too cruel.

After about five minutes, Violet had worked her way through the dark to the road that led from the castle to the town. She had been on it last year when they came to see the general's victory parade. She tried to remember what she could about it. She knew there was a bridge she had to cross. She prayed that it was not guarded.

She was wrong. Two soldiers manned each side of the bridge. She considered moving off of the road and climbing down the banks of the wide stream that the bridge crossed, but it was too late, one of the soldiers had seen her.

"*Look, a girl!*" he shouted out to his companion. "*Come here, little girl and give us a kiss! What are you doing out on a night like this?*"

Violet kept moving towards him, shuffling her feet in short steps like a Chinese girl might do. She scoured her brain for the right answer to give him. When she was just upon him, he brought his rifle down from his shoulder and held it across his chest barring her way.

"*I asked you a question, my little flower. What are you doing out here on such a rainy night?*" His voice made him sound young, maybe nineteen or twenty.

Violet knew that the man couldn't see her face well and so she tried to disguise her voice to make it sound like that of a young Chinese girl. "*Please let me pass, I'm in a hurry,*" she said as sweetly as she could.

"*Not until you tell me your business. I'm a corporal and in charge of this bridge. No one can pass without my permission.*"

Fear made Violet shake. It was a good thing he couldn't see her. She tried to keep the fear out of her voice.

"*I've just come from the castle. There was a big party. I'm going home,*" she said.

"*I happen to know that all the maids sleep in the castle,*" the corporal said. "*So don't tell me any lies. You're going to meet someone, aren't you?*"

"*Yes! Yes!*" Violet said quickly. "*A boy. A soldier like you. Please don't tell any one!*"

The other soldier had sidled over and he was standing to her left. If she ran, he would catch her in a few seconds.

"*Aha!*" the corporal said. "*I thought so! Who is the lucky man?*"

"*I can't tell you that, he'll get in trouble,*" Violet answered him. She could make up a name, but the corporal might know all the soldiers stationed locally and find her out.

"*Hey, leave the girl alone,*" the other soldier said. "*It's raining, can't you see? She soaking wet. She'll catch her death of cold.*"

"*Whoever this fellow is, he must be something special to tempt you out on a night like this,*" the corporal said. "*And you must be something special for him to risk a punishment so he can be with you. Are you something special? I can hardly see you in the dark.*"

"*Come on, Ching,*" the other soldier said. "*Let her pass. Don't be an ass.*"

"*I'm the corporal here, not you!*" Ching spat back. "*I decide who crosses the bridge!*" Then to Violet he said, "*I'll let you across if you give me a little kiss, okay?*"

Violet was afraid that if she got too close to him, he would see who she was, or at least see the gold embossed collar around her throat. But she had to risk it. "*Okay,*" she said. "*But just one.*"

Ching laughed. "*Okay! Just one!*" he replied.

He handed his rifle off to the other soldier and put his arm around Violet's waist. He pulled her body close to him and captured her lips. His tongue darted into her mouth. Violet was repelled by his act, but kissed him back all the same, putting her hands on his shoulders and holding him tight. After about twenty seconds he came up for air.

"*Now I know why your boyfriend is waiting up for you so late!*" he exclaimed as he released her.

"*Here's your rifle,*" the other soldier said. Ching took it into his hands.

"*Okay, you can go. But if I'm still on duty when you return, I want another kiss on the way back!*"

"*Yes, yes, anything,*" Violet replied.

Ching turned to the soldiers at the other end of the bridge. "*It's okay!*" he yelled. "*She can pass!*"

As Violet began to move off, she heard his voice ask her, "*Hey! What's your name?*"

"*I'll never tell!*" Violet called back. And she laughed.

军阀 外家
CHAPTER EIGHT

Violet scurried past the guards at the other end of the bridge and headed towards the town. She had been worried that the men would notice her bare feet, but it wasn't her feet they were looking at.

The town was another half mile away from the bridge. The road was wet and muddy, the fens on either side having overflowed from the near torrential rain. Great bolts of lightning and deep, rumbling thunder seemed to increase the drama of her escape. She was filled with both exhilaration and dread. It had been a close run thing at the bridge. But, perhaps, she thought, it was a sign that God would be protecting her on the journey. She couldn't help but pity the soldiers in the morning when her escape was discovered. Although the warlord might not have them all beheaded, Corporal Ching would not be a corporal any more, that was for sure.

She met no one along the road into town. The lights in most of the houses and other buildings were out. She passed a tavern where there was still revelry ongoing and she heard a man's deep voice call something out to her as she passed.

Violet had spent many hours looking down at the town from the seraglio balcony and knew which way to go to get to the docks. She wondered whether she should try and do something about shoes before she tried to find a boat. She knew that every second counted but also realized that she wouldn't get very far on bare feet.

Along the way to the docks was a house that she recognized. She had spent many hours at night looking at it from the third floor of the castle. She hadn't been able to see much from that far away, but she always noted the lights at night and often wondered, as she waited for them to go out, what sort of people lived there, what kind of life they led. She knew that it was a family because she had seen them coming and going. She realized that if there was a family there, there might be shoes.

The house was set back from the street. All the lights were out. She crept up to the porch and saw several pairs of sandals by the door. There was a pair of men's, three pairs that looked like they were children's and one other pair that she decided belonged to the lady of the house. She quickly sat on the highest step to the porch and put them on. They were a little small, but they would do. As she got up to head for the docks, she said a little prayer of thanks to the woman and asked for her forgiveness for stealing her shoes.

The dock was several blocks away. The town had grown since Violet had become the warlord's prisoner. The streets on the outskirts were wide and seem well planned, but the closer you got to the docks the narrower and more crowded the streets became. She passed what seemed to be a dry goods store. It was darkened, as were all the stores. Violet realized that she would need some food for her journey and stepped up to the window to look in. She saw barrels of rice and beans and dried fruit. Hanging in the window was a string of what looked like dried sausages. Her belly was already demanding sustenance.

The food was so close and yet so far away. For a moment, she considered breaking the glass and grabbing what she could, but she realized that it would make too much noise. On an off chance, she tried the door, but it was locked. She debated going around the back and seeing if there was another way in. A bolt of lightning and a roll of thunder reminded her of the perilousness of her journey and the need for haste so she decided against it. With deep remorse, she continued on her way to the docks.

When she arrived at the last building before the wharf area, she paused. There was likely to be a night watchman.

She looked both ways carefully and then crossed the broad street. There were a number of barges tied up and a large steamer. The riverboat that General Wang used to make his trips to Shanghai was there and there were some lights on it. She dashed past it and headed to where she saw some junks and smaller boats.

She knew that she would never be able to navigate even a small junk by herself. She knew nothing of sails and whatnot. It would have to be a small rowboat like the ones they used to row when she was a girl on the lakes back home. There were several piers and she walked up and down a few of them nervously looking out for the watchman. Some of the junks served as home for their owners. Knowing that there were people on board them made her very nervous. One of them might wake up and need to empty his bladder or something and see her. On the other hand, there might be food aboard that she could steal. She thought about exploring one, but then thought better of it. It was too dangerous.

She had gone up and down six or seven piers and seen nothing she could use. She was beginning to get desperate. Then, on the last pier, she saw a little rowboat tied up next to one of the junks. It was perfect. The only way to get to it was to climb on the bigger boat and then let herself down the side. It was risky, but worth the gamble.

She stepped carefully onto the junk. She had to make a little leap to clear the gunwale and she made a loud sound as she landed. She stood stock still for a moment. She could hear a man snoring loudly from inside the cabin. There was no other noise except for the rain hitting the deck. Believing she was safe, she tiptoed to the port side of the boat and looked over the side. There was the rowboat. The oars were still in it. Using the rope that held the bow of the rowboat to the bigger boat, she lowered herself down. The rowboat kept moving below her and she tried to keep it still by using her tippy toes. The rowboat clattered against the side of the junk making a loud noise. She froze again. The snoring had stopped but there didn't seem to be any activity. She waited about 15 seconds before trying to maneuver the rowboat to where she could step into it again. This time she got it.

Her foot found the plank across the bow of the boat and she carefully planted it. When she felt she was stable, she tried to put her other foot down. The rope she was holding onto was slippery and wet and it just slid out of her hands. She fell backwards into the rowboat knocking the oars about and causing the boat to collide once more with the side of the junk. This time it made an even louder sound.

An angry voice came over the side.

"*Who's there? What are you doing?*"

Panicked, Violet scrambled to untie the bow line. It was tied tight and slippery and she had trouble with her longish nails getting a grip on it. She looked up and a man's head peered over the side of the junk.

"*Hey, who are you? What are you doing?*" it called out angrily. A chasm opened in Violet's belly. Her fingers pulled and tugged at the knot, trying to get it free. She heard another voice, a woman's.

"*Husband, what's happening? Why are you yelling?*"

"*Someone's trying to steal our boat!*" he answered.

"Aieeeeee!" she yelled. "*Do something about it! Don't just stand there!*"

"*Help! Help! Thief! Thief!*" he yelled.

"*What are you doing?*" the woman shouted.

"*I'm calling for help,*" the man said.

"*Get in the boat and stop him, you old fool!*" the woman insisted.

"*But he might be a robber! He might have a knife!*"

"*Ohhhhhhh! You coward! I'll do it!*" she yelled.

Violet was overwhelmed with panic. A vision of being hauled back to the castle, all trussed and beaten flashed through her mind. "Oh, please! Please! Please help me get the rope loose!" she pleaded to heaven.

Just as the old woman started to haul the rowboat closer to the junk using the bow line, Violet got it freed. The rowboat banged up against the side of the junk once more. She kicked at the bigger boat with her right foot and the rowboat fled away from it. She quickly jumped back, grabbed the oars and took a seat. Three pulls and she was clear.

"*Oh! He's getting away!*" the woman called out. "*Stop! Thief! Stop! Oh, you old fool! You let him get away with our boat!*"

As Violet rowed away she could hear the man and woman arguing. Several other voices joined them and here and there oil lamps were turned on. The piers at Yeuyang were built into a little cove and it was a good quarter mile before she would be in the river proper. She pulled and pulled on the oars with all her might frantic that someone would come in pursuit of her. She was afraid too that somehow the fact that a boat had been stolen would get back to the castle and someone would get suspicious. Her only hope of escape was to put several hours between her and her inevitable pursuers.

It took about fifteen minutes for her to row to the entrance to the cove. So far, no one had emerged from the docks to give chase. Her back was to the river as she rowed. She didn't see that the heavy rains had caused the river to swell and that what was normally a calm, laconic flow had turned into a torrent. When the nose of the boat entered the heavy stream, it picked up speed and it was off.

The heavy current came as a shock to Violet and almost pulled the oars right out of her hands. She was adroit enough to immediately pull them from the water. She turned and tried to see where the boat was headed. The river water looked black all around her. She could only see a few feet ahead. It was still raining hard and the water dripped off her forehead into her eyes. She pulled the oars into the boat and turned so that she was seated facing the bow. She held onto the gunwales and sat back for the ride.

She knew that big boats plied the river here with impunity and so she was not afraid that her little rowboat would hit any snags or rocks as long as she kept to the middle. She deftly used the oars to right the boat each time that it threatened to spin off towards one bank or the other. There was no way to estimate how fast she was going, but she knew that she was going much faster than she could have rowed. Any fear that she had of capsizing or running aground was easily offset by the thought that she was free, finally free. No more Whore Number Four, no more whips and chains, no more nights serving the warlord's drunken guests. And most importantly, no more warlord! She was Violet Howard once again! It would be a perilous and arduous journey until her new found freedom was secured, but she just knew that she would make it.

Shortly after her sleigh ride had begun, the rain finally let up. After about two hours, the river banks turned from high and narrow to low and wide and the current slowed. The sun was just starting to break and the clouds overhead to dissipate. Violet realized that she had to get off of the river. There was no way she could travel by daylight. She kept her eyes out for some break in the riverbank where she might turn into so that she could hide the boat and get some rest. She was wet and cold and tired. When she saw a promising opening, she broke out the oars, slowed the boat and steered towards it.

It was perfect. The high level of the river due to the storm had created a little lagoon. She was easily able to row the boat into it. It was surrounded by high reeds. She rowed across the small lagoon far enough so that she thought she would be safe and then beached the boat.

Suddenly all the tension and spent energy caught up with her. Her body felt leaden. She crawled out of the boat and pulled it high enough on the bank so that it would not float away and then lay down to rest for a minute or two. She fell immediately asleep.

When she awoke, it was almost midday. At first she wasn't sure where she was. She had been dreaming of her life in the seraglio. The former head chaperone, Zhu, was beating her. She had been crying and begging her to stop. When she realized that she was lying on a riverbank many miles from the castle, she was relieved.

She was thirsty and hungry. And dirty and wet. Her long hair was a tangled mess. She remembered her cut foot and looked down at it. There was a deep gash, but the bleeding had stopped. Then she wondered about her hurt ankle. When she looked at it, she realized that it was swollen. She would have to try and keep off of it as much as she could.

But she did need to find something to eat. Anything at all to keep her energy up. She was sure that she could go without full meals for several days, but she also knew that she needed to be alert and on her toes or she would certainly be caught.

Rising to her feet, she shucked off her damp clothes and laid them on some bushes to dry in the midmorning sun. She then set off to find some berries or perhaps even a fruit tree. When she placed her weight on her ankle, she nearly fell, the pain was so exquisite. The bank of the lagoon was heavily wooded and she looked around for a stick she could use as a crutch. She saw one the perfect size and she hopped over to it. It was a couple inches around, about five feet long and had a large knot growing out of the side. She found that when she put it by her side, she could hold on to the knot with her hand and lean on the stick for support.

She hopped around the woods for a short distance. She came to a little clearing and spotted just what she was looking for. It was a series of blueberry bushes! She rushed over to them and began picking and eating the tart berries like they were going out of style. Her hands soon became stained blue with the juices. The blueberries served the double function of slaking her thirst, at least immediately. She knew that she would need to do more than eat some berries to keep herself from becoming dehydrated, but realized that this would have to do for now. She wanted to put off drinking river water as long as possible, leery about its quality.

When she had had her fill, or at least as much as she could eat in one sitting, she hobbled back to the boat. She set herself down against a tree and raised her injured ankle on a rock. It was going to be a long wait until darkness.

After a while, she dozed off. She awoke with a start when she heard the unmistakable sound of a large ship's engine. Mingled with it was the sound of large paddles running through the river. She realized at once that it was the warlord's riverboat.

She knew that her best bet was just to stay out of sight, but curiosity got the better of her. She got up and hobbled over to the riverbank and knelt down naked in the reeds. She was just able to see the river through them. Sure enough, within a minute, the large river boat came into view. Black smoke was pouring out of its stack. She could see soldiers stationed on her decks peering into the riverbanks. A couple of them, officers, were standing on the upper deck and looking out with binoculars. She had known that it wouldn't take long for them to connect the stolen rowboat with her. It was just bad luck that she had been forced to pick a day for her escape when the steamboat was in dock. She comforted herself by the thought that there were miles and miles of riverbank and that only so much could be seen from the ship's deck.

She knew too that there would be other boats looking for her, so the fact that the riverboat had passed did not mean that she was safe. She watched the riverboat pass down the river and returned to her perch.

The day passed slowly. She drifted in and out of sleep, resting for the night ahead. Her thoughts drifted to the ordeals she had suffered during her four years of captivity. At times she cried. She cried too for poor Iris and Tatiana, wherever they were and whatever suffering they were enduring. She cried for the lost years.

One consolation was that she was free of the despised lock she had worn on her loins for almost two years. She ran her hand over her pudenda, reveling in its freedom from encumbrance. She was even delighted that she could feel a slight stubble on her love lips, for it was the first day in four years that the eunuch had not shaved her there. And it was the first morning in which she did not have to suffer the indignity of being brought to orgasm by him. The only physical reminder of her captivity was the black collar affixed to her neck. Yes, there was much danger ahead, but there was much to celebrate.

When dusk came, she readied herself for the continuation of her journey. She loaded her belly up with berries and donned her clothes. Her ankle was still swollen and the cut on her foot had begun to throb a little. She worried about infection. There was nothing she could do about it. She could not put her sandal on her injured foot so she left them both off.

It was, to her great relief, a moonless night. When she was sure that her little boat would be obscured, she pushed it out into the lagoon. The water had fallen somewhat from the night before and she had to drag it over the mud to get it fully into the water. Her legs and feet became besmirched with mud up to her knees.

Finally, she was on her way again. The current was laconic compared to the previous night. She knew that she could not row her way all the way to Shanghai so she interspersed rowing with just letting the little boat drift in the current, keeping its straight by an adjustment with the oars here and there.

Here and there she passed anchored junks. She smelled cooking from some of them and her belly ached for food. It was not long before her thirst returned and she finally succumbed to the necessity of drinking water from the river, scooping some up with her hand. Otherwise the night was uneventful. She passed several villages and towns on each side of the river and stayed as far away from them as she could. At one point, she passed the riverboat. It was anchored on the side of the river and all lit up. There were search lights aboard and so she scrunched herself up as low as she could get in the boat while she passed it. At one point the beam from one of the searchlights passed over her, but whoever was manning it did not see her.

When the sky revealed that dawn was near, she found another little cove and brought the boat into it. She was ravenously hungry and tired. She hid the boat as best she could and went on a search for some berries or fruit, still hobbling along on her little crutch. She was not as lucky as on her first day. She did find some berries growing from a bush, but she did not recognize them. They were bright red and smooth and round. She did not dare eat them for fear of getting sick.

That day seemed much longer than the first. She kept her eye out for the riverboat. It passed her early in the day. Several junks came quite close to the shore and she assumed that they were part of the general's fleet and that they were scouring the river banks looking for her. She had found a pretty good hiding place and felt safe.

In the midafternoon, about two o'clock, she heard voices coming down the riverbank. She had been asleep and they were almost on her when she awoke. She scrambled into some bushes to hide. It was an old man and a young boy of about eight or nine years old. They were carrying fishing poles and were engaged in an animated conver-sation. They were almost past her when the boy spotted her.

"*Look! Look, Grandfather, a woman is hiding in the bushes!*" he yelled. They stopped and looked at her. Violet's blood ran cold.

The old man was tall and spindly. He had long grey hair and was wearing grey cotton pants and shirt. The boy was similarly dressed. His hair was black and cut short.

"*Come out, little lady,*" the old man said. "*We won't harm you.*"

Violet saw little reason to keep hiding. Fearfully, she rose and hobbled out to them. She had washed out her pants in the river water earlier, but they were still stained brown from the mud. Her hair was matted. She was tired and gaunt. She knew that she looked terrible, but she put on as good a face as she could.

"*Please don't tell anyone about me,*" she begged plaintively. "*They're looking for me and I don't want to go back. Please!*" She broke into tears.

"*So that's why the boats keep coming back and forth!*" the old man said. "*Don't worry, we won't say anything. Who are you?*"

Violet explained who she was and why she had run away. Interspersed with her story, she begged and pleaded with them not to betray her. She realized that there would be a big reward for whoever turned her in. The two appeared to be poor peasants. A little bit of money would mean a lot to them.

When she finished her tear filled monologue, the man shook his head. "*A sad story,*" he said. "*Don't worry, we are no friends to the warlords and soldiers. They come and take what they want and who they want. They force the men to work for them and despoil the young women. Your secret is safe with us.*" And then, looking her over, he asked her, "*When did you last eat?*"

The very question made Violet's stomach growl. "*Two days ago,*" she answered. She had espied the plump sheepskin bag hanging by a strap across the old man's chest. "*And I'm thirsty too.*"

"*I'm a thoughtless old fool,*" the man said. He slid he bag off of his shoulder and proffered it to her. Violet took hold of it greedily. She pulled the stopper free from its mouth and lifted it to her lips. It was some kind of heavenly fruit juice. She drank until her belly was full and handed it back.

"*Oh, thank you,*" she said. "*I thought I might die of thirst.*"

The boy had a pouch slung across his chest and he opened it up. "*Here, have some of our wheat cakes,*" he proffered. Violet took two of them and downed them in an instant. A wave of warmth came over her.

"*Why don't you wait?*" the old man said. "*We're sure to catch some good fish. I'll cook some for you.*"

"*Oh, that would be lovely,*" Violet answered.

She sat in the shade of a large tree while the man and boy fished from the riverbank. After a while, the boy came over to her and sat nearby. He had all kinds of questions about the warlord and what is was like to live in the castle. Violet regaled him with some of her stories, leaving out the more lascivious parts. The boy was fascinated. At various junctures he decried the evil warlord and vowed to avenge her. When Violet told of the huge battle with the forces of the Nationalists, he changed his tone and seemed thrilled by the general's heroics.

The old man caught four plump fish that looked to Violet like trout. He cleaned them on a flat rock and then cooked them on sticks. Violet devoured the fish with ravenous glee. The old man told some tales of his village that made Violet laugh and laugh. His name was Qi and the boy's name was Qiang, which meant 'strong'.

When darkness was about to fall, the old man announced that he had to go back to his village. "*They will be suspicious when I do not come back with any fish, but I am considered a foolish old man and there won't be too many questions,*" he said. "*The boy will keep your secret, won't you Qiang?*"

"*Oh, yes, Grandfather. I won't tell anybody, not even Mother.*"

The old man smiled. "*So, you see, you will be safe. I will pray for you and light some incense before the family altar.*"

"*Thank you,*" Violet said. "*You have saved my life. I was so hungry that I thought I might eat some bark off of the trees.*"

"*It was our pleasure to aid you. And, in the years to come, the boy will have a great story to tell, how he saved the beautiful lady.*"

Violet smiled. "*And I will always remember your kindness,*" she said.

The old man and the boy both gave her a hug and went on their way. There had been enough fish left over that he had been able to wrap some in some broad leaves so that she could take it with her. They gave her all of their wheat cakes too, and the rest of the pouch of juice. After they had eaten, the old man had found some medicinal plants and had squeezed some of the sap from them in her wound. He tore a length of his pants and wrapped her foot with it.

Violet was sad to see them go. They were a side of China she had never seen. When they were out of sight, she waited until it was a little bit darker and then continued on her journey.

That night was much better than the night before. Her spirits had brightened. She felt stronger. The river had narrowed a bit and the current had become a little faster. She felt like she was making good time. She did not pass the riverboat that night, but she passed several junks anchored in the shallow water near the riverbanks.

She remembered her terrible journey upriver four years ago, a helpless, confined prisoner. She had seen none of the landscape on that trip, having been blindfolded any time she was allowed to come out on deck. She could see little of it now in the darkness. "Some day I will travel up this river in style," she promised herself.

She hid her boat in some reeds the next morning and spent the day sleeping in the shade of some trees. She had finished the last of the fish and the juice. By the time she was ready to go in the evening, she was hungry and thirsty again. The cut on her foot had stopped throbbing and her ankle seemed to be getting better. As she pushed the boat onto the river, she wondered how far she had come and how far she had to go. The trip upstream had taken ten days, but that had been against the current. She wasn't traveling much faster than the current now, but it had to be quicker than the way up.

At about three in the morning, she passed the riverboat again. It was anchored in a little cove and was pointed upstream. She felt comforted that it would be going in the other direction in the morning.

Towards dawn, she began to look for a good place to beach the boat. Unlike the areas she had been passing through, the riverbanks here were low and there wasn't much cover. She began to become worried. It was getting lighter and lighter. When she saw some fishermen getting their boat ready for the day's work, she knew that she had to get off the river. She pulled the boat to the right bank and got out. She had a dilemma. If she left the boat where everybody could see it, one of General Wang's junks might come by and spot it. If that happened, she was doomed. She could let the boat drift downstream, but there was always the chance that it would get hung up on a snag in the river. Then they would know how far she had gotten. There was only one solution: she would have to sink it.

She started to cry. She was tired and hungry and afraid. It didn't seem fair that she would have to abandon her boat. It had been like a friend to her. Now she would have to travel on foot. After a short while, she recovered herself. It had to be done. She waded out into the river as far as she could go and began to rock the boat back and forth. The gunwale on the boat was very low and it did not take long for it to begin to fill with water. When the water reached about half way up, it began to sink. When it fell below the surface, it vanished from sight.

Violet crawled back up to the riverbank and dragged herself over to a small stand of trees. She lay down and was fast asleep within moments.

She awoke in the middle of the day. She realized that she would have to make time now that she as traveling on foot. She would keep as close to the riverbank as she could so she would not lose her way and she would be careful to try and not be seen by anyone. Three times that day, she had to skirt small fishing villages, detouring into the countryside and then carefully working her way back. She was getting hungrier and thirstier every step of the way. She eventually came across a free flowing stream and she filled the sheepskin with water and drank her fill.

By nighttime, she was at her wit's end. Her ankle had begun hurting again and she was limping badly. The cut had opened up. It was getting harder and harder to see her way and twice she took nasty falls. When she came to a village, she just did not have the strength to work her way around it. She decided that she would sneak in and try and find something to eat.

It was more like a little town than a village. There were people on the street and stores and taverns lit up. She tried to hide her face and seem as inconspicuous as possible. When she passed a restaurant, the smell of the cooked food overwhelmed her. She decided to take a risk. She went to the rear of the building. Restaurants were always throwing away food and she hoped to find their trash bin. Sure enough, there was a large barrel in the back. It was filled with bones and roughage from vegetables. It was dark and hard to see, but she was able to scrounge up some bits of fish, some rice and some partly eaten turnips. She had never had such a wonderful meal.

She still had water in her pouch and she was able to wash it down.

When she was full, she limped on her way, staying in the shadows as best she could. She passed a tavern that was all lit up. There was obviously a party inside. There was laughter and loud voices. A drunk came stumbling out and ran into her.

"Ooooouuuuf!" he blurted out. He grabbed at her. "*What have we here?*" he asked loudly. "*A lovely apparition! Come and give me a kiss, little woman!*" He threw his arms around her and tried to put his face on hers.

"*Let me go! Let me go!*" she shouted. He continued to grope her and try to place his lips on hers. He stumbled and they both fell onto the ground. They rolled around a bit and then Violet pushed herself free. She ran away as fast as her feet would carry her.

"*Come back! Come back, sweetheart!*" the man called out.

Her heart beating a mile a minute, Violet did not stop running until she was clear of the town.

She slept that night in some bushes. It started to rain about half way through the night. She huddled up as best she could. She became terribly cold and she started to shiver. Luckily, it was not the harsh rain of the night she had fled the castle, but a soft, misty rain that stopped about an hour later.

When she awoke, her clothes were all wet. She got up and struggled on her way.

She continued thusly for two more days. On the first, she was not so lucky as the previous night and she did not find any place to get some food. She found some berries on the second day and wolfed them down. On the second night, she found another town and was able to eat out of several trash bins.

She was getting more and more tired. The little she had to eat was not enough to keep up her strength. On the third day, she had to stop several times and rest for an hour or more before she could go on. She became increasingly despondent at the possibility that she would never reach salvation. She had not been able to find a clear running stream from which to fill her water skin and she had to fill it from some swampy, murky pools. By the late afternoon of the third day she had become feverish. Her ankle was becoming worse and worse and it was excruciatingly painful to step on the cut on her foot. She was so hungry that she thought several times of turning herself in at several of the villages she passed. She was forced to cross several large rice fields and she tumbled several times off of the slender dikes which divided them into the brackish water. It had rained again during the morning and she was soaked to the bone all day.

Finally, she could not take it any longer. She had to admit defeat. She had no idea how far she had come and how far she had to go. Anything was better than the constant hunger and weariness. Her hair was matted beyond all recovery and she was filthy from head to foot. At the next village, she decided to risk being captured. She had to eat and she had to rest somewhere else but in a muddy field. She trudged along the dirt road that led into the village. She passed several villagers who just stopped and stared at her like she was some form of demonic apparition. She didn't even have the strength to ask them for help.

Then she saw it. She had to blink her eyes several times to make sure that it was real. It was a church. Not a temple, she had passed by a few of those. This was a real church with a steeple and a cross prominent at the top. It was not a big church, more like a chapel, but it was an undeniable sign of Western civilization. She stumbled towards it, thanking God for her delivery. There were two wide, wooden doors guarding its entrance. Crosses had been carved on them. With a mighty effort, she pulled one of the doors open. There were plain, wooden benches instead of pews, but the church had a large stained window exhibiting the crucifixion and an altar at the front. The floor was made of brown tile and the coolness of it felt heavenly on her feet.

Just by the altar was a tall, heavyset man. He was dressed in black pants and a black shirt. He had grey hair surrounding a prominent bald spot. He did not react to the opening of the door. He seemed to be cleaning the brightly polished wooden altar.

Violet hobbled about half way up the aisle. The man seemed to notice something and he turned around. When he looked at her, he became wide eyed. In a distinctly English voice, he said in Chinese, "*Beggars go to house! No come in church! Go now!*"

Violet's mind exploded in exaltation. In English she said softly, "My name is Violet Howard. I'm British." And then she collapsed to the floor.

军阀 外家
CHAPTER NINE

Violet awoke in a comfortable bed. Daylight was streaming in through the window. It had frilly, lacey curtains on it, yellow and white. The room was painted a soft yellow. A modest, wooden dresser stood against one wall and a full length mirror hung on the back of a closet door. A vase of flowers sat on the bedtable to her right next to a little porcelain figurine that looked like a young, distinctly European shepherd boy tending his flock. Over the door, which was closed, hung a simple, black crucifix.

She took all this in in an instant, trying to figure out where she was. She could have been in a guest room in any cottage in England. Then she remembered. This wasn't England, but it was a little island of it. She was at a mission in China. She had heard the English accent of the minister. She put her hand under the nice, soft, woolen blanket and found she was wearing a cotton nightgown. She looked up again and saw, sitting across from the bed, a little pigtailed Chinese girl. She was dressed in a plain, pale blue frock and was smiling at her. "You wake now! I go get missy!" she announced excitedly in English. She ran from the room.

A minute later, the door opened and a tall, thin woman, of about thirty years, not too far from Violet's age, came in. She had long brown hair that descended past her shoulders. She was wearing a yellow blouse primly buttoned up to the neck and a blue cotton skirt that went down to her ankles.

"Oh, thank god, you're awake at last," she broke out as soon as she saw Violet. "I've been so worried about you."

Violet didn't really know what to say. "How long have I…." she managed to squeak out.

"You've been asleep for a little over 14 hours. You had a terrible fever. I'm so glad you're awake," she repeated. "Let me get you some tea. Would that be all right?"

"Tea, yes…." Violet said in return. The idea seemed very nice indeed. "English tea?" she asked. "With cream?"

"Of course, of course," the woman answered. The little girl, she seemed about 7 or 8 years old was hiding behind the woman smiling. She was missing a front tooth. "Jie, go tell Cookie get tea for missy, chop chop!" the woman said to the girl. She clapped her hands for emphasis. The girl's smile broadened and she left.

"My name is Delia Brown. My father runs this mission. He's the one you saw in the church. He's down in the infirmary now seeing some of the Chinese children. He'll be back in a little while."

"My name's Violet Howard," Violet returned. "I've been…."

"Now you can tell us the whole story a little later," Delia interrupted. "I think that you could use some more rest. Drink your tea and then I'll come back and see you in an hour or so. All right?"

"All right," Violet answered.

"Oh, I need to tell you, I'm sorry about your hair. I saved as much as I could."

"My hair?" Violet asked. "What's the matter with my hair?" She put her hand up to try and feel it. It was gone, at least most of it. It was cut down to just a little above her shoulders.

"I gave you a bath as soon as you were brought into the house. A couple of the Chinese women helped me. Your hair was a tangled, knotted mass. It would have taken a century to work out all the knots. I'm sorry, but I couldn't let you go to bed like that. I had to cut it off."

For a second, Violet was upset at the loss of her beautiful, long, brown hair. Then she thought of how upset the eunuch, Li Pao, would have been, and she laughed. "That's all right," she said. "I'm just grateful for your help."

The door, which had remained partially open after the girl, Jie, had left, now swung slowly open the rest of the way. It was Jie and she was holding with both hands a delicate tea cup and saucer. The cup was white but embellished with little hand painted roses along the brim. The tea was a beautiful, murky tan.

Violet sat up in the bed. Her head spun and she had to close her eyes.

"You see," Delia said. "You're not all well yet." She moved towards the bed and helped Violet prop herself up on the large, fluffy pillow. "That's better," she said. "Now, just enjoy your tea and get some more sleep. I'll send up some hot soup for you later."

Delia smiled and left the room.

The little girl stayed and handed the tea cup and saucer up to Violet with both hands as if it were an offering. She smiled again when Violet took it.

"*And how old are you?*" Violet asked in Chinese.

The girl's eyes widened as if she had just heard a talking horse.

"*What's the matter?*" Violet asked playfully. "*Has a cat got your tongue?*"

The girl's hand flew up to her mouth as if to check if a cat had really stolen it. Then she laughed. "*I'm six years old!*" she announced proudly. "*You speak Chinese!*" she added.

"*Yes I do,*" Violet answered. "*It's so I can talk to pretty girls like you.*"

The girl blushed. "You drinkee tea," she said in English.

"I drinkee tea," Violet repeated.

It was one of the best cups of tea that she had ever had. It tasted like Earl Grey. The cream was delicious. All of a sudden, Violet realized that it was all over. She had made it. She was saved. She was lying in a bed that was a little piece of England, sipping tea. She had had a conversation with another Englishwoman, in English! There was no one to beat her for it. No one to beat her ever again. Tears came to her eyes. The cup in her hand started to wobble in its saucer. She took hold of it with both hands until it stabilized and then she took another sip, just to make sure that it was all real.

When she finished her tea, she felt a wave of fatigue pass through her. She lay back down in the bed and was fast asleep in an instant.

It was dusk when she awoke again. Another pretty little girl was sitting on the straight back chair in front of the bed. She had identical, long, black pigtails, but her face was fuller and she seemed a little older. Unlike Jie, she did not smile. She was dressed the same, in a pale blue frock that came down over her knees.

"I must tell Miss Delia that you are awake," she said in almost perfect English. Before Violet could respond, she had stepped formally but gracefully from the room.

Delia came in a few moments later. "I see you're up again," she said. "Do you feel well enough for some soup?"

"Soup would be delicious," Violet answered.

The tall, dour girl was standing behind the Englishwoman. "Lucy, please tell the cook that Miss Howard is ready for some soup."

"Yes, Miss Delia," Lucy answered. She turned abruptly and left.

Delia came over and sat down on the bed. "I'm afraid that we couldn't remove your collar," she said. "We tried to cut it with a very sharp knife, but there seems to be some kind of metal inside it. Father said that we will need to get some kind of metal sheers or maybe a hacksaw."

Violet's hand went up to her throat. She hadn't even noticed that she still had it on. She shuddered when she touched it. Her eyes filled up with tears. She looked at Delia. "I was his prisoner, you know. For four years. It was awful."

Delia grabbed Violet's hand and patted it. "There, there, now. It's all over. You're safe with us."

"Thank you very much," Violet answered.

Lucy brought back the soup. Violet hadn't realized how hungry she was. When Delia offered to spoon it to her, she declined. She had had four years of spoon feeding by her maids. She wanted to serve herself.

It was a delicious onion broth. It felt so good going down into her stomach. She was just finishing it up when there was a knock on the door. Violet looked at Delia. Then she remembered that she was back in a culture where her privacy would be respected. "Come in," she called out.

It was Rev. Brown. He was wearing a black shirt with a Roman collar.

"Am I disturbing you Miss Howard?" the man asked.

"Not at all," Violet replied. "Please come in."

"I'm so happy to see you looking so well," the reverend said. "You were quite a sight when you came into the church."

"Oh, yes, I'm sorry for frightening you," Violet replied.

"Not at all," he protested. "We are all happy to be of assistance." He looked at Lucy who was standing primly by the door. "Lucy, I have some things to talk about with Miss Howard. Would you please go see if Cookie needs any help with dinner."

"Yes, Reverend Brown," she answered politely.

When she was gone, Rev. Brown sat in the chair opposite Violet's bed. "We've noticed the reference on your collar," he began. "Cookie translated it for me. I dare say we've all heard of General Wang. He has a very evil reputation around here. His soldiers raided a village a few miles from here two years ago. It was awful. Now tell me, is General Wang looking for you?"

Violet told him the whole story, from her kidnapping in Shanghai, to Robert's betrayal of her and so on. She left out the more salubrious parts in deference to his vocation, but she left it no doubt what being General Wang's concubine meant.

"My, my," was all Rev. Brown said after she was done. He sat in thought for a moment. "The city of Yeuyang is four hundred miles from here as the river flows," he told her. "Getting this far is quite an accomplishment. Our little village is about 120 miles from Shanghai. There's a truck that comes from there every other week to bring supplies and mail. You've wandered a few miles from the river, I'm afraid."

"Can the truck take me to Shanghai?" Violet asked. "When is it due?"

"Yes, the truck can take you back to Shanghai. It's due in three days."

"Oh, that's so wonderful!" Violet exclaimed. She felt like getting up and dancing.

"I think that that's enough for now," Delia announced. "She's still very weak, Father. Let's just let her get some rest."

"Very well," the reverend replied. "Perhaps we'll see you in the morning at breakfast."

They did see her the next morning at breakfast. Delia, after changing the bandages on her foot, gave her one of her dresses to wear. Delia was a little plumper than Violet, so she had had one of the Chinese women take it in. Other than being a little confining up front, it fit perfectly.

Breakfast was a wonderful affair. And so was lunch and dinner. Violet spent most of her time catching up on the world from Delia, reading some of the newspapers from Shanghai that came every other week and teasing little Jie.

The mission had an orphanage and Jie lived there. She was one of the brightest students and so she got to work in the manse. Lucy, whose Chinese name was Liu, was a little over twelve. It was hoped that she would win a scholarship and go to England to study. She was very bright and very proper. She was slightly disdainful of Violet. Violet detected a resentment against her submission to the war-lord and her subservience to the old, feudal ways.

"Rev. Brown says that someday soon all China will be united under Dr. Sun Yat Sen," she told Violet. "We will have a democracy and a republic. Then we will kick all the foreigners out!"

Delia was coming into the room as Lucy was speaking. "Now, Lucy," she remonstrated. "That's no way to talk to a guest. And I've told you, the foreigners are here to help China. If it wasn't for the foreigners, there would be no trains, no steamboats and much much more. Someday China will prosper, but it will be with the help of Britain and countries like ours."

Lucy gave a little, "Harummpf!" and stormed out of the room.

Delia smiled.

Violet awoke on the third day full of excitement. It was the day that the truck was to arrive to take her to Shanghai. It had been a wonderful three days. She was beginning to feel like a real person again. It was like a heavy weight had been removed from her. She felt like laughing every moment.

Lunch was a little celebratory affair. Rev. Brown had been away on business the day before and he was back now. For some reason, he looked a little glum to Violet. "Is everything all right, Reverend?" she asked.

Rev. Brown had been staring out the window to the little sun room where they were having lunch. He snapped out of his reverie and answered Violet's question.

"Yes, thank you for asking," he said. "Everything is quite all right. I have a great deal of responsibility, you know. This whole village. There are three hundred people who live here. Most of them are women and children because the men are all away working or taken for soldiers. This country is very dangerous."

"That's why I'm so glad to be leaving here today," Violet answered, "to relieve you of the burden of hiding me. If General Wang ever found out I was here, there would be hell to pay. Even now, his boats are probably still scouring the river for me."

"I'm well aware of that Ms. Howard. I'm hoping that you remember us fondly. We can only do what we can, you know."

"I will always remember your hospitality, Reverend Brown. And yours too, Delia. I will think of you when I'm back in England."

The reverend's head perked up as if he had heard something. "Please excuse me a moment," he asked.

Violet nodded yes to him and watched him walk out of the little cottage that served as the rectory to his mission. She turned to Delia. "I'm sorry to be taking one of your best dresses," Violet told her. She was wearing the same light green dress she had been given the other day. It had a modest bodice and nice pleats. Delia had even given her some of her underwear, something that Violet had not worn for four years. And shoes too. Not real high heels, of course, but black with a properly prim, thick two inches.

Rev. Brown came back in. "It's time to go, Miss Howard," he announced. Violet had not heard the truck, but she was so anxious to get going that she made no note of it. She rose and thanked Delia again. Little Jie was crying and Violet leaned over and gave her a big hug, promising to send her a nice present from England. To Lucy, she gave a more formal handshake and made her promise to look her up in England if she won that scholarship. She gave Delia a big hug and a kiss on the cheek. "I'll never be able to thank you enough," she said. Delia had tears in her eyes.

"Come on now, Miss Howard, you've got to hurry," the reverend told her.

Violet nodded and headed for the door. She had no luggage or baggage to bring with her. She only hoped that the Consul's Office in Shanghai would be able to help her with getting some more clothes and a boat ticket back to England.

Rev. Brown was standing at the door waiting for her. When she passed him, he placed his hand on her back as if he were escorting her out. It was a bright and sunny day and it took Violet a moment to adjust her eyesight. She took a few steps and then she gasped.

Arrayed in front of her in a little semi-circle were ten of General Wang's soldiers. Along with them was Major Won, Wang's second in command.

"Oh my god!" Violet screamed. She turned to run and saw that there were two soldiers behind her who had been hiding by the sides of the door. She looked at Rev. Brown. "What have you done?" she demanded.

"I'm sorry, Miss Howard, but it's as I told you. I'm responsible for this village. If General Wang ever found out that we had assisted in your escape, his men would come and burn the village to the ground. They would kill all the men and rape and kidnap all the young women, selling them off as whores, not to mention my own daughter. He would leave the old women and children to starve to death. That's what would happen. I couldn't allow that. Too many of the villagers knew you were here. It would have gotten back to General Wang one way or another."

"You bastard!" Violet yelled. She ran at him to attack him, but the two soldiers stepped forward and grabbed her arms.

"God has his plan, Miss Howard," the reverend said, "and we all have our crosses to bear. I'm very sorry. Goodbye." He turned and stepped back into the rectory.

"Noooooooooooooo!" Violet yelled. She struggled to release her arms from the grips of the soldiers, but they were too strong for her. She kicked and squirmed and fought desperately for her freedom. She felt hands grab at the back of her dress and then violently rend it in two.

"No! No!" she screamed. "Don't let them do this! Don't let them take me!"

Within a few moments, the men had torn the beautiful, light green dress from her body. She was thrown to the ground and fierce, male hands ripped the white cotton underwear that Delia had given her apart. Her shoes were pulled off and the brassiere that she wore for the first time today was ripped from her body.

Strong hands held her to the ground on her back, gripping her arms and legs tightly. She felt her thighs spread and pulled back, revealing her sex. "Oh, my god, they're going to rape me right here!" she thought miserably. But that was not what they were about. Major Won stepped into her view and pulled something from his tunic pocket. Violet recognized it right away. It was the lock she had worn on her loins for two years, the one she had been so happy to have been liberated from. He was going to put it on her again.

"*Please don't! Please don't!*" she begged. "*Please let me go! I don't want to go back! You can't! You can't!*"

Major Won also had in his hand the thin, silvery cable that was used to bind her labial lips close together. Violet watched as he knelt down between her thighs. She tried to free them from the grasp of the men. She pulled and tugged and shook, but they held her firmly in place. When she felt the cable being passed through the holes at the bottom of her love lips, she screamed. "*Don't do it! Please! Please!*"

She broke into deep, heartbreaking sobs as she felt the cable being threaded through the other holes. She let out a loud sob when she felt her labia being pulled tightly together. And she gave out a deep, delirious moan when she felt the lock attached and then released to fall on her pudenda.

She had no more chance to beg and plead, because one of the men forced a long, thick leather gag into her mouth. She shook her head wildly as she felt it being buckled at the back of her head. Hands pulled her wrists and ankles together and bound them with leather thongs. One of the men produced a long, thick bamboo pole. In a trice, they had affixed her wrists and ankles to notches at either end.

Major Won gave out a sharp command. The men formed into ranks. Two men picked up the ends of the pole and hoisted it onto their shoulders. Major Won spat out another harsh order and the men were off.

Violet squirmed and twisted her body frantically as she was carried along. Her arms and legs were stretched to the extreme, leaving a few inches between her torso and the bamboo pole. Her body bounced with each step, her naked breasts jiggled, and the lock on her mons bounced up and down. "Oh my god! Oh my god! I can't believe this! It isn't real! It can't be!" she cried to herself. But the bonds that held her wrists and ankles firmly, the heaviness of the despised lock as it lay on her love lips, the offensive, degrading gag they had placed in her mouth all told a different story.

Several of the villagers were standing by the side of the road as she passed. They had expressions of indifference on their faces. One of the women, elderly with stringy, grey hair, spit at her and called her "*Whore!*"

Once they had gone a few hundred yards, Violet gave up her struggle. She knew that it was fruitless. She began to worry about her upcoming reception back at the warlord's castle. Her stomach quailed and her blood ran cold as she thought of the punishments the warlord would arrange for her. "It's not fair!" she called out in her mind. "It's not fair! It's not fair!" Tears streamed down her face.

Rev. Brown had told her that she was a few miles from the river. The soldiers covered the distance in about an hour. All the time, Violet's body bounced and danced. When they got to the fishing village, the men marched to the docks and came to attention. Violet dangled from the pole helplessly, her naked body for all the villagers to see. Desperately, she tugged and pulled at her bindings. Her head was hanging downwards and she looked and saw one of the general's junks pulled up at the dock. A sailor, dressed in light brown pants and shirt, came down the gangplank and stepped over to where Violet was hanging helplessly. He and Major Won spoke for a moment. The man grinned and nodded his assent. Violet could see them talking but could not hear what they were saying.

The sailor nodded again at Major Won and then turned to his ship. He barked an order and two men came running down the gangplank. They relieved the soldiers who were holding Violet aloft of their burden, turned and went back the way they came.

Violet often had nightmares about her trip up river when she had been kidnapped. To have been held in such unforgiving bondage for so long, without any real human contact, going off to an unknown fate had been a horrifying experience. Her mind rebelled against having to experience it again. "*No! No!*" she tried to yell. "*Not that! Please! No!*"

Her voice emerged as a jumble of muffled sounds. The sailors brought her on deck and then quickly over to the hold. One man went down the ladder first and then the other, taking Violet with them. Once all the way down the ladder, they lowered her to the deck.

They were obviously waiting for something. A few moments later, the first sailor, the evident captain, came down into the hold. Violet saw that he had something in his hands. In the left was a hammer, in the other what looked like large, metal staples. He proceeded to bang the staples into the deck. He did four in a large square, about three feet apart. He hammered a fifth into the deck between the two nearest the hatchway. When he was done, he nodded to his men.

The men began to release Violet from the pole. They untied her wrists and ankles. As they dragged her over to where the staples had been hammered into the deck, Violet began to understand what they were for. She struggled valiantly as they began to tie her down, kicking and screaming, trying to flail her arms. Her wrists were tied tightly to the first two staples, forcing her elbows and palms onto the deck. Her legs were spread behind her and her ankles tied off to the other two. Then the captain came up to her. Violet was crying and struggling against the ties. Smiling at her, he tied one end of a cord to the ring in the front of her collar and then pulled the other end through the staple in between the ones that bound her wrists. Violet felt her head being pulled downwards. She tried with all her might to resist it, but the man had been a sailor all his life and was quite strong. When her neck was lowered almost all the way to the deck, he tied off the cord to the staple.

Violet was essentially bound on all fours. Her rear end was in the air and her legs were splayed apart, making available and vulnerable her lower orifices. The only motions she could make was to raise her hips up and down or shake them from side to side.

"*Noooooooo!*" she tried to cry again. "*Please don't do this! Please!*"

The men stood there taking in her distress for a while. They remained silent. She heard the sound of a cigarette being lit and soon smelled the tell tale smoke. She could not look up at them. She could only raise her head a few inches upwards off the deck. A wave of revulsion flowed through her. "*Pleeeeeeease! Pleeeeeease! Don't leave me like this!*" she begged through her gag. "*Pleeeeeeease!*"

She heard footsteps coming down the ladder. Whoever it was handed the captain something. She could not tell what it was. And then he stepped behind her. She felt a certain tenseness fill the air and she realized what was about to happen. "*Noooooooo! Pleeeeeeeease!*" she begged. Only muffled sounds emerged from behind her gag. There was a whistling sound and then a lash of fire crossed her rear cheeks. "Ohhhhhhhhh!" she moaned. "Ohhhhhhh-hhhhhh!"

She pulled and tugged at her bindings in a vain attempt to escape her punishment. But her body was bound firmly in the most appropriate position for this exercise. The whip came down again and again and again. Violet howled at each blow. Her muffled voice echoed throughout the empty hold. She thought that she was free of the whip, that she would never have to suffer the kiss of leather ever again. Despair flooded her. She cursed the Browns, cursed the sailors, cursed the warlord, cursed her fate. Each time the whip fell it was like a rough edged blade was scouring her skin. Each time, she let out a bloodcurdling scream.

Finally, it was over. She heard the captain sternly order his men, "*Up!*" That was the only word that was said. She was barely aware of their leaving until the last man started up the ladder. She could just see his sandaled feet as he started his way up. A few seconds later, someone closed the hatch, plunging her into darkness. A few moments after that, she felt the boat being poled away from the dock. When the current took them, she felt the junk surge. They were on their way. She laid her head on the deck and began to sob.

She was left that way for several hours, plunged into absolute darkness. She went through various phases of emotional discord during that time. When she was brought up river the first time, she had no real idea what would happen to her except for her direst fantasies. Now, if she didn't know precisely what punishment the warlord would order meted out to her, she certainly knew its nature and ferocity. Her brief period of liberation, getting to know and feel what it was like to be a free woman again, tore at her as she realized that she was now almost certainly irretrievably returned to bondage.

She would never be given the chance to escape again. All of the stars had to be in the precisely correct configuration for her to get away this time. The odds of it happening again were infinitesimal. While at the mission she had dared to dream of a normal life again for herself, a return to England. She would take up teaching the piano again. She would go for walks whenever she wanted, visit shops, go to parties, have friends of her own choosing. And most importantly, be able to choose for herself when and if she would allow anyone access to her body again.

Instead, she was being returned to the status of an abject whore. The ancient Chinese villager who had spat at her had had it right. She was a whore.

She couldn't understand why God had let her down so miserably. She had prayed and prayed that her bid for freedom be successful. And he had denied her. Why? Why was this happening to her? What had she ever done that would deserve the terrible fate that awaited her?

And to have been betrayed by a man of God, that was the worst of it. And an Englishman, too. Not to mention his daughter, Delia. The tears that she had in her eyes when Violet said goodbye now stood out as a sign of her guilt at her treachery. "How could one woman do that to another?" she asked herself miserably.

The way she was bound, she was unable to lower her hips or bring back her legs. She couldn't raise her head more than a few inches off of the deck. Her arms were splayed wide, bound into immobility. The most that she could do was to rock herself backwards and forwards. She had started to do that unconsciously, just to give herself the illusion of freedom. But when she did, she set the infernal lock that imprisoned her loins in motion, causing it to sway and bump back against her tightly bound love lips. Her stomach curdled at the thought that it was there again. She yearned to rip it from her body, regardless of the injury to herself. Even when she kept stock still, she could feel its weight. It ate at her consciousness. It was like the warlord had reached out these many hundred miles and touched her with his foul hands. He had taken repossession of his property. What was it that General Chi had said? Yes, she was merely the delivery service for it. It was the most important part of her, denied to her own touch, but subject to the attentions of whomever her master deigned to offer it to.

She could feel the sway of the ship as it tacked upstream, hear the water of the river rushing by the hull. She could hear the footsteps of the men above decks and sometimes their voices as they called to each other. It had taken ten days to reach the castle the first time. This time it would take about a week. She faced seven days of cruel bondage and cruel isolation. Already the minutes were slowly dragging by, seeming like hours. Every once in a while she would tug fruitlessly at her bonds, shake her head and scream into her gag, just to break up the terrible monotony.

When the hatch opened, light flooded the hold. A man was coming down. The hatch closed behind him, but he was carrying a lantern. He hung it from a hook in the overhead. The flickering light made everything seem grotesque. All she could see were his feet, but she was sure it was the captain.

He squatted down next to her and looked at her for a while. He grabbed her hair at the back of her head and lifted her face up so that he could gaze at it. It was the captain. Violet looked back with a sincere and virulent hatred. He just laughed.

He reached a hand under her chest and took hold of one of her breasts. Her breasts were swinging free due to her confines. He stroked and squeezed it. His hand was rough and strong. He reached across and seized the other, pinching its nipple until Violet gave out a little squawk.

She was repelled by the man's touch. She was helpless to resist him. Self pity at her powerlessness and anger at his callous use of her welled up inside her.

"Don't touch me, you swine!" she yelled from behind her gag in English. "Leave me alone! Leave me alone!" She shook her head and body in emphasis at her effete demands.

The man's hand left her breast. He stood. He stepped behind her. She sensed him picking something up from the floor. She heard a familiar whistle.

"Crack!" the whip sounded as it scoured her already wounded rear cheeks. "Crack! Crack! Crack! Crack!" it went in quick succession. Violet screamed from the pain. Her body quaked. "Ooooooooouuuuuuuuu!" she moaned. "Aaaaaaaaaiiiiiiie" she screamed.

After five brutal strokes, the man tossed the whip back onto the floor. He came back around to Violet's front and squatted before her once again. She was still sobbing from her injuries. He grabbed her hair again and lifted her face. "*No talking!*" he said to her.

Violet nodded her head eagerly. She had learned her lesson. She wouldn't talk. Not for seven days.

Satisfied at her commitment to compliance, the man let go of her hair and resumed caressing and teasing her breasts. Violet's skin crawled as he touched her. The first time she had made this journey, the men were apparently under strict orders not to touch her sexually in any way. That was apparently not the case this time. She recalled the conversation the captain had had with Major Won and his amused laughter in response. What had the major told him? Did he give the captain free license to abuse her? Was she to spend a week as the man's helpless toy, the repository of his spume? How many of the other men were to be per-mitted access to her, she wondered miserably.

Her fears were heightened when the man withdrew his hand from her breast and then ran it gently down her naked back. It didn't stop at the edge of her spine, but continued onwards and took measure of her proffered, red lined rear globes. Violet tried to avoid his touch by shifting her hips and rocking forward, but the man gave her rear a vicious slap that resounded through the small room. Violet just hung her head and cried.

He continued the exploration of her flesh. He caressed and pinched her fleshy hindquarters and then ran his hand up and down her trembling, pale thighs. Her skin thrilled at the contact, sending her a wave of unwanted pleasure, stoking her desires.

Violet knew what was going to happen. He was going to fuck her. Four years of habitual sexual use, often many times a day, had trained her body to respond to the least caress. The heat of the man's rough hand on the inside of her thighs, on her buttocks, over her back and down again triggered the spark of incipient lust within her. When he ran his hand over her imprisoned pudenda, her body shivered and she had to suppress a moan. He did it again and again, stroking her softly and expertly. His right hand was caressing her bound quim while his left slithered back and forth over her rear and back. It then reached under her and seized a breast, massaging and caressing it, teasing its now hardened tip.

Violet could not help the moan escaping her lips. She heard the man chuckle and she despised herself for her slatternness. When he began to tickle the stiffened button at the apex of her sex, she gave out a great sigh and pressed her pussy against his hand.

That was, apparently, his signal. He moved behind her. She felt his hand tug at the lock that hung from her loins and the heard it click as he unlocked it. She felt it as it slid over the thin, silvery cable ends. She moaned when she felt the cable bring pulled through the holes in her labia. She shivered when she felt them freed.

The captain paused in his assault of her while he shucked off his coarse, cotton clothes. When he was naked, he shuffled up behind her on his knees and probed his stiffened cock against the entrance to her womb. Using his right hand to hold it steady, his left resting on her hip, he poked the head of his prick inside her. Filled with revulsion and self hate, Violet tried to avoid being pierced by shifting and rotating her hips. The only effect was the immediate, harsh slap she earned on her buttock. She whined and ceased her gyrations, hanging her head in despair. When the cock slid easily into her moist, hot channel, she gave out a deep, lustful moan.

The captain rode her for a long time, slowly drawing his rigid piece in and out of her crevasse. Violet could not resist joining his motions, pushing back to meet each languid thrust, clamping her well experienced sleeve tightly against his cock and pulling her hips back. The soft, flickering light of the lamp made the room seem demonic, like she had been transported to a lower level of hell. The man behind her seemed like a ghostly demon intent on punishing her soul.

When she came for the first time, she clamped her hands into fists, bit down harshly on the thick, offensive gag in her mouth and moaned. Her mind yearned to halt somehow the exquisite torture of the conscienceless prick abrading the walls of her sensitized canal, but her body celebrated the sensations, demanding more and more. Her powerlessness to prevent the man's callous and determined use of her, his ability to bring her to a shattering climax against her will, filled her with despair and self contempt. As her juices rose again, prefatory to another climax, she groaned with self pity and succumbed.

The man's pace began to quicken, his hands, which had a firm, impassioned grip on her hips, clasped them tighter. He began to issue forth staccato, satisfied groans. With self loathing, Violet prepared to receive his spunk. It would conjoin with the spunk of the hundreds of other men who had polluted her. She issued a loud, pitiable groan of misery and anguished protest. And yet, when she heard the man's groans accelerate and meld into one long, continuous expression of physical pleasure, when she felt his prick begin to throb and jerk within her womb, when she experienced for the thousandth time the well known suffusion of warmth that signaled his discharge, her body exploded into a cataclysmic series of spasms as her hot, demanding tunnel clamped tight against the invader, contracting and expanding in body wracking pulses of pleasure.

When he was done, the man resumed his languid strokes within her as he recovered his breath and his body cooled. His motions delivered a series of exquisite aftershocks to her canal, causing her body to shudder. When he softened and withdrew, Violet pressed her forehead down on the deck and sobbed.

As an expression of his satisfaction with her performance, the man caressed her flanks and ran his hand over her swollen, still trilling love lips. He rebound her cunt, this time threading the infernal, glittery steel cable from top to bottom so that the lock hung from the lower portion of her outer labia, giving him easier access to it Violet groaned with dismal unhappiness when she felt the tell tale click of the lock sliding closed. The lock swayed back and forth gently when he released it, pulling on the tightly drawn cable, sending reverberations of pleasure throughout her.

The man stood, gave her a pat on her still proffered rear haunches and redonned his clothes. Then, taking the lantern with him, he stepped up the ladder to the main deck. He banged harshly on the hatch three times. Violet heard it unfastened. The hold flooded with light. The man stepped up out onto the deck and the hatch reclosed, plunging her into darkness once more.

Thus began her week of torment. The captain used her frequently during the day and night. Sometimes he came down and fucked her, spilling himself alternately in her womb or her bowels. He would kneel in front of her, loosen the cord that bound her collar to the deck and use her mouth, plunging his meat down her throat and emptying his balls directly into her belly. Other times, he would merely manipulate her pussy to pleasure with his hand or mouth, driving her into shuddering completions of lust.

She was fed as she lay on the floor. He forced her to pee as she knelt there, her thighs splayed wide. She was brought up on deck, naked, blindfolded and bound twice a day to empty her bowels and for a short period of exercise. But most of the time she spent alone, fastened to the floor in the dark, cursing her fate.

At night, after the men had consumed their evening meal, the crew would have their turn. They would come down, alone, or in groups of two or three, and use her mouth and rear for their pleasure. Her loins would remained locked. The captain had apparently retained the pleasure of its use to himself.

Once, early in the voyage, she had revolted when one of the men was preparing to pierce her nether hole, by shifting and gyrating her hips, moving his target until the man gave up in frustration. Even his repeated, harsh slaps on her rear did not deter her. Her victory was short lived. After the man left, the captain and another man came down. He knelt in front of her. He had brought with him a long, thick cucumber and a bowl of greenish paste. He loosened her gag and, after dipping his finger in the paste, slid it between her lips. Her mouth erupted into fire at once. She cried bitter tears as she watched him dip the cucumber into the paste, coating it heavily. She screamed and begged for mercy, promised obedience, sobbed and cried while she struggled at her confinements. The captain ignored her outbursts. While the other man held her hips still, the captain spread her rear cheeks with one hand. He pressed the tip of the cucumber against her anal ring and then plunged it in. Her insides erupted into immediate, tortuous heat.

She cried and begged for him not to leave her that way. Returning to her front, he merely squeezed her cheeks until her mouth opened and returned her gag to its place. She knelt in agony for hours. Her anus burned as if someone had taken a lighted match to it. She did all that she could do to expel the offensive object, but to no avail. Later, when one of the men came down to remove it, she gave him no trouble when he penetrated her there, despite the awful, wrenching, burning sensations she experienced as he possessed her.

By the time they reached their destination, Violet was a miserable shell. Despite her fear of the further punishments that awaited her, she was relieved that her hellish journey was over at last. Her body was limp as they dragged her onto the deck. They bound her hands behind her back and, still gagged, thrust her into a tiny, steel cage. The cage was hoisted by two men down to the dock and loaded on a waiting cart. It was the middle of a bright, sunshine filled morning and, as was undoubtedly intended, her naked, confined body was visible to all.

The warlord's rebellious prisoner had been returned. The message was clear. No one escaped the wrath of General Wang.

Violet felt nothing but numbness as the ox led cart plodded its way to the castle. She closed her eyes to block out the sight of the curious crowds that formed to gaze at her. She only began to shed tears when the cart was halted at the outer gate to the castle so that it could be formally admitted. Once the inner gate was passed, her cage was unloaded from the cart and placed on the ground.

She waited there for a long time. She watched with apprehension as a gibbet was mounted in the center of the cobblestoned courtyard. She watched with dismay as the general's troops assembled into formation, forming a large square. When the general emerged from the castle, resplendent in his best dress uniform, her stomach quailed and she whined with fear.

Two men marched solemnly to her cage. They opened it and dragged her out. She was led to the gibbet. Her hands were freed from behind her only to be bound in front and then affixed to the extended arm of the gibbet. Her gag was left in place.

There was a moment of silence. She had begun to sweat as a disabling fear permeated her. She saw the fierce, cold determination in her master's eyes and quailed. She heard a rumbling, the sound of wheels traversing the cobblestones. When she looked back at the entrance to the castle, she saw her beautiful, black piano being pushed into the square by two of the general's servants. They abandoned it there and scurried back into the castle.

There was the roll of a drum and then two soldiers emerged from the assemblage. They were carrying axes. When they reach the piano, they attacked it.

Violet sobbed with misery as she watched the beautiful instrument being demolished. Each cruel cut of an axe was like a dagger in her heart. The piano clinged and clanged as it was chopped into pieces. The strings sang as they were severed, the last sound they would ever make. Her eyes flitted back and forth between the destruction and the warlord's impassive, imperious face. She pulled at her bound hands above her, sobbing inconsolably at her loss.

When the men were done, they stepped back. Another soldier emerged from the formations. He was carrying a gallon sized, steel can. He approached the wreckage and began to pour the liquid contents onto it. He stepped back. A soldier carrying a torch stepped out and, advancing in precise, measured steps, brought it to the awaiting warlord. The general took it from him and then stepped solemnly towards the wrecked piano. When he tossed the torch onto it, it erupted into a huge tower of flame.

The fresh wood crackled and popped as it burned. The fire roared. Its heat was intense, making the air around it shimmer. For a full minute, as the flames consumed her former source of joy, the assemblage remained silent and still.

The, as if on a prearranged signal, one of the men stepped out of the formation and marched to the general. He had in his hand a coiled whip, and when he reached General Wang, formally presented it to him. Wang looked at it coldly for a moment and then he proceeded to unbutton his crisp, green, bemedalled tunic, revealing the crisp, white blouse underneath, and hand it to a soldier standing behind him. He took the coiled whip in hand, waved the presenting soldier away and stepped towards her.

Violet watched with horror as her master unfurled the heinous instrument. It had a thick handle and tapered to a slender tip. Its end was knotted. When loosened to its full length, it measured at least seven feet long.

Violet began an involuntary whine. Her hands writhed in her bonds and her eyes flooded with tears. She tried to beg for mercy, but her throat was so dry that no sound emerged. Her skin prickled and her stomach soured. She felt a chill go though her. She raised her eyes toward heaven and prayed for deliverance.

When her eyes returned, she looked into the face of her master. It had lost its cold indifference and had erupted into a fierce scowl of anger and hatred. His arm reared back and he threw the whip forward, pulling back on it at the last moment. It made a loud, 'Crack!' as it snapped back in the air. Violet's whines intensified. She closed her eyes and tried to shrink within herself. She bit down fiercely on her gag.

General Wang glared at his victim. He had suffered over a week of anguish after her escape. His anger and wrath had been building up exponentially since he had had word of her capture. She was the symbol of all he hated within himself, his weakness, his longing for love. At the same time, she was the avatar of all the forces that were surrounding him and threatening his kingdom. The Nationalists had sent another note expressing their ultimatum. British gunboats had been seen on the river, darting back and forth within range of his guns. General Chi's patrols had been increasing their pressure from the south, testing his defenses. And this woman, who had once been at the center of his heart, had caused him to lose face before his subjects, his men, the world. He rued the day he had ever seen her. And now she would pay for his suffering.

He flung the long, thin whip back and then brought it forth. It hurried relentlessly towards its target and snapped loudly when he pulled it back. It struck Violet on her belly and she gave out a long, agonized scream. A fiery, red wound emerged immediately. He stepped around her quickly, faster the she could react, and let the whip fly again. This blow caught her on her right buttock. Her whole body convulsed and she screamed again. He threw the whip a third time, targeting her plump, swaying feminine mounds. The tip engaged her right breast, making it jump. A deep reddish gash blossomed forth and her screams became intense and otherworldly.

He continued to circle her, lashing forth again and again. Violet screamed and danced and writhed. Her mind was on fire, her body electrified with pain. The burning piano raged on and on making her feel that she had been cast into the fires of hell itself. The whip tore at her flesh again and again until it seemed like her body was one, continuous wound.

After the tenth lash, he stopped. He was out of breath. His shirt had become drenched with sweat. His anger had been satiated. His victim hung lifeless in her bonds, her damaged body swaying. He stared at her for a long time. All of a sudden, he was overwhelmed with grief, grief for all that he had lost, grief for all that might have been. He tossed away the whip. His eyes were brimming with tears. He turned and fled into the castle.

Major Won marched formally into the middle of the square. He raised his right knee high and then stomped his boot hard onto the cobblestones. His voice called out loudly his order for the men to come to attention. The rumble of hobnailed boots striking the ground rolled through the courtyard. Rifles snapped onto shoulders. He called out another order. A single drum began a deep, mournful beat. The formations commenced an orderly, somber march from the courtyard, forming into a single column of eight men across, and paraded out the gate. When they were gone, all that was left was the dangling, moaning, naked English concubine and two sentries posed at attention on either side of her.

军阀 外家
CHAPTER TEN

General Wang did not bother sending Violet to his dungeon. After hanging in her bonds for several hours, her wounded body displayed for all passers by to see, the eunuch emerged from the castle. He looked at her with pity. He had not been surprised at the near success of her escape. Although he had done all he could to prevent it, he had secretly wished her luck on her journey. He had been saddened by news of her capture.

He looked upon her ravaged form and pondered the vicissitudes of fate. The gods worked mysteriously. Which one, he wondered, what savage deity, had condemned this woman's gentle soul to such torment? Was there some ultimate purpose that would be served? Or were the gods merely playing with her, amusing themselves at her misfortunes?

He ordered two of the servants two cut her down. They carried her limp body into the fortress and brought her directly to the seraglio. Her tearful maids, who had watched her torture from the seraglio balcony, received her and brought her into her room.

New security arrangements had been ordered for the recaptured prisoner. Black bands of steel reinforced leather were sewn with hard steel wire around her wrists and ankles. Like with her collar, the ends were soldered together, making the bands virtually irremovable. Each band had a thick, golden colored brass ring so that her limbs could be locked together or attached to a chain. Orders were that she be continually affixed to some unmovable object. Steel rings had been hammered into the floors and walls of the seraglio and all over the living areas of the fortress at strategic places to accommodate her confinements. There would be no more escapes. Violet had been right about that.

It took two weeks for her to recover from her punishment. The eunuch had her body rubbed with special salves the old woman herbalist had devised to prevent scarring from her wounds. Violet had developed a severe fever and her maids nursed her around the clock, cooling her body with wet cloths, stroking and comforting her.

Li Pao, bordering on insolence, had declined the warlord's order to bring her to him, citing her need for a full recovery. Her sister concubines, who had suffered woefully in her absence, took up the slack, suffering intense, additional torment as a result.

When Violet was brought into the warlord's presence for the first time, her wristbands locked into the ring in the front of her collar, she shivered with fear despite having been given a double dose of the lust producing witch's brew. The warlord forced her submission to him, driving her to unwanted explosions of lust and emptying himself in her three times, once for each orifice.

After a month, the seraglio returned to its routine for its prisoners. The eunuch shaved their loins and brought them to climax every morning. They made languid love to each other during the day, and they served the warlord and his guests at his whim.

Violet had descended into indifference at her fate. Although she fervently engaged in bouts of passion with her sisters and maids as if rabidly hungry for the sensations of physical pleasure, she remained uncommunicative and aloof the rest of the time. Only little Wen, her youngest and most diminutive maid, received anything like affection from her. From time to time, Violet would stroke her face gently, giving her a wan smile, and then lean over and devour her lips with ferocious lust.

Her use by the general was brutish and nasty. She trembled each time she was brought into his presence. He beat her repeatedly and used her ruthlessly. He kept her loins locked up except when in use and doled her out to one guest or another almost every night he did not compel her to his presence.

It was in the fall that the Kuomintang forces struck. Wang had been assiduously preparing for war the whole summer. Through a German agent, he had purchased more machine guns and another armored car. He had purchased on the black market five hundred thousand rounds of ammunition for the English rifles that had been captured in the big battle two years before, and crates of shells for the 6 pounders. He had even established his own air force, although it consisted of a single World War One surplus German made Fokker D VII biplane. The Fokker had been the ultimate in German aerial technology at the end of the Great War. It was fast at 125 mph and carried twin, synchronized 7.92mm Spandau machine guns. It was not rigged for bombs but was excellent in an aerial surveillance capacity. He had three pilots trained and they alternated patrolling the skies.

He had put five thousand peasants to work building fortifications and trenches. The approaches to the likely invasion routes had been mined, with machine guns and cannon trained on the projected killing fields. Telephone lines had been strung to remote observation posts. He had expanded his standing army to 2,000 men and trained 5,000 more militia. He had purchased German Mauser rifles for them all. His cavalry had been expanded to six battalions. At Li Pao's insistence, he created a medical corps and a central military hospital to tend to the expected wounded.

The first warning had come from his spies in Nanking. The Nationalists had started two divisions of their best troops on the march. It was an overwhelming force. During the ten day march necessary to get them in position to strike, Wang called out his militia and, in a series of fiery speeches, exhorted them to defend their homeland. His airplane reported to him the enemy column's daily progress.

On the first day of battle, the Kuomintang forces attacked in three waves. They had come not through the slender pass through which they had attacked two years before, but in the open plain ten miles to the west.

Wang had been ready for them. His six pounders smashed the attacking formations to pieces while his machine guns raked the survivors. It was only the third wave that reached his lines. In hand to hand combat, his troops drove them back.

During the day, three British made Spads, biplanes sold to the Nationalists by the British Army, made their appearance over the fortress. The day marked the first recorded aerial combat in Chinese history. Alerted by Wang's forward observation posts, his Fokker had taken to the air and gained its maximum altitude just at the moment that the Spads appeared in the sky above the castle.

The Spads each came equipped with a 250 lb. bomb. As they dove in a single line to make their run, the Fokker descended from high above them. The first two Spads unloaded their bombs. One struck the center of the fortress inner courtyard, killing seven men who had been standing there gawking while the bomb descended on them. The other landed in the garden, sinking into the soft soil and deadening the effect of its shrapnel. Its blast blew out all the windows on the first and second floors in the rear of the castle.

The third Spad never got the chance to complete its run. The Fokker came hurtling across its path of travel, its twin machine guns barking. The Spad's tail was shot clean off and the plane commenced a wild spin to the ground terminating in a brilliant ball of orange.

Meanwhile, the other two Spads had climbed again and launched themselves against Wang's plane.

All eyes on the ground were in the sky that day. The entire town of Yeuyang stormed out of their stores and homes to watch the magnificent machines dance and circle around each other, machine guns blazing. The concubines, Violet included, jammed themselves onto the balcony, their eyes pinned upwards to record the extraordinary event. Wang too was watching, and at each pass the planes made at each other, his heart formed in his throat.

On its fifth pass, the Fokker's bullets danced across the engine cowling of the second Spad, resulting in a torrent of black, billowing smoke. It glided away, disabled from the fight, and crash landed several miles distant. Its pilot was captured by some peasants and turned over, battered and bruised, to Wang's forces.

Just as the Fokker was pulling out of its attack dive at the second Spad, the third caught onto its tail. The two planes flew in ascending and descending gimbals as the Fokker tried to shake its pursuer. In a remarkable maneuver, the Fokker flew straight up and then made a large loop, turning upside down for several seconds and came down on the tail of the Spad. The Spad maneuvered away. The planes each made wide turns away from each other and then flew straight at each other, machine guns blazing. After they passed, the engine of the Fokker exploded into smoke. It made a long, dulsatory circle, winding earthwards and then crashed into the Yangtze.

The Spad turned back and made a victory pass over the castle, dipping its wings up and down. It then headed back to the Nationalist lines.

Wang was disconsolate at the loss of his warplane. But it had done its job. It had forewarned him of the attack and it had knocked two of the Spads from the sky. The third one limped back to its airfield, but was too damaged to take any further part in the fighting.

On the day after the initial Kuomintang attack, General Chi attacked from the south. Wang was ready here too. Chi's forces had to advance across a wide field that was hemmed in by a vast lake on one side and a thick swamp on the other. They crossed the field in ragged formation. Chi's army was officered by corrupt, venal men, and the foot soldiers were treated brutally and with scorn. They were ill fed, ill paid, ill equipped and ill trained. The moment they reached the center of the plain, Wang's armored cars sprung out from hiding. They cut the men down like stalks of wheat. The remnant cast aside their rifles and fled for their lives. Chi's army retired from the field for the duration.

But in the north, the fighting went on. Three days were spent in relentless artillery duels that wore on the nerves of the men in the trenches. The Kuomintang attacked again on the fourth day, this time breaking through Wang's line in three places. They were forced back by his cavalry. Casualties were heavy and streamed back to the hospital. Ammunition was running low.

On the morning of the fifth day of fighting, two British gunboats attacked Wang's gun emplacements on the Yangtze. The duel lasted all morning, the ships darting in and out of range again and again, their six inch guns blazing. His forces fought gallantly, striking the British gunboats with direct hits several times. But the gunboats were unrelenting. Their range and accuracy was greater then the French 75's Wang had mounted on the escarpments above the river. One and then another and then another gun was put out of action. When his men were down to one gun, the gunboats slipped by the fortifications. Two barges full of Kuomintang troops followed suit, landing on the north shore. Within an hour, they were assembled on the plain above the river and were on the march towards Wang's fortress.

When Wang got word of the breach of his defenses, he hurriedly formed a flying column of his best battalions. He had enough forces in position by the river, mostly militia, to stem the tide of the Kuomintang advance for a while, but knew that they would ultimately be overrun. He personally took command of the relief forces and, duplicating the heroics, in nature if not in scale, of history's most famous generals, marched them throughout the night, a journey of 35 miles with full packs, and delivered them just in time to repel an all out Kuomintang assault.

But that was the beginning of the end. For the next three days, increasing pressure on his lines necessitated retreat after retreat. His troops, even the militia, maintained their discipline unto the end. They fought fiercely for every inch of soil. But when his battalions were reduced to companies, companies to platoons and squads to a mere handful of men, it was all over.

In a dramatic effort, worthy of the finest military formations, Wang conducted an orderly retreat over the Yangtze, saving most of his remaining units. The Kuomintang were able to push their guns to the edges of the escarpments overlooking the river and bring his fortress within cannon range.

On the morning of the tenth day of fighting, just after the rise of dawn, a single gun of the Kuomintang force rang out. A shell floated over the river and crashed into the roof of the fortress. It collapsed the ceiling in the third floor of the north wing, wrecking the floor below it.

Wang had begun the night before alone in his salon. He had started out drinking, but soon tossed the bottle away. He would not spend what was inevitably his last night in his castle in a drunken stupor. His men had put up a heroic fight against overwhelming odds. But his empire and the fledgling Republic of North Hunan was doomed. A little after midnight, he went out and visited with his remaining troops. They were a battered lot. He went to unit after unit, thanking them for their bravery and assuring them that their suffering was at an end. There would be no more fighting. He visited the hospital, appalled at the carnage he had wrought. There were only two doctors and little medicine left. He had sent out his troops to raid the opium dens of Yeuyang and they had returned with some opium with which to relieve the pain of the wounded. But it was not enough. The maids from the fortress had been recruited as nurses and they were scurrying about with bandages, severed limbs, the bodies of the dead.

His visions of glory had come down to this. It all had turned on the cut of a deck of cards that infamous night during General Chi's visit. It was then that he had lost the good graces of the gods. He had had it so long, had had so much success and luck, that he had fooled himself into believing that they would never abandoned him. They had given him a great gift in the person of the English concubine, but he had squandered it. His men had paid the terrible price.

He had not slept that night. Li Pao was busy making arrangements for the evacuation of the fortress. A string of carts had been assembled and he was loading gold from the fortress vaults into them. Space was made for his wives and concubines. He would not be leaving without them.

When the first shell struck, Li Pao was ready. At the general's instructions he ordered that their flag, the fierce red dragon on a field of brilliant yellow, be lowered. A large white flag, sewn together from sheets, was hoisted up instead. The fighting was over.

Li Pao headed the surrender delegation which met under a tent on the north side of the river. He made sure that all of the militia members who had been captured would be released and allowed to return to their homes. He secured medicine and bandages for the hospital. Wang's regular forces would surrender and be incorporated into Kuomintang units. The town of Yeuyang would not be looted.

General Chi was there, gloating over the victory. But he was not in charge. It was General Li Chiang of the

Kuomintang forces. He dictated liberal terms. General Wang would be allowed to vacate the fortress, taking with him all the gold and goods he could carry. His wives, servants and concubines could accompany him along with a small bodyguard. He was to swear allegiance to the Nationalist Government and retire to Chengdu, General Chi's capital, where he would be, ironically, under General Chi's protection. General Chi would insure that Wang did not enter into any conspiracies to retake his domain.

Attending the surrender conference was Colonel Emmet Parker, the British soldier who had been at General Wang's birthday celebration two and a half years ago. He and his commanding general had come in search of Violet, sparked by rumors that had reached Shanghai. Violet had been forced, under threat of painful torture and death for herself and the young American concubine, Iris, to pretend that she was General Wang's willing companion. Colonel Parker had not been fooled, but his general, disdaining Violet as a compromised whore, vetoed any further efforts on her behalf and had reported back to the British Consul that the woman in General Wang's seraglio was not Miss Harris after all.

Parker became apoplectic when he learned that General Wang was to be allowed to take his concubines with him. "But he's holding a British subject against her will," he told General Li.

General Li's response was that concubines were essentially like wives and that under Chinese laws, they were Chinese citizens. In any case, he told him, he had made the deal and that was that.

Violet had been well aware of the fighting. She had been hoping and praying that it would lead to her delivery. The maids kept coming back to the seraglio telling of misfortunes at the front. Then they were recruited into the hospital and there was no news at all.

The shell which had destroyed much of the third floor of the north wing of the castle had caused an uproar in the seraglio. They had heard the explosion. The castle had shaken to its foundations. An hour or two later, word got back to one of the chaperones that General Wang had surrendered. Violet was overcome with glee. Her glee turned to misery when the eunuch came into the seraglio the next morning. He was accompanied by a number of General Wang's soldiers. They were carrying cages.

Violet screamed and raged, but the men soon had her subdued. It was easy to lock the rings of her ankle and wrist bands together. She was gagged and hooded, her wrists confined behind her back, and forced into one of the cages. Seeing the demise of Violet's resistance, the others went peaceably.

About ten o'clock that morning a column of ox led wagons started out on the road to Chengdu. Violet sobbed and sobbed as the movements of her cart jolted her from one side of her tiny cage to the other. Her heart had been so set on her liberation that it was almost too much for her soul to take.

Colonel Parker had watched as the cages containing the concubines were loaded onto the ox carts. Because they were hooded, he could not be certain which one contained Violet Harris. He burned within at his helplessness to save her. It was the second time he had failed. His heart was heavy with pity for her fate. Now that she was being taken to Chengdu, she would even be further removed from any power he had to redeem her.

Once the last cart had left the fortress, Colonel Parker saw squads of General Li's men rushing in carrying loads of explosives. General Li was nearby and he sought him out.

"What are your men doing?" he asked.

"They are mining the fortress," General Li replied in English. Despite his many years in China, Parker had never picked up the language.

"You mean you're going to blow it up?" he asked, incredulous.

"Of course," Li replied.

"But the castle is over 500 years old!" Parker exclaimed. "It's an historical treasure."

Li smiled. "500 years in China is not what 500 years is in England, Colonel Parker," he said. "Here, it is the blink of an eye."

"But why? General Wang is gone! You've captured it! It's a terrible waste!"

"It is very simple, Colonel," Li answered. "No fortress, no warlord."

"But, inside there are countless treasures, vases, ornaments, paintings, rugs. They are part of China's national heritage! You can't destroy all that!"

Li just shrugged his shoulders.

"Please," Parker begged, "give me 100 of your men and two hours. We'll have the castle cleared out in no time. I'll save everything."

Li turned to him. "I'll give you 50 men and one hour."

Parker went to work immediately. One of Li's lieutenants spoke passable English and he supervised the men at Parker's directions. They scurried in and out carrying arm loads of treasures. They went from room to room. Parker had promised the men 10 silver dollars a piece if they worked quickly.

Some of Wang's servants were still left and they guided the men to the store rooms where even more treasure was kept. General Li had allowed a number of the army's wagons to be pulled up to the fortress and had ordered some other men to load them.

He was, in fact, astounded at the amount of loot that emerged. It suddenly occurred to him that they were worth hundreds of thousands of dollars if not millions. His attitude changed and he gave them an additional hour to work. Later, when they returned to Nanking, he sold much of the goods on the black market, making him a millionaire, and kept a small portion of the better pieces to decorate the huge mansion that he built.

When the men reached the third floor, they encoun-tered a locked door. Parker corralled the lieutenant and he had one of the servants explain that it was the seraglio. Parker ordered the men to break the door down. They quickly explored the outer rooms, recovering numerous items of value. Then they broke down the door to the inner seraglio, where the concubines actually lived. Parker was astounded at the sumptuousness of the rooms. His heart broke when he thought of Miss Harris confined here for so many years.

They went from room to room. One of the rooms was different from the rest. There were three bedrooms walled by rice paper. This one was surrounded by walls of plaster and had a wooden door.

When he entered it, he had the distinct impression, guided by what he did not know, that this was Miss Harris's room. Everything was a jumble, clothes strewn all over the floor. He went to a closet and opened it. There was not much in it. But there was one thing on the bottom that caught his attention. It was a large, well decorated, bamboo box. He opened it. Inside were several notebooks. He opened one. There was elegant Chinese writing on one side and a French translation on the other written in a distinctly feminine hand. It was one of Violet's books of poetry. In the haste of the evacuation, they had been left behind. Cognizant with French, he stood and read the first poem. It spoke of love and longing, the product of a lonely heart and a beautiful mind. A tear came to his eye when he realized that Miss Harris had undoubtedly written it.

The lieutenant came into the room. "Come quick! Come quick!" he said. "General Li say two minutes, that all!"

"Okay," Parker replied. He scooped up the journals and fled.

* * * * * * * * * * * * * *

Life in Chengdu went downhill pretty quickly. At first, with the eunuch's assistance, General Wang tried to keep up appearances. He bought the most elegant mansion he could find. He dressed daily in his military uniform. There were lavish parties. He energetically sported with his concubines. A special room had been set off for them, isolated from the rest of the mansion and they, especially Violet, remained closely guarded prisoners.

The problem was that he had been sending most of his gold to banks in Shanghai. They were under the custody of his sons. At first, they sent him regular stipends to subsidize his life style. Over the year that followed, the stipends came less and less frequently and grew smaller and smaller.

Wang had taken to drink. He had always been a hearty drinker, but now he became drunk every day. He would start drinking in the morning and be passed out in his cups by the early afternoon. He would rebound for the evening and carouse with some hangers on unto the wee hours. The next day, he would start all over again.

To Li Pao's credit, he did not desert him. The eunuch supervised the household staff and regulated the concubines as thoroughly as he had before. Other than the fact that Wang's use of them started to become fewer and farther in between, their life went on as usual. Violet still spent her time chained constantly to this or that, and she and the other women were recruited now virtually every night to serve the warlord's guests.

When the money began to run out, and Wang became so indolent that he ceased being a force in the house, his wives took over. They supplemented their income by renting out the concubines every night, turning the mansion into a virtual whorehouse. They sold off all the goods. The maids were let go. One by one, the concubines were sold off until only Violet was left.

It was a year almost to the day from his defeat that Wang fell ill. It was apparent to all that he did not have the will to live. His wives were philosophical about his illness. While he was alive, their duty was to remain with him. Once he was dead, they could move to Shanghai and live in luxury with their sons. While they did nothing to expedite his death, they did little to prevent it.

On his last day, the household staff, such as they were, were called in to say farewell to him. Violet was one of the last ones brought in. At first, she stared numbly at his diminished form. His chest was rising and falling weakly. His skin was wan. His face was hollow. He was wheezing heavily. When she came in, his eyes were closed. She had long ago suppressed all of her emotions. She had no pity for him now. The memory of all the things he had done to her, all the years she had lost, more than five in all, came rushing into her mind. A fierce hatred filled her, the first emotion she had felt since the day of her brutal whipping after her recapture.

She was standing no more than three or four feet from the bed, dressed in a threadbare silk gown, her hands chained together. Li Pao was standing near the bed stoically. She could see the emotion in his usually cryptic face. Wang's wives were at the foot of the bed.

The withered warlord opened his eyes. They flitted weakly at the crowd around him. He saw his English concubine standing near him. A wave of pleasure and then sorrow passed over his face. He reached out his spindly, emaciated arm. His lips moved but no sound emerged. His face contorted in exasperation and then he tried again. With all the force left to him, he called out in an anguished voice, "Violet!" And then he died.

Violet burst into tears. She collapsed on the floor. A vision of their few happy days together flowed through her mind. Her heart ached with what could have been. He was a man unlike she had ever known, would ever know. What terrible forces had kept them apart? Why was she suffused with sorrow when she should be full of joy? He was a proud, fearless man who deserved a better end. It would have been far better had he been killed on the battlefield. China had lost a visionary. Despite his cruelty and his iron rule, his subjects had loved and respected him. They had fought for him to the death. If he had been given another five years, he might have been master of all of China.

The room was silent but for Violet's violent sobs. Li Pao watched her with a broken heart. He looked back at the peaceful face of his master. "How did I fail you?" he asked his ghost. "Please forgive me."

It was the eunuch who moved first. Wang's wives were sniffling at the foot of his bed, their emotions drawn out by Violet's grief. He approached the weeping concubine. "*Up!*" he commanded. Violet did not respond. "*Up!*" he commanded again, his voice louder and more imperative.

Violet turned her head. She was still a slave, she knew that. Her master's death would not liberate her. No, in fact, it would make her lot much worse. General Chi had been an occasional visitor to the former warlord's mansion. He had bought her use several times, reminding her that her ultimate fate was to be owned by him.

She took hold of herself. She would not spoil the dignity of her master's death chamber by making a commotion.

Slowly she rose to her feet. Li Pao ordered her to follow him and she obeyed.

There were three days of mourning. General Wang's wives, Li Hua and Yu Jie, called Violet into the large receiving room of the mansion and informed her that arrangements had been made to sell her to General Chi. Since no business could be conducted during days of mourning, he would take possession of her the day after General Wang's funeral. Li Pao led the disconsolate concubine back to her chambers.

The funeral was a dismal affair. It was raining lightly and it took three attempts to light the funeral pyre. The wood and charcoal burned slowly, creating a vast cloud of smoke. It was like the general did not want to leave the mortal realm. That night, Violet sat alone and unhappy in her room. Wang's widows were all packed and ready to begin their journey to Shanghai the next day. She was having terrible visions of what life with General Chi would be like, recalling his terrible torment of her. She was not crying. She had cried herself out for General Wang.

About an hour after dark, Li Pao came into her room. Her ankle was chained to a ring in the floor. It was long enough so that she could lie on her bed. Her wrists were joined in front of her. All the maids were dismissed and Li Pao had been taking care of her by himself for the last several weeks. He came over and unlocked the chain from her ankle. "*Come with me,*" was all he said.

Violet followed him. She was surprised that he had not chained her ankles, as was normally done when she was transported from place to place over the last five years. She put it down to his disturbance at the loss of his master and the fact that he, too, would be departing the next day and had become slack in his duties.

Wang's wives still made occasional use of her and she speculated that they intended to have one last fling. But they did not head down the wing where the wives' bedrooms were. They headed to the back of the house. They went through the empty kitchen and headed for the back door. A stab of fear went through her as the thought entered her mind that perhaps General Chi had come for her early, that some lackey of his was waiting in the back yard of the mansion to spirit her away to his palace. When they reached the door, Li Pao turned and, to her surprise, unlocked her bound wrists. He told her, "*Strip!*"

Violet made to obey. Even her tattered kimono had value, she thought. He was probably going to sell it for travel money. Unhappily, she drew the silky covering off of her body, standing nude in the man's presence for the last time.

The eunuch ordered her to lie on the floor and raise her knees. When she had done what he said, he produced the key to the lock on her loins from a pocket. He crouched down and undid the lock. He slid it off of the cable that confined her purse and then drew the cable free. He had given up on the use of the ben wa balls some time ago when the warlord had stopped using her.

Violet's hatred for the callous eunuch grew within her. Now she knew what he was up to. He had agreed to rent her out to someone. She would be a whore to the last. She glumly rose when he ordered her up. He pointed to a box on the floor next to where they stood. "*Open it,*" he commanded.

Violet, curious, went over and opened the bamboo box. There were clothes in it, a peasant woman's blouse and pants, some sandals and a conical, straw hat. She looked at the eunuch quizzically. "*Get dressed,*" he said.

Violet obediently donned the clothes. When she had placed the hat on top of her head, tying its strings under her chin, he opened the door and told her to come with him. Tentatively, Violet stepped through the doorway. She had never been out of the house since they had arrived in Chengdu.

There was a slight chill to the air. There was a half moon just on the horizon and the stars were all out. It was a beautiful night.

To Violet's surprise, there were two horses there, a rider on one of them. They moved restlessly, clattering their hoofs on the stones below them.

"*Keep those horses quiet!*" the eunuch hissed. The man did not respond, but gathered the reins of the second horse closer to him.

Violet looked at the eunuch with wonderment.

"*You know how to ride a horse, don't you?*" he asked.

Stunned by the question, Violet nodded.

"*This man is to be trusted,*" he said. "*He will take you north to Yeuyang. There is a junk there awaiting you.*" He pulled a small bag from his pocket.

"*There are ten gold coins in here. Give the captain three of them. The rest is yours. The captain will take you to Shanghai. You are free.*"

Violet was stunned. Free? She was free? Just like that? She couldn't believe it. It had to be some kind of cruel joke.

The eunuch spoke again. "*You have a great soul, Violet Harris,*" he said. He had never used her name before. "*I had my hopes that you would become a mate to my master and sit by his side. You could have done wonders for him, filling the void in his heart, making him a complete man. But it was not to be. I couldn't stand by and let you become the property of General Chi. The gods would have punished me. As it is, I have lost my master and am adrift in the world. When General Chi learns what I have done, he will have me beheaded. So be it. It is my fate. Your fate is to live and give your soul to the world.*"

Violet was speechless. Long ago, she had speculated on some ulterior purpose of the eunuch in his treatment of her. But the last two years had been so terrible that she had forgotten it. She looked at the horse. It looked beautiful. She held out her hand to the eunuch and took his hand in hers. "*Thank you, Li Pao,*" she said. "*I will never forget you.*"

The eunuch shook her hand and then gave her the bag of coins. "*Do not tarry. Ride all through the night. If the general's wives discover you are gone, they will raise the alarm. Goodbye and good luck.*"

Violet clutched the bag of coins to her. Ten gold coins was not much remuneration for five years as a whore. But they would have to do. She placed the bag in a small saddlebag on the side of the horse and then swung herself up. It had been a long time since she had ridden; she had learned as a young girl. She was sure that it would all come back to her. She turned to her guide. "*Let's go,*" she said. And they were off.

They rode all through the night. They stopped three times to rest the horses. The guide spoke little to her except to give directions. He had brought a bag of wheat cakes which they ate while the horses rested. He had a flask of brandy and gave some to her. It was the first hard liquor she had drunk in five years.

The sun was peaking over the horizon when they arrived in Yeuyang. The guide brought her around the outskirts of the town so that she would not be noticed. A mile away, up on a hill, she could see the wreckage of the castle. It had been blown into rubble. Her heart ached for what she had lost there and for Iris and Tatiana too. She would come back, she vowed. She would save them.

The junk was all ready to go. She presented the three coins to the captain, but he waived them aside. "*General Wang is dead,*" he said, "*but I still serve him. He would have wanted you freed. It is my privilege to have you as my guest.*"

Violet smiled warmly, the first time she had smiled at anything for a long time. The crew cast off the lines holding the boat to the dock and poled it away. The wind took hold of the sails right away and within a minute they were in the river. As they headed downstream, Violet looked up at the destroyed castle. So often had she looked down the other way wishing that she were on one of the ships plying their way downstream. And now she was here. At long last. When they turned a bend in the river, the castle became just a memory.

The journey was laconic and pleasant. The crew were all courteous and kind. She ate with them, laughed at their stories, stood on the deck during the day and watched the vast, immensely beautiful scenery float by. She had traveled the river three times and yet had never seen it. Despite all that had happened to her, she realized that she loved China. She would never leave it. There had to be some way she could stay. She thought of Sister Therese and the orphanage in Yeuyang. How nice it would be to come back here and live and work with them. When the captain had refused her passage money, she had given it and the rest of the gold to her guide with instructions to deliver it to the French nuns. *"I don't need it and I don't want it,"* she said. It would go a long way to replace General Wang's past subsidy to them.

It was on the fourth day that her idyllic journey came to an end. They were rounding a river bend. A large motor boat was plying its way in their direction. It had a golden sun attached to its mast. It was a Kuomintang patrol boat. There was a machine gun mounted on its bow. When the captain saw their junk, he veered the boat towards them and ordered the machine gun manned.

Four soldiers boarded the junk. At first they ignored her. Violet tried to keep herself small, like the peasant woman she was supposed to be. The soldiers were callous and rude. They were ostensively looking for opium smugglers, but really out to see what they could extort from river travelers. They searched the boat. The captain of the junk offered the men a wad of paper money, but they disdained it. The captain was wearing a watch and they took it. The hold was full of rice and they ordered the sailors to put ten bags onto the patrol boat.

Finally, the leader of the boarding party came up to Violet. "*What a pretty wench,*" he said churlishly. "*Are you their whore?*"

"*No, sir,*" Violet replied obsequiously. "*I'm just a traveler on her way to Shanghai. I'm going to meet my husband.*"

The soldier took hold of her hand and looked at it. "*You do not have the hand of a peasant woman,*" he said. "*Your hand is nice and smooth like a whore's.*"

Violet gingerly tried to pull her hand back.

He pulled her blouse up her arm. "*I see that you are wearing a fancy bracelet,*" he said, looking at the confinement that was still around her wrist. "*And your skin is pale and white like a whore's,*" he commented. "*Let me take a better look at you.*" Violet was wearing the straw hat she had been given by the eunuch, trying to hide her face. The soldier whipped it off. "*And you do not have the face of a female pig,*" he said. "*You have the face of a whore.*"

Violet's stomach grew tense and her heart began to beat rapidly. She had a queasy feeling throughout her body. This was not going well at all.

The soldier was staring at her face, studying it. "*In fact,*" he said. "*You do not look Chinese at all! You are a foreign devil! What's that around your neck?*"

When the patrol boat had been approaching them, Violet had taken a cloth and wrapped it around her neck to hide her collar. The sailors had tried to take it off, but they hadn't any tools strong enough. "*Nothing,*" Violet said desperately. "*It's nothing.*"

The soldier took hold of the cloth around her neck and ripped it off. The bright gold ideograms emblazoned on the collar jumped out at him.

"*General Wang's concubine!*" he announced gleefully. "*She's General Wang's whore!*" All the other soldiers surrounded her to gawk at her.

"*Are you running away my little whore? I heard that General Wang is dead. Did his wives sell you off to a whore-house and you ran away? I'll bet there is a very big reward out for you.*"

"*No! No!*" Violet screamed. "*Let me go! Let me go!*"

The sailors on the junk made as if to move at the soldier, but the other soldiers lifted their rifles and clicked rounds into their chambers. "*My captain will want to talk to you, my little whore,*" the soldier said. "*Say goodbye to your friends.*"

"*No! No!*" Violet screamed. She tried to resist the soldier. He took hold of the hair at the back of her head and pulled at it savagely.

"*You're coming with me whether you like it or not, whore!*" the man said.

Violet screamed and yelled as she was dragged towards the patrol boat. Two men took hold of her body and wrestled her on board. She writhed and twisted and turned in an effort to resist them. They dropped her on the deck of the patrol boat like a sack of rice.

The captain of the patrol boat was standing over her. "*What have we got here?*" he asked, amused.

"*She's General Wang's concubine, Captain,*" the original soldier said. "*She's probably run away. I'll bet they're searching for her high and low. She's a good looking whore.*"

"*General Wang is dead,*" the captain said.

"*Yes,*" the soldier replied. "*She was probably sold to a worehouse and she ran away. They'll pay big money to get her back.*"

"*Undoubtedly,*" the captain acknowledged. Then he looked at her more closely. "*She's not Chinese!*" he said.

"*No, probably one of those Russian whores who were traveling down the river escaping the communists. Or maybe she was taken from Shanghai. I hear that there are thousands of them there.*"

Violet was still lying on the deck where she had been plopped. "*I'm not Russian!*" she shouted. "*I'm British!*"

The captain laughed. "*So you say. So say all the Russian bitches when we capture them. Prove it, I say!*"

"*How could I prove it?*" Violet demanded. "*Do you speak English?*"

"*Not a word,*" the captain acknowledged. "*But my general does. We'll take you to him. If he says you're British, so be it. But if not, he'll probably give you to us to play with for a while and then return you to your owner. As our leader, Dr. Sun Yat Sen says, 'The key to an orderly republic is the sanctity of private property.'*" He laughed.

"*Take her below and tie her up,*" he ordered. "*I don't want her jumping overboard.*"

Violet struggled as they brought her below decks. They threw her into a small cabin. Two of the soldiers held her while a third went to get some rope. When they pulled her arms behind her back, they saw the brass rings embedded in her bracelets.

"*Ah, look!*" one of them said. "*She's all ready to be tied up! How convenient!*"

They fastened her rings together with a strand of strong rope and then did her ankles. They then tied her ankles to her wrists, putting her in a hog tie.

"You bastards! You bastards!" Violet yelled in English. "Let me go! Let me go!" She couldn't believe what was happening. She had almost made it! Just like the last time! They would take her back to Chengdu! She would become General Chi's property, his whore! And before that, they would rape her! It couldn't be happening! It couldn't!

"*Gee, she makes a lot of noise,*" one of the soldiers said.

Another one handed him a rag. "*Here, stuff this in her mouth. That'll shut her up.*"

Giggling like a little school boy, the soldier pushed the dirty rag at Violet's face. She protested and struggled, but another one took hold of her jaw and forced her mouth open. The rag went in. They ran a rope around her head over her mouth several times and then tied it off behind her so she couldn't dislodge it.

When they were done, naturally, they needed to inspect their prisoner. They had heard the captain. There was a chance that she might be turned over to them, that is after the general and the captain were through with her. They just wanted to get a peak at her treasures.

One of the men pulled up her blouse, exposing her pure white breasts and the men took turns manhandling them. One leaned over and put his mouth to a teat, suckling it. Then they pulled down her pants and stole a look at her hairless mons.

"*Look, no hair!*" one of the men said. Hands stroked her skin, testing its smoothness.

"*It'll be heaven to fuck her,*" one of the men said. "*I'll bet she knows all the tricks.*"

The other two men agreed.

The voice of the captain called down the passageway. "*What are you dunderheads doing down there? Get up on deck!*"

The men murmured acknowledgements and sorrowfully pushed Violet back over onto her belly. They shut the door to the cabin and locked it from the outside. As they were heading back up the ladder to above decks, the boat's motor came to life and it roared away.

Violet cried and cried and cried. Her hopes for freedom had been dashed again. Why was God being so cruel to her, she asked the heavens. What had she ever done?

The boat took a good hour before it docked. Two of the soldiers came down and freed her ankles and then pulled her to her feet. They had an old rice sack with them and they put it over her head and tied it around her neck. Then they brought her up the ladder to the upper deck.

She was hustled off of the boat and into an awaiting car. It drove for about a half hour and then came to a halt. She was dragged out of the car, up some stairs and into a building.

"*Tell the general I have a present for him,*" the captain said.

A man's voice answered politely and Violet heard a telephone being lifted off the hook. A young, male voice said, "*I'm sorry to bother you general, but Captain Chung is here and he has a woman with him.*" There was a pause. "*Yes, sir,*" the voice said. And then, "*You can go right in, Captain.*"

Violet was marched forward and into a large room. The men had taken her sandals when they had tied her up and she felt the thick rug on her feet.

A deep voice said, "*What's this all about, Captain Chung?*"

"*A woman, sir. We found her on the river. She says she British, but I think that she's an escaped whore. She wears a collar that says she's General Wang's concubine. Since he's dead, she was probably sold to a whorehouse and then escaped. There's bound to be a reward for her.*"

"*Let me see her,*" the general ordered. The sack was pulled from Violet's head. The room was dimly lit by an overhead electric lamp. The general was broad chested and his hair was grey. He had a small beard. His tunic was off and he was dressed in a white shirt, finely pressed. There was a wide, green pad on the desk in front of him covered with piles of papers. The telephone was to his left. The room was well decorated, with an ancient vase on a small table to Violet's right. There were two easy chairs on the other side of the room, to her back. There was a narrow tower of books on shelves built into the wall behind the general.

"*Take that rag out of her mouth,*" the general ordered.

The rope was untied from around Violet's head and the rag pulled out. Violet sputtered and coughed. "*I'm a British subject,*" she managed to croak. "*You can't do this to me!*"

"*We will see about that,*" the general said. "*How do you come to speak Chinese so well?*"

"*I was General Wang's prisoner for five years, that's how,*" Violet shouted. She was struggling, but the captain had a firm grip on her arm.

"*So you admit that you were his concubine?*"

"*Her collar says so, General,*" the captain blurted out. "*Take a look!*" He pressed Violet closer to the general so that he could read the golden ideograms on her collar.

"*So I see,*" the general said. "*You're undoubtedly right. She probably belongs to some whorehouse. General Wang was living in Chengdu. That's where she should be returned to.*"

"*No! You can't do that! I'm a British subject!*" Violet yelled. "*The British are your allies! You can't do this to me! Please! Please! Please send to Shanghai! Someone there will vouch for me! I'm sure of it! Send a message to the British Consul! He'll tell you! I was kidnapped five years ago and made into General Wang's concubine! I was his prisoner for five years!*"

Having exhausted her outburst, Violet burst into tears. The men watched her for a moment. Then the general spoke to her again. "*I don't even know if you speak English,*" he said.

"I do! I do!" Violet answered in English. "Ask me anything about Britain! Anything! I'll tell you! I'm British I tell you!"

The general paused again. Violet could see that he was thinking. Then he spoke. "All right. I'll tell you what I'll do," he said in English. "It's possible that you're British as you say. It's also possible that you are Russian and you learned English from an Englishwoman. You say you were a prisoner for five years. That would give you plenty of time to learn all about Britain. I'll send a message to the British Consul in Shanghai. I have a packet going to Shanghai in a couple of days. It'll take about a week until it gets back. If he vouches for you somehow, sends someone who can identify you or a picture, then I'll release you. If it turns out that you are lying, I'll have you whipped and sent back to Chengdu. *Take her away,*" he concluded in Chinese.

Violet sobbed as she was brought out of the room. She recalled her last contact with British authority. She had met with the British general and the colonel. The general bought her story about being General Wang's willing mistress. The colonel knew better, she was sure of it. If he somehow got word that she was a prisoner here, he'd rescue her, she was sure. If not, who could tell what would happen. There was always the possibility that he was no longer even stationed there. The only other person who knew her in Shanghai was Robert and he was the one who had betrayed her into slavery in the first place. If Robert got word that she was here, he would probably come himself to make sure that she was sent back to Chengdu. He couldn't risk her telling everyone what had happened!

Robert had been an occasional visitor at General Wang's castle. He was the general's partner in the opium business. He had gotten himself a plane towards the end and he used to fly up very couple of months. While he was there, he always abused her unmercifully. He taunted her about her fate, plowed her fore and aft, until General Wang locked her pussy up at least. Later, when General Wang disdained the use of it, Robert would fuck her there and then, laughing, bind her back up. He often beat her.

The last few times, he brought his wife, Lady Preston with him. She had become engaged to him after she had been kidnapped. She had been quite a prize. She was younger and prettier than Violet and her father was dripping in riches. She had laughed when she first met Violet, standing naked and bound in the general's salon. She made Robert have her suck his cock. Then they took her to their bedroom where they both abused her for several days.

She was worse than Robert, much crueler. She too would have a lot to lose if Violet ever got free. She would have a lot to answer for. Her blue blood friends would shun her if they knew that she was a sadistic lesbian who had repeatedly taken a whip to an unwilling Englishwoman, had conspired to keep her a dismal sex slave. Her family probably had very strong connections at the consulate. If she got word that Violet had escaped and was a mere hundred miles or so from Shanghai, she would prompt Robert into immediate action.

Violet spent a dismal week in a primitive lockup. It was a converted peasant's hut made of stone. They kept her hands bound to her collar the whole time, even serving her her meals in a dirty bowl on the floor. She had to beg her guards to unfasten her hands so that she could use the filthy bucket they provided to her as a bathroom. They watched and laughed as she relieved herself in it, locking her hands back up immediately once she was done.

Her only amenity was a small, barred window. If it wasn't for that, she would have been kept in continuous darkness. She could just look out of it if she stood on her tippy toes. Naturally, she couldn't do that very long. But just the occasional peek lifted her spirits. And to be able to hear the noises outside, the voices of the people of the fishing village that served as the patrol boat's base of operations, the sound of the general's car going to and fro, the birds singing, all the sounds of an active town.

When she thought of the possibility that she might be sent back to Chengdu, she shivered with fear. She wondered whether the general had sent word there. If word got back from there first, before word got back from Shanghai, she was probably doomed. They thought that she was the property of some whorehouse. If they learned that she was owned by the powerful General Chi, that would be another story altogether. They wouldn't wait for word from Shanghai. They would just ship her back.

Other times, she believed that she would be saved. She had never lost her faith in God, even though it seemed that he had deserted her. She prayed many times every day as she waited.

Sometimes she would cry bitter tears. All of her faith would leave her. Lying in the darkness, on the thin, cotton pallet they had given her as a bed, she would lay awake, thoughts of despair running through her head.

On the tenth day of her confinement, early in the afternoon, she heard the lock to her little prison turning. She had already had her lunch and no one had been in to see her since the beginning of her confinement except her jailers, and them only at meal times or when she begged to use the toilet. Her heart went aflutter. Her pulse quickened. She knew that word had come, but was it from Shanghai or Chengdu? Was it Robert or Colonel Parker who had gotten the news? Would she be saved or would she be damned?

The door swung slowly open. It was bright outside and the light from the open door blinded her for a moment. She blinked until she could see clearly. The door swung closed, making the light dim again. She couldn't believe her eyes.

It was Robert!

She collapsed to her knees and began to sob. "Oh, no!" she whined. "Oh, god, no!"

"Yes, Violet, it's me," Robert said. He was dressed jauntily. He had knee high, polished leather boots on and a thick leather jacket. His hair was mussed like it had been blowing in the wind. He had a scarf around his neck. He smiled at her cruelly.

"It's pleasant to see you again. You look well." At this he let out a hearty laugh.

"Please, Robert," Violet begged. "Please don't let them send me back. I'll do anything that you ask. I won't tell anyone what you did. I promise. Please, please!" She was crying. Her hands were folded upon her chest, locked there in an attitude of prayer. She knew that she presented a pathetic appearance. Her peasant's clothes were dirty and ragged. Her hair was knotted and thick with grime. She hadn't bathed in almost two weeks. They had fed her a thin gruel and she had lost about 10 pounds. "Please, Robert," she repeated, her voice not much more than a whisper.

"You know, it's really a matter of dumb luck that I'm here," Robert said, his voice polite and pleasant. "Apparently your claim to be a British subject was received by the British Consul about a week ago. The note said that a former concubine to General Wang was claiming to be a British subject. She said her name was Violet Howard and that she had been kidnapped and forced to become General Wang's slave. The Consul paid no mind to it. You see, that British general who came up to Yeuyang two years ago was pursuing rumors that an Englishwoman had become General Wang's prisoner. When he came back, he reported that it had all been a mistake. The woman in question was an imposter, not an Englishwoman at all.

"When word came in of your claim, the Consul ignored it. It wasn't until I had dinner with him last night that I heard about it. He mentioned it casually between the main course and the dessert. Because he knew that you had once been my fiancé, he thought I might be interested. I was surprised to hear about you. I naturally volunteered to fly up and see if you were the real thing, put the matter to bed, so to speak. He was happy to accept my suggestion.

"So I'm here to identify you. Of course I won't. As far as I'm concerned you're some Russian whore who once had contact with the real Violet Howard who was unfortunately kidnapped off the streets of Shanghai five years ago and hasn't been heard from since. God knows what happened to her. I mean, in addition to you and me, and Lady Preston, of course." He laughed again. He took a cigarette out of a golden case in his vest pocket and lit it. The aroma filled the room quickly.

"You know, it smells like a pigsty in here, Violet. You used to be more punctilious with your person. But then again, I forgot. You're not Violet Harris. You're some Russian whore." He laughed at his joke.

Violet sobbed and sobbed. She couldn't believe what had happened. She was doomed. Instead of finding her way back to Shanghai and freedom, she was going to be sent far, far away, to Chengdu, where she truly would never be heard from again. She would die there. General Chi would visit the worst punishments on her. He had told her about boiling people in oil. When he was tired of abusing her, that is probably what he would do.

"Please, Robert," Violet moaned. "Please don't do this to me. I'm sorry for throwing you over. I'm sorry, believe me."

"I'm glad your sorry, Violet, because that has been the point of all this. I had General Wang kidnap you and turn you into his whore for that very reason. And you're going to continue to be sorry, for the rest of your miserable days. I hate you with every ounce of my body! You dared to refuse me! You would have made me the laughingstock of all Shanghai!" His voice was rising now. He had lost his insouciant coolness. His face had turned red.

"Who were you anyway? You were some poor relation to the Royal Family! Your father was a drunkard and a degenerate gambler! You had no one to turn to, no one who wanted you! I offered you the chance to be my wife! Begged you to reconsider! Humbled myself before you! And yet you spurned me! You told me no! On the day you were kidnapped, the day I brought you to the park so that General Wang's men could seize you, my heart leapt with joy as I watched the car whisk you away! I've enjoyed seeing you every time I visited General Wang's castle, using you like the whore you are!"

He stopped and collected himself. He took a brisk puff from his cigarette and stomped it out on the floor. Calmer now, he said, "And, by the way, so has Lady Preston. We joke about you all the time. I'll have to find out what whorehouse bought you in Chengdu and make arrange-ments to pay you a visit. We both will. Goodbye, Violet! Till then! My time is up. After all, it shouldn't take too long for me to decide that you're not Violet Harris. We don't want anyone getting suspicious, do we? So, farewell."

He made a motion towards the door. It swung open. He stepped back in surprise. A uniformed, British officer came in. It was Colonel Parker!

Violet stared in amazement. It couldn't be true, could it? Was she really seeing what she thought she was seeing? Could it be possible? How?

Colonel Parker spoke. "If those kind of things were permitted these days, Lord Preston, I would challenge you to a duel right now. You are the lowest form of person there is on the earth." He slapped Robert viciously across the face. Robert stepped back, his face red.

"Y,you," he stuttered. "How? Why? I, I…."

"I'll tell you how, Lord Preston," Parker spat out at him. "When we returned from Yeuyang two years ago, General Witherington made his report to the Consul. He reported that the woman we saw in General Wang's castle was not Violet Howard. And if it had been up to him, that's where things would have stayed. But I spoke to the Consul privately. I told him that we had, in fact, met with Violet Howard. That she was being held against her will by General Wang, forced into the most despicable acts, treated like the meanest whore. He believed me. But what could he do? General Witherington's report was official. Besides, Miss Harris had said, although I convinced the Consul that she was forced to, that she had willingly become General Wang's mistress and concubine. We couldn't very well send the army after her under those circumstances, could we?"

Parker paused to take a breath. Then he continued. "When word came that Miss Howard was a prisoner here, the Consul sent for me immediately. I was up to coming here at once. The Consul had a different idea. You, Lord Preston, have been a wart on our community for a long, long time.

We're all aware of your involvement in opium smuggling, that you were General Wang's business partner. But we never had proof. The Consul told me that I should wait a few days until he had an opportunity to arrange to have dinner with you.

"When his plans were laid, I took a gunboat here. I briefed the local general on what was happening. He was dutifully cooperative. We knew you would fly up immediately when you learned that Miss Harris was here. I got here first. The gunboat is upriver now hidden in a cove so you wouldn't see it when you flew in. It will pick me up later today.

"I've been listening at the window the whole time you were with Miss Harris. So has the general. He'll sign an affidavit as to what he heard. I'm a live witness. Your days in Shanghai are over, Lord Preston. You'll resign your peerage, settle half your fortune on Miss Harris and return to England or word will be spread of your perfidy. I wouldn't be surprised if the government in England would insist on your prosecution. Kidnapping is still a hanging felony in Britain, my old man. Or had you forgotten that?"

Robert was speechless. So was Violet. She began to cry.

"Get out!" the colonel said to Robert. "Get out before I thrash you to within an inch of your life! The Consul is awaiting your return to Shanghai. If the proper measures haven't been taken by the time I return, I'll give my report to the British papers!"

Robert nodded anxiously and began to leave.

"Oh, and Lord Preston," Parker added, grabbing hold of his collar, "what I said goes for Lady Preston as well. Half of her fortune. Got it?"

Robert had turned pale. He murmured an affirmation and dashed from the room.

Colonel Parker turned to Violet. She was trembling and crying. She too had turned pale.

"Miss Harris," Parker said, stepping towards her, "let me help you up. I'm going to take you home."

* * * * * * * * * * * * *

By the time that Violet and Colonel Parker reached Shanghai, Robert and Lady Preston had deposited the sum of 225,000 British pounds in the local branch of Barclays' Bank to Violet's account and set sail for England. It wasn't exactly half of their holdings, but Violet was more than satisfied. They had also deeded to her their mansion on Hungkow Road in the International Settlement. Ironically, it was the same house that Violet was originally to have lived in with Robert had they been married five years ago, before all this happened.

Invitations poured in from all the high society crowd for Violet to attend this or that soirée or party, but Violet shunned them, receiving only a few visitors, just enough to communicate politely her wish to be alone. All press inquires were rejected. All Violet wanted, after all these years, was her privacy.

In the beginning, day after day, Violet woke up trembling and frightened, unsure of where she was. During the day, she spent many lonely hours trying to gain acceptance in her mind that it was indeed all over.

Of course, it was not all over for either Iris or Tatiana. The American authorities were notified about Iris' fate, but they were powerless to do anything about it, not knowing where she was or who was holding her. The Soviet Government representative exhibited no interest in Tatiana. Colonel Parker was able to track down her relatives. All that was left in Shanghai was a distant cousin. She was a bar girl, ironically, at the Blue Cantina, where Violet had first met General Wang. She was thankful for the news, but what could she do?

Colonel Parker was Violet's lifeline to the world. He arranged for the servants for the mansion, arranged for a piano to be brought for Violet's enjoyment, deflected all press inquiries and visited her every day. He returned to her her books of poetry, urging her to seek a publisher for them. Violet hesitated, not only because they were so private, but also for fear of whipping up more sensationalism about her story. She could never be sure whether the poems were accepted for publication for their merit of because of the caché of their origins.

Violet begged Colonel Parker to bring her back to Yeuyang so that she could begin the process of tracing the fates of her two lovers, but Parker thought it still too dangerous. Even though she would be traveling with a representative of His Majesty's government, there was always the threat of General Chi's men seizing her and returning her to captivity.

This problem was assuaged a few months after Violet's return to Shanghai.

It seemed that General Wang had been right about the perfidy of the Kuomintang government. General Chi had surrendered his independence, recognizing the suzerainty of the Nationalists in Hunan. In exchange, he had been made governor of the province. That lasted less than a year and a half. His army was incorporated into Kuomintang units. Most of his officers were cashiered. In September, 1926, six months after Violet's rescue, a formerly obscure Kuomintang general named Chiang Khi-chek assumed control of the Kuomintang movement, President Sun Yat Sen having died. One of his first actions was to replace General Chi as Governor of Hunan with one of his own men. Without his army, Chi was unable to do anything about it. He was found dead one night in his bedroom. A heart attack was the official diagnosis, but there were many who said that he had been poisoned.

After Chi's death, Parker felt it safe enough for Violet to begin her search. They returned to Yeuyang by riverboat. Violet's first stop was the French orphanage. Sister Therese was overwhelmed with joy to see her. The gold Violet had left the orphanage had been a boon to them, but it was almost exhausted. Violet immediately made arrangements for a regular, liberal stipend to be provided for them.

The first stop in their search was with Fu Ming, the procurer, to whom both Iris and Tatiana had been sold. A little gold, and a threat from the Kuomintang District Commander, produced results. Iris was traced to a brothel in Chengdu, not far from where General Wang's mansion had been. Violet bought her contract. Their reunion was deeply emotional. They both wept and wept. Poor Tatiana was never found. They traced her through several brothels. She had been ultimately purchased by an agent for a private buyer whose identity was not revealed. Her whereabouts was unknown.

Iris was reunited with her family. She declined to stay with them and came to live with Violet in Shanghai. Violet had created a foundation with her fortune to benefit Chinese orphanages and Iris became the director of it. The foundation operated up until the outbreak of World War Two, when the Japanese invaded and seized Shanghai. Iris and a young American banker with whom she had fallen in love made it out on the last ship to escape the city. They settled in San Francisco where they were married. Iris had three children and lived a happy life until her death in 1976.

Violet and Colonel Parker became very close. When he proposed marriage to her, Violet demurred, to his great sadness. Instead, she fulfilled her wish to return to Yeuyang and work for the French orphanage there.

The years between 1928 and 1941 were the happiest of Violet's life. She never took vows as a nun, but she lived with them as an acolyte. She loved teaching and caring for the children. She often gazed up at the wreckage of General Wang's castle fortress. Sometimes she shuddered, recalling the agonies she suffered there. Other times she looked on it wistfully, remembering the man who had owned her and the brief period of happiness she had shared with him.

It was in 1941 that Li Pao's premonition of her great soul came to fulfillment and God's plan for Violet became known. The Japanese had been advancing steadily up the Yangtze, burning and pillaging as they went. Orphans flooded the French mission. Sister Therese had passed by then. The remaining French nuns were recalled by their order due to the dangers of the war. Violet stayed to manage the orphanage with the help of the native sisters who had converted to Christianity.

The Japanese reached the escarpments looking over Yeuyang in December, 1941. They immediately sur-rounded the city and commenced a bombardment. It became apparent that the city was going to be destroyed. Violet organized the children and, together with the Chinese sisters, slipped them through the Japanese cordon and then led them on a march through the mountains to Chengdu. It took them ten days. They were battered by heavy storms and bitter cold. It was only Violet's strength of will that saw them through. A number of the 150 children who began the march died along the way along with two of the sisters. When they reached Chengdu, a new orphanage was founded by her which operated throughout the war. Thousands of children passed through it and owed their lives to her.

When the war was over, she returned to Yeuyang and refounded the orphanage there. The French nuns returned. When the communists took over the country in 1949, the French nuns fled again, but Violet remained. She surren-dered her British passport and became a citizen of the new People's Republic. She was the only foreigner in Hunan for many years. The authorities, although suspicious of her aristocratic background, accepted her and allowed her to continue her work.

In 1957, during the great Chinese famine, she did her best to keep the children fed. It was a terrible winter that year.

In the spring of 1958, she contracted typhus and died at the age of 64.

Colonel Parker had never forgotten her. He too escaped from Shanghai. He was evacuated to Australia and then shipped back to England where he was promoted to command of a regiment of fusiliers and took part in the Battle of France in 1940. He was evacuated from Dunkirk and was assigned a division with which he fought through Africa with Montgomery. His division was returned to Britain after the fall of Rommel and took part in the invasion of France in 1944.

Parker retired after the war. He never married. Violet had kept up a constant correspondence with him with up to the outbreak of the war and had shipped off to him for safekeeping all of her volumes of poetry, her verses made during her captivity and afterwards. They were published after her death to great acclaim and won several literary prizes. A volume was published in China in 1984.

Parker, an old man, returned to China and Yueyang in 1962. He received special dispensation to visit from the Chinese government as a part of the general thaw of relations with Great Britain. He was shown Violet's unkempt grave in the French sisters' cemetery by the head of the orphanage, which still flourished. Tears in his eyes, he adorned it with a simple bouquet of flowers.

Yeuyang has grown into a great city. If you go there, on the southern outskirts, in one of the city's famous parks, there is a monument to Violet that was paid for by the subscriptions of the men and women whose lives, as children, were touched by her. It is in dark bronze. Her figure is at the southern end of the monument. She is striding forwards, a thin cloak wrapped around her. One hand is pointing the way of Chengdu. In her other hand, is the hand of a child.

The end.